C000175452

Here to
Slay

Also by Radhika Sanghani

The Girl Who Couldn't Lie (Usborne)

Published by Knights Of
Knights Of Ltd, Registered Offices:
119 Marylebone Road, London, NW1 5PU

www.knightsof.media
First published 2024
001

Written by Radhika Sanghani
Text copyright © Radhika Sanghani, 2024
Illustrations copyright © Jade Deo, 2024
All rights reserved
The moral rights of the author and illustrator have been asserted.

Set in Bembo Std / 12.5 pt
Typeset by Georgina Charles
Printed and bound in the UK

A CIP catalogue record for this book will be
available from the British Library

ISBN: 9781913311742

Here to Slay

Radhika Sanghani

To all the teens who slay

Chapter 1

I can't believe this is happening. But it is.

The entire class is staring at me, and Mrs Patel is forcing them to sing 'Happy Birthday.' I can't look up. It's too much. So I just stare at my scratched wooden desk, my cheeks burning up, even though my dark brown skin means I'm the only one who knows it. They're getting to the 'dear Kali' bit, and my stomach is churning with dread.

I keep my eyes firmly down, wishing I was anywhere but here. I can still see everyone smirking in my peripheral vision. Hayley and Rihanna rolling their eyes at each other as they sing obediently, fully aware of just how cringe this is. Joe King (his actual name) singing loudly and deeply, his voice as sexy as always. And then he practically booms 'dear Kaaaa-liiiiiii' and I don't know whether to be thrilled that my crush of five years knows my name, or totally mortified he's being forced to sing it out loud in our RE class.

Finally, the nightmare ends, and everyone claps politely. I shoot Mrs Patel a look that sums up exactly how I feel, but only when she's turning the other way. I'm not *that* brave. But I am still annoyed.

Just because Mrs Patel and I are the only Indians in the whole of South Bridge Secondary, she thinks that makes us friends or allies or whatever. It doesn't. I don't need her drawing more attention to the fact I'm different to everybody else with my skin, irritatingly thick black hair, and the curries my mum gives me for my packed lunch. All I want is to fit in. That's my 16th birthday wish. To get through the rest of the day – and ideally the rest of the year – without anybody noticing me. It hasn't gone well so far, but now the singing's out of the way; things should be back on track.

'In honour of Kali's birthday, I've decided to theme today's lesson around the Hindu goddess that she's named after,' beams Mrs Patel. I stare at her in horror. This is *not* what I meant about getting through the day without being noticed. 'According to Hindu mythology, Kali is the goddess of death, destruction and doomsday. The three Ds!'

That's it. I give up. If it wasn't bad enough that I'm named after the scariest, ugliest Indian goddess in existence, Mrs Patel just felt the need to divulge it to the entirety of Year 11. There is no way Joe King will *ever* ask me to the Summer Dance now.

'Doomsday!' It's Joe himself. He's cracking up with laughter, and if it wasn't about me, I would've been as well. 'Kali's named after the *doomsday* goddess?'

'Awkward,' says Hayley, glancing over at me. It's not often I agree with Hayley – though obviously I would never tell her that; I'm not ready to commit social suicide – but right now, she's got a point.

'Calm down everyone,' says Mrs Patel, clapping her hands for attention. 'You'll understand more when I explain the creation story of Kali.' She gives me a pointed look, before clearing her throat dramatically. 'It begins with the ancient Hindu gods. They were battling a demon called Raktabija, which translates to Blood-Seed. He was incredibly powerful, and if a drop of his blood touched the ground a clone of his would instantly appear.'

I stare at her in surprise. I had no idea that this story even existed – or what it has to do with the goddess I'm named after.

'Every time he or a clone was slain, there were new clones to deal with,' she continues. 'It meant the gods were close to losing their battle against him and his army of clones, so they decided to work together. They combined all their divine energy to produce one super-being who could destroy the demon once and for all: the goddess Kali.'

I gasp aloud. I'm obviously not a fan of the goddess I'm named after – the three Ds? Seriously? – but it is cool she's a super-being with the ability to destroy demons.

'Whoah!' Joe's eyes are wide. 'Did Doomsday kill them all?'

'She did,' affirms Mrs Patel. 'She swallowed Raktabija's army whole, so none of their blood touched the ground, and then she defeated him by cutting off his head and drinking up his blood to ensure no more demons would enter the world!'

That is *not* where I was hoping this story would go.

'Ew!' cries Hayley. 'She drank his blood?! That's seriously gross.' She faux-gags while Rihanna laughs in agreement.

I slump down into my seat in resignation. Any remaining hope I had of getting through the day without more humiliation has officially disappeared. The most popular girls in the whole year know I'm named after a blood-sucking goddess.

4

How could things get any worse?

'I've printed out a photograph of Kali so you can all look at it for context,' announces Mrs Patel, who is fast becoming my new nemesis. 'Jack, hand them out.'

This was definitely worse.

Jack – Joe's best friend – howls with laughter as he looks at the image, before trying to control his mirth as Mrs Patel glares at him. I know what's coming, and I force myself to breathe deeply before I look at the sheet that Jack hands me with me a smirk. It's worse than I remembered. Kali, in full A4 size, with her charcoal-black skin, bulging three white eyes (she has an extra one on her forehead) and enormous red tongue. The tongue that she uses to lick up demon blood.

'Kali is not cute,' declares Rihanna. Then she looks at me and her hand flies to her mouth. 'The goddess, I mean! Not... uh... I don't...'

'I can't believe you're named after a demon hunter,' says Joe, looking right at me. Oh my god. He's talking to me. On purpose. 'That is seriously crazy, Doomsday.'

I gape, speechless. The boy I've had a crush on since Year 7 has just given me a nickname. And it's Doomsday. Is this as bad as it sounds, or... is it progress?!

I wish I had a best friend to over-analyse this with,

5

but ever since Tanya left to go to Greece last year, it's just been me. So, I do what I always do, and turn away with an embarrassed smile, hiding behind my curtain of thick, dark hair.

'So, are you ready for the archery competition on Saturday?' Rihanna asks Joe.

'Yeah, I've been practising,' said Joe. My ears prick up. I didn't know Joe was going to be in the archery competition. I didn't even know there was one. That's how involved I am in school extracurriculars.

Hayley winds her hair round her fingers as she smiles at Joe. They used to go out. But they broke up last year. Hayley always said it was her choice and, judging by the way she's fluttering her lashes at him, she's changed her mind. 'I bet you'll be amazing!'

'Well, I've been practising too,' said Rihanna, shaking her braids confidently. 'So the competition is officially on!'

'Can't wait!' squeals Hayley. 'I've already chosen my outfit.'

I roll my eyes and turn back to the front as Mrs Patel calls out for attention. 'Right, I'd like you all to write an essay on Kali for homework please. 500 words on who she is and what she represents.' Just then, the bell rings and everyone starts rushing out of the door, chatting together, bags clashing. I move to follow them, but Mrs Patel stops me. 'Happy birthday again, Kali. I just wanted to say… good luck. With everything. You'll be okay.'

I blink at her in confusion. 'Good luck with… my essay?'

'Yes exactly!' she says, her face clearing. 'I think you'll find you may have more in common with the goddess Kali than you think.'

I can't think what she's referring to other than the fact that we both apparently now go by Doomsday – oh, and that Rihanna thinks neither of us are cute.

Chapter 2

I am *so* over today. By the time I get off the school bus and drudge down the quiet suburban roads to my house, all I want is to be alone in my room. I thought things were peak in RE, but the rest of the day was just as bad. Joe, Hayley, Rihanna and Jack – the popular crowd – kept finding reasons to reference 'doomsday' in class. Then they'd all look at me and stifle laughter behind their hands. I preferred it when none of them acknowledged my existence.

It used to be different when Tanya was here. Back then, I always had someone on my side. We were allies – I stood out because I was brown, and Tanya did because she was neurodivergent. We both knew what it was like to not fit in, so we spent all our time together, having sleepovers at each other's houses every weekend, and eating our lunches in the library together. That's how we met, on the first day of Year 7. We were both so terrified by how scarily grown-up our classmates seemed (they'd already *kissed* people. We hadn't even started practising on our hands!) that we separately decided to hide out in the library and eat our lunches there. We found each other in the Teen Fiction corner, reaching for the same feminist fantasy novel. We became best friends right then and stayed that way for the next four years.

Until Tanya's dad got a fancy job for a Greek airline and moved the whole family there to 'connect with their roots'. Tanya used to call me every day at the start, showing me their outdoor swimming pool, and telling me about life at her international school. But then she made friends. Lots of them. And the phone calls stopped coming.

She still messages once in a while – mainly sending reels and memes – but it's not the same. She's moved on, and I'm stuck here at South Bridge, where everyone already has best friends, lab partners and lunch buddies. Except for me. I don't even have my *period* yet and I'm 16 now. Hayley and Rihanna got theirs in Year 7, naturally. They announced it on their socials. It's why I try to just get through the days as quietly as possible, so I can come home and curl up with my fantasy books and video games. Everything makes so much more sense to me when it's not reality.

I turn down the corner of my road and halt in surprise. There are strings of fairy lights sparkling outside our house and I can hear the cadence of people's voices over upbeat music. I feel a glimmer of excitement. Have my parents planned a surprise party for me?! I never have parties – normally, I'd just do a birthday sleepover with Tanya, but now that she's gone the plan was to go for a family dinner on the weekend to my favourite Indian restaurant. But it looks like my parents have decided to give me a Sweet Sixteenth after all. It won't be anything like the one Hayley had (think caterers, a DJ and a black-tie dress code; I saw it on her socials) and everyone there will be related to me. But there'll probably be chilli paneer, and best of all? They'll all be there for *me*!

My heart flutters as I push open the porch door and walk into our three-bedroom semi. The voices are coming from the back garden. I pad down the hallway grinning despite myself – family parties can be boring, but this is still better than doing my homework in my room – and bump straight into my mum. She's wearing a gorgeous indigo saree, with her hair in a pretty bun, and she's holding a giant box. Her delicate, threaded eyebrows rise in shock.

'*Beta*, what are you doing here? You'll spoil the surprise.'

I laugh. 'It's okay Mum, don't worry. It's still amazing!'

'Yes, yes,' she says, ushering me through the glass doors into the garden. 'Let's hide out here, so that when Radha comes we can all jump out and shout 'congratulations!''

I stare at my mum in confusion. 'Wait, *what*?' Radha is my older cousin. She's the 'perfect one.' She got top grades, won a scholarship to Oxford, became a doctor, and now she's marrying a lawyer. It's the Indian dream, and on top of that, she's undeniably beautiful. Naturally, I hate her.

In my defence, I didn't always. We used to play together when I was younger. Back then, I practically worshipped her. But the older we got, the more my mum would start to compare us and tell me to 'be more like Radha', even though she's an entire decade older than me as well as genetically gifted. And then Radha began to change. She'd ignore me at family gatherings, scrolling through her phone instead, choosing to hang out with the adults instead of taking her customary spot at the head of the kids' table. She's still my cousin, but it's been a long time since I thought of her as a friend.

And now she's stealing my birthday.

I find myself squeezed in between a load of aunts and uncles, dressed in musty-smelling sarees and shirts. A masa pinches my cheeks while my favourite mami whispers, 'happy birthday Kali!' At least someone remembered. But then the lights turn on and everyone leaps up, shouting: 'Congratulations!!!'

Radha – dressed in a brand-new lilac sari, meaning she obviously knew this was happening – feigns shock. 'Oh, my goodness!! A surprise engagement party! Thank you so much!' Her fiancé Kevil steps into the garden behind her and swoops down to give her an over-the-top kiss.

'You deserve it baby!' He beams. 'I can't *wait* to marry you. You're the best thing that's EVER happened to me!'

Everyone claps at his show of love while I resist the urge to make a face. Kevil is so obsessed with Radha, it's embarrassing. I know he must be smart if he's a lawyer, but the way he goes on about her just makes him sound dumb. Radha could do way better.

And then she turns to look at me. 'But this isn't just my day, or Kevil's. It's Kali's too! Happy 16th Kali!' She smiles at my mum, who brings forward a giant

12

birthday cake with candles. It must've been in the box she was carrying. And then everyone starts singing 'Happy Birthday' to me for the second time that day.

I know that this is what I secretly wanted from the second I saw the fairy lights. But that was when I'd thought everyone had come here just for me. Only, as always, I'm the afterthought. The real centre of attention is Radha. This party was for her, and now she's making sure everyone knows it. This birthday cake is not a sweet cousinly gesture. It's a passive aggressive move to show *she's* the one standing in the spotlight, and I'm on the outside.

I blow out the candles quickly, squirming away from all the happy birthdays so I can run away to my room. But my dad intercepts me by the glass doors and gives me a big hug. 'Happy birthday Kali! I'm so proud of you! 16 already!'

I smile awkwardly. I don't know why he's proud of me; I have absolutely no talents at all, my grades are startlingly average even though my lack of a social life means I should probably be a top student, and my looks are as mediocre as my grades. But that's my dad for you. Perpetually cheerful and an eternal optimist. Unlike my mum who's always busy running around in a state of semi-stress, even when the only drama at hand is what we're going to eat for dinner.

I slide away from his hug and escape to my room as fast as I can. I'm still mortified that I got things so wrong. Of course, my parents weren't throwing a huge party just for me: it's all for Radha. The daughter they wanted all along. I know that sounds self-pitying, but it's true. She's always in our house, making my dad roar with laughter, having endless heart-to-hearts with my mum, and showing everyone how much better she is than me. It's been that way ever since she was my age, and her mum died of cancer. Her dad remarried shortly afterwards, and Radha lived with him and her step-mum Kavita. Kavita isn't the clichéd evil stepmother, but she does have the personality of a damp dishcloth. So, Radha ended up spending most of her free time at our house, and my parents adopted her in all but name. I know she's been through a lot, and it wasn't easy watching her dad move on from Seema Masi to the dishcloth in only six months. I am genuinely glad Radha could seek refuge with my parents. I just wish there was still space for me.

Finally, I make it to my room. I close the door

behind me in relief, taking in the reassuring poster of Ms Marvel and the familiar scent of the vanilla candle Tanya gave me when she left. After a day from hell, I'm grateful to be alone in the one place I feel truly safe. I chuck my bag under the desk where my laptop sits, ready to collapse straight onto my bed. But, instead, I freeze.

Because there, sitting on top of my badly-made single bed, is the most horrific thing I have seen in my entire life. I blink to make sure I'm not imagining it. But it is still there. It's the size of an adult man but like no person I've seen before. Instead, it has taut blood-red skin, crazy big muscles like a bodybuilder who downs protein shakes, and one giant eye in the middle of its head. An eye that is looking straight at me.

I made a tight, strangled sound as the demon – because that's the only word that accurately describes it – opens its mouth to reveal pointed yellow teeth. I retreat in horror as I realise it's *grinning* at me.

Before I know what's happening, the demon stands up on my bed, its head grazing the ceiling, and widens its mouth so I can see a black hole of nothingness behind its teeth. It starts salivating, frothing at the sides, and reaches out its arms. Claws spring out of its hands, and it bends its legs as though it's about to launch itself right at me.

Oh my god. It's going to kill me.

I panic and grab the first thing I can see. My fountain pen from my desk. I don't think. I just launch the fountain pen as hard as I can, right at the demon's face. Somehow, miraculously, it pierces its eye.

'AAAAAAAHHHHHH!'

The demon makes a bloodcurdling sound as it falls onto my bed. It writhes around, clutching its eye, blood spurting onto my freshly washed duvet. I'm frozen to the spot, unable to do anything but gawp at the nightmare in front of me. It goes on for what feels like forever, and then, after a final gruesome shudder, it suddenly stops. The demon is lying on my bed, motionless.

Everything inside of me is telling me to GET OUT NOW in case the demon bursts back to life. But I need to know if it's truly dead. I screw my hands into fists, trying to summon every ounce of courage within me as I gingerly walk towards the demon.

I can do this. I take a step. And then another. I force myself to go even closer, but just as I'm about to take another step, the demon disappears.

I freeze in confusion. But it's completely gone.

16

The body has dissolved into thin air. Or evaporated. Or something that science can't explain. All I know is that there was a dead demon lying on my white duvet, but now the only thing that's left on it is a load of dark red blood stains.

My mum is going to *kill* me. Unless a demon gets there first.

Chapter 3

It turns out that there is no logical 'next step' after you've just killed a demon. Especially when its body has disappeared so you can't technically confirm that said demon is dead. I'm just praying that it is, because otherwise it might come back. And there's no way I'll be able to kill it *twice*.

I have absolutely no idea what to do. I stand staring at the bloody mess on my bed for way too long. But then I realise that someone could've heard the demon's scream and be on their way up to my room. Right now. I cannot afford to have my parents see this – they'll freak out. They would never believe the truth; they'd just think I'm insane. *I'm* not even sure I believe the truth. Which is why I need to tidy up and make sure they never find out.

I sneak out to the corridor to get a bin bag, and then I shove all my bedding inside. I'm not sure if I'll be able to replace it without my mum realising, but the

18

risk is worth not having to sleep on demon blood. I sneak down the stairs with the bag, pausing every time I hear a sound, peering round corners before I move, like I'm James Bond. I make it to the hallway without anyone spotting me, but then a bunch of aunties all pour in from the living room and I'm cornered in the hallway, clutching the bin bag. I wait for them to ask me what I'm doing, nervous sweat collecting on my brow.

Only, nobody does. They're all too busy gushing about how beautiful Radha looks, where her saree is from, and how handsome Kevil is. Nobody pays any attention to me at all. Even when Puja Auntie literally walks into me, she just pats me on my head absent-mindedly. 'Sorry, *beta*, didn't see you there. Aren't you *dai* for taking the rubbish out?' I don't feel like the good girl she thinks I am; I just feel stupid for trying so hard to be James Bond about this when nobody even *notices* me.

But I have bigger things to worry about, like hiding the demon evidence. I dump the bin bag outside, then slide back upstairs to the bathroom so I can wash the blood off my hands. I feel like Lady Macbeth in the Shakespeare play we studied last year: 'out damned spot...

will these hands ne'er be clean.' But unlike Lady Macbeth, I'm not trying to wash away any guilt with the blood. That demon attacked me, unprovoked. It broke and entered into my room, which is definitely a crime, then it snarled at me whilst unleashing its claws, which was a clear act of aggression; if I hadn't pierced its eye with my pen, who *knows* what it would have done?

Suddenly, a wave of nausea hits me and I reach out to steady myself against the wall, light-headed and dizzy. There's an ache in the depths of my stomach too. It must be all the stress of what's happened. I sit down on the loo to ground myself, forcing myself to breathe deeply. Then I decide I may as well pee while I'm there, so I pull down my knickers. And that's when I see it.

Blood. And I don't think it's demon blood.

After all this time, my period is finally here. I don't know how to feel. I've wanted this for as long as I can remember. I've felt positively abnormal ever since Tanya got hers two years ago. The worst was when I turned 15 and Mum took me to see the doctor about it. Dr Gupta – this old Indian man who I've known since I was five years old – started asking me intimate questions about the inner workings of my body. It was all mortifying. Especially when he took my blood, and the tests came back *normal*. I'd been hoping to find out what was wrong with me so I could take some medicine, get fixed and start moaning about hormonal acne like Hayley and Rihanna. But there was no official reason for my womb's decision to delay functioning properly. In Dr Gupta's words I was just a 'late bloomer' – and in medical terms, I had 'amenorrhea' which basically meant the same thing. He acted like it wasn't a big deal (clearly showing he'd never been a teenage girl before), then told me to come back if my period hadn't started by the time I turned 16. I guess that's one appointment I no longer need.

But this doesn't feel as momentous as I thought it would. I've waited for blood for so long, only now, it isn't even the first drop of blood I've dealt with in the last hour! Not to mention everything else I've been through today. Like my crush calling me Doomsday whilst my RE teacher ruined my life, my parents throwing a party for my perfect cousin on *my* big day, oh, and killing a DEMON in my bedroom.

I reach for the sanitary pads under the sink. There aren't any tampons in there because my mum doesn't use them, so I guess I won't either. I unpeel the backing on the wings of the pad, just like the Period

Lady made me do in the assembly she gave us in Year 7. Back then, I totally messed up the demo, and the wings didn't attach properly to the knickers, so when I gave them back to the Period Lady, the pad floated away onto the floor. Everyone found it hilarious, and for days, Hayley made jokes about my flying sanitary pad. But she'd have nothing to laugh about it if she could see me now — I've evidently learnt from my mistakes, because I attach the pad perfectly, with zero drama.

I throw the wrapping into the bin, pull my knickers up and flush the loo. Done. It all feels so anticlimactic. Maybe because I've been preparing for this day ever since that assembly. Or maybe it's because my big moment of womanhood has been usurped by a demon.

I walk out of the bathroom, ready to go back to my room and do some serious journaling about what's just happened. I have a *lot* to process. But before I get there, I crash straight into Radha.

'Kali! Where have you been?'

'Uh… the loo.'

Radha frowns and steps closer to me. I can see her perfect, flawless skin and I can't help but inhale her sweet floral perfume. She inspects my less flawless skin before scratching my cheek with her long nail.

'Ow!' I cry out. 'What are you doing?'

She peers down at a speck on her perfectly shaped peach-coloured nail. 'Is that *blood* on your face?'

I freeze. Demon blood. It must be. 'Um… I… just got my period.' It's the first thing that comes to my mind. Besides, Radha already knows about my amenorrhea, because she's the one who told my mum to take me to the GP. Yet another thing I can thank her for.

'Oh! Finally!!' She beams at me, looking weirdly pleased about the fact that my womb lining is officially shedding. 'Congratulations! But…' She pushes her long wavy hair behind her ear. 'How did you get it on your *face*?'

Valid question. 'I… had to change my bedsheets. It got everywhere.'

She looks at me in alarm. 'You must have a very heavy flow. Do you have super absorbent tampons?'

My face must show that I have no idea what she's talking about because she shakes her head and starts rummaging around her handbag. She hands me a pack of tampons. 'Take these. I forgot your mum probably doesn't use tampons, does she? Indians, I swear. Kavita used to think a tampon would take my virginity. Completely mad – and sexist. Don't believe anything they tell you, okay? This tampon is not a big deal. It just slides in there, collects the blood, and means you don't have to walk around essentially sitting in your blood all day. I'd recommend you get a menstrual cup too. Similar vibes but better for the environment. These will do in the meantime though, okay?'

I nod wordlessly. I don't think I've ever seen Radha so passionate before.

'Good.' She flicks her hair behind her ears, regaining her composure. 'Let me know if you need anything.'

Obviously, I would never do that. But I nod politely before walking away. I'm going to need to raid the airing cupboard in search of new bedding before my mum comes up. And then I've got some serious Googling to do. I'm hoping the internet will be able to tell me exactly why a red one-eyed demon just appeared – and then disappeared – on top of my bed.

Chapter 4

I wake up with a start. I'm covered in a slick layer of sweat, and it's not just because the only bedding I could find in the cupboard was a thick winter duvet. It's down to the nightmare I had about killing a one-eyed demon with my fountain pen. Then I realise I'm lying beneath said thick winter duvet *because* my normal duvet isn't here. It's covered in blood at the bottom of the bin. I reach for my fountain pen and, as I feared, the nib is bent.

That's when I realise it wasn't a nightmare: it was all real. The horror. The killing. The bloody sheets. And then the hours of Googling late into the night, trying to find out more. I was there for hours, but I couldn't find anything except sci-fi blogs, ancient legends, and the Blood-Seed demon that Mrs Patel taught us about. Which reminds me that I haven't done the essay she assigned us. And, seeing as my alarm has started to go off, I won't have time to either. I groan as I pray that, for once, our shared brownness will work in my favour and Mrs Patel will let me off.

★★★

'Kali, stay behind please,' says Mrs Patel. 'I need to talk to you.'

My stomach sinks. Looks like I won't be let off after all.

'Bad luck, Doomsday,' smirks Hayley, her tote bag swinging against my shin as she barges past. Great. Joe King's nickname for me has become official.

I walk up to Mrs Patel's desk apologetically. 'I'm sorry. For forgetting to do my homework. I can make it up on the weekend.'

'Please do. I think it will be… helpful.'

'Right.' I don't know what she's trying to help me with now – embrace my roots? Own my cultural identity? Whatever it is, I don't have the energy to deal with it. Not while I'm still trying to find out if this demon is going to reappear or not.

'And… Kali, do you know any other girls called Kali? Your age. Or older. Because I think it would be really beneficial for you to speak to some.'

Wait – she won't make allowances about my

homework, but she wants to find me a mentor?!

'Uh, I'm fine about my name Mrs Patel. I don't need to speak to someone else who has it to make me feel better. Besides, hardly any Indian girls are called Kali. Most parents *don't* name their precious baby daughters after the doomsday goddess who licks up demon blood with her tongue.'

A shadow of something passes over her face. But, before I can figure out what it is, she's smiling at me sadly. 'No, they don't. But a few do. And… it's not my place to get into this. But if ever anything, um, unusual happens to you, I really suggest you find some other Kalis.'

She emphasises this last sentence so heavily that I stare at her in surprise. Surely, she can't mean… I bite my lip, before trying to figure out how to subtly ask my teacher if she knows I was attacked by a demon. 'When you say unusual…'

'Just reach out to some other Kalis,' she interrupts briskly. 'I can't say any more, I'm sorry. But please. Find other Kalis. And also, Kali? You're doing really well. I'm proud of you.' With that, Mrs Patel gives me one last look – a creepy combination of worry and maternal pride, ew – then picks up her oversized handbag, walking out of the classroom.

I'm left standing there on my own, in my scratchy navy skirt, white shirt and trainers, wondering if it's just me or does Mrs Patel know more than she's letting on?

***

It's 5.05pm and I've pretty much survived the whole day without any demon-related disasters or social humiliation. Considering how yesterday went, this feels like a major achievement. Especially because Joe King and I had the most incredible moment imaginable.

I still can't really believe it happened, but there I was in the hallway, when I saw him struggling to get a protein shake out of the vending machine. I know that vending machine well – Tanya and I used to go every day before the school had a health kick and swapped everything delicious for weird nut bars – so I stalled by him, working up the courage to ask him if he needed help. But before I could, he turned around and said 'Hey!' To *me*. With a *smile*.

A smile from Joe King is no small thing – my whole body turned to jelly and I got butterflies in my stomach – so naturally I couldn't reply with words. But it gave me a boost of bravery, and I went up to the machine and kicked it hard. The protein shake fell down. And then Joe's smile got *even bigger*. His cheekbones were practically touching his eyebrows when he grabbed his shake and said: 'Doomsday to the rescue! Thanks!' Whilst looking right at me, the whole time.

It was the most romantic moment of my life to date, and I got actual shivers. 'Doomsday' might not be the nickname I would have chosen, but the point is that my crush knows who I am, he has a personalised name for me, *and* I rescued him. Life could not have been better if it tried.

So, as I walk home from the bus stop, I'm feeling pretty positive about things. It looks like yesterday was just an abnormal blip, and life as a 16-year-old is actually going to be quite good.

And then a brick comes flying at me.

I duck instantly, as it narrowly misses the top of my head. I race to hide behind a giant hedge, instinct kicking in. I have no idea what just happened, but I can't resist peering out, heart beating, to see where the brick came from.

The demon.

Of course. He's back. Snarling, red, scrunched-up

face, and a singular giant eye. I gulp in fear; my worst nightmares are coming true. I don't know what to do. I grapple around my bag, trying to find a fountain pen. But I can't even find a biro. What do I do now?!

The demon opens its mouth and makes a low, guttural animal sound. It fills me with terror. But something – adrenaline – kicks in and I realise I need to do something. As the demon starts to come towards me, my fingers grasp something sharp. My keys. I launch them as hard as I can. The chances of them hitting the demon's eye are practically zero. I can't even hit the ball in a rounders game; I'm the only person in the whole year who almost failed PE. But somehow, my keys fly straight into the centre of the demon's eye. I hold my breath, praying that it will collapse like it did last time. And it does!

I watch, trembling, as it falls onto the ground, writhing in agony, clutching its eye. And then it suddenly stops, motionless. I think it's dead – but that's what I thought last time. What if it disappears and then comes back again? Will I ever be free of this crazy demon?! I take a tiny step closer, arming myself with a twig from the ground. The demon *looks* dead. Red blood is sprouting from its eye, just like last night, and dripping down its body. A couple of drops fall onto the ground.

I don't know what to do. Can I trust that its body will disappear? And if it disappears, does that mean it will come back again? Just as I'm deciding whether to go over and snatch my house keys back, the body vanishes. Exactly like last night. One minute it's there, solid 3D flesh and blood. The next minute it's gone. I've never seen anything like it… but then again, I'd never seen a live demon before yesterday. Quickly, before it comes back, I run over to grab my house keys, wiping the blood on the hedge. I shove the keys into my pocket as I run away. All I want is to get home, lock myself in my room, and never leave again.

But then I hear another snarling sound. I turn around in total dread to see that it's BACK. And this time, it's brought a friend.

They are identical. And they're coming straight for me. I don't even think. I just run. As fast as I can down the roads I grew up on. I want to turn around to see if they're still chasing me, but there's no point. I know they are. I can feel it in my bones. Then I hear a rasping sound. They're getting closer. I don't know what to do. I can barely breathe as I run faster than I ever have in my whole life, at a speed I never even knew I was capable of.

If I had known, I might have done better in cross-country.

I can sense the demons getting closer. But I can't think of what to do, other than keep on running. So I do. Then I spot the private path to the Marshalls' garden and quickly dive in, knowing that I can use their back gate to cross through the neighbours' gardens to get home. As I approach their gate, a cold wave of horror pins me to the spot. Their gate is *locked*. I've walked into a dead end and the demons are right behind me.

I have no choice but to duck down behind a wheelie bin. This is the worst hiding place in the world. A five-year-old child would find me in less than a minute. But I have no other option – I can't go back the way I came, or I'll be walking straight into the demons' path. I stay there, breathing deeply, as I hear the demons turn into the alleyway. Oh my god. They're metres away from me. I can hear their loud breath, and weird grunting sounds. They've going to find me, and kill me, or eat me, or... wait. Is it me or are the demons *leaving*?!

I hold my breath as I slowly peer around the side of the wheelie bin and see that the demons are walking away. They haven't found me! It didn't even occur to them to look behind the bin! For the first time, I realise that these demons are kind of stupid, and I am beyond grateful. My whole body exhales with relief as I hear them continue to retreat, back the way we came.

I'm safe, but I don't trust that it's over yet. If I was a demon, I would hide out on the street, waiting for me to think it's clear and then come out. This could all be a trap, with them faking their stupidity. So I keep waiting, until I'm so desperate for a wee that I have no choice but to get up. Slowly, cautiously, I creep out of the Marshalls' path back to the main road, checking constantly to see if the demons are there.

But they're not. The demons really are dense – they've gone. I take full advantage of this and race home before anything else happens. I slip through the front door and sprint up to my room without my parents noticing. I open my bedroom door, my heart still pounding heavily, praying there won't be a demon inside.

Chapter 5

There isn't a demon in my room, but I am still not okay. It's one thing to be attacked by a demon once – but to be attacked *twice*?! Two days in a row? And then have MORE demons pop up?! I'm freaking out right now. I am going to need *so* much therapy when this is over. If I can find a therapist who believes I'm talking about literal demons not metaphorical ones. But now is not the time to focus on my future therapy. I need to figure out exactly what is happening to me, so I can work out how to stop it.

I presumed it was the same demon who attacked me when he threw a brick at my head. But then I saw two identical demons chasing me, which means that there could be multiple versions of this thing. I shudder at the thought and force myself to come back to the facts at hand. I grab my phone and sit up straight on my bed, ready to take notes and figure out what the hell is going on.

So: I was attacked by Demon 1 on my birthday. I thought it didn't die and came back today. But maybe it *did* die, and Demon 2 – the brick thrower – was a new demon. Both disappeared, but then Demon 3 and 4 appeared. And they're still out there. They could be coming for me any minute. Demon 1 knew where I lived; maybe he spread the word?! This is not a comforting thought and I hastily double-check my window is locked. I don't know what else to do to try and protect myself. Should I leave my curtains open in case these demons are like vampires and can't deal with the sun? But the demons attacked me in broad daylight… Maybe I need a cross, like the one Hayley wears, to ward them off? I don't have one though; would an 'Om' pendant do instead?

I feel so powerless over this situation. I close the Notes app on my phone and start Googling again: 'demon + blood + red + one eye + disappear'. But this time I add in the word 'identical.' The first thing that comes up is the Kali legend Mrs Patel told us about. I groan – as if I need reminding *again* of the humiliating story with Raktabija and Kali's blood-sucking tongue. And then I gasp, bolting upright. In the legend, Raktabija produces clones whenever a drop of his blood touches the ground.

What if Raktabija is the demon who is attacking me?! Or at least, his clones. That could explain why two more popped up today right after I killed Demon 2. His blood went all over the ground! But Demon 1's blood went everywhere when I popped its eye with my fountain pen on my birthday and no more clones appeared then. Except Demon 1's blood didn't touch the *ground*. It was all soaked up by my duvet…

I gulp in horror. If I'm right, then the clones of the demon who *all the Hindu gods couldn't defeat* is after me, Kali Kadia. I might have the same name as the goddess Kali, but unlike her, I don't have magic powers. And there's no way I'm going to lick up a demon's blood with my tongue. I can't defeat these demons! So why are they coming for me?! Just because I have the same name?! Have they got confused?!! This is a complete and utter disaster. I don't know what to do.

I force myself to breathe. I need to come up with a plan. I have to speak to Mrs Patel – she's been weird with me ever since my birthday. She wanted me to look into Kali's story to 'help me', she kept wishing me luck *and* she wanted to check I was okay today. Not to mention her comments about something

36

'unusual' happening to me. It's just so frustrating that today is a Friday; I have to wait for the whole weekend before I can speak to Mrs Patel at school on Monday. And judging by the number of demons who have been attacking me lately, I may not even *make* it to Monday.

Then it hits me. I don't need to speak to Mrs Patel right now because she's *already* given me advice: to speak to other Kalis. I need to start finding some right now. Because if my gut is right, then I might not be the only Kali this is happening to.

***

It's taken two hours of trawling through socials, but I've finally found one. A Kali. Just like me, she's 16, and she only lives one town away. But unlike me, she's seriously cool, has hundreds of followers and definitely isn't being chased by demons. Or at least, I can't see any sign of that on her socials. I scroll through her photos one more time. I can't get over how badass she looks. She wears all black, has loads of piercings and I think she might even have *tattoos*. Also, she goes by 'K', not Kali. That's why it took so long to find her.

There really aren't a lot of people called Kali out

there. There are a few white people with the name in America, but hardly anyone brown, and I have a feeling I need to speak to brown Kalis. I did come across one Indian model called Kali who lives in New York, but I was way too intimidated to message her. Also, judging by her Insta account, there is no *way* she's fighting demons in her spare time. She's too busy sipping martinis in rooftop swimming pools.

K, however, is not. She's obsessed with martial arts, indie films, and political activism. I think she's in the same year as me because she's also doing her GCSEs, though she goes to the private school nearby. And she's obviously Indian, not just because she has the same skin colour as me, but because there are loads of photos of her wearing Indian outfits. I was surprised to see someone as cool as her was proudly showing off her culture – at South Bridge, it was the opposite of cool to do anything that marked you as different – but K is clearly an exception to the rule. Which means she is obviously the Kali I should reach out to.

But what exactly do I message her? 'Heyyyy so, my Indian RE teacher thinks we should chat. By the way, have you ever been attacked by a demon? Lol, jokes, me neither!'

It's just *weird*. But then again, maybe it's not as weird as what I've been through lately. So, with a deep breath, I start composing a message.

It takes me 20 minutes and 25 drafts, but by the time I hit send, I'm proud of what I've written.

'Hi. I'm also called Kali.'

If she knows, she'll know. And if not, well, she'll think I'm a bit strange. And seeing as that's what most people already think, it will make no difference to my life. I put my phone away and get ready to sleep. I have no idea how I'll ever relax after the last 48 hours, but my body is exhausted. So, I turn my light off and then—

'Unggh!'

There's a grunting sound coming from behind my door. I bolt upright and seize the fountain pen by my bed. But then the door budges open and through the crack of light flooding in from the hallway, I see my dad. My shoulders lower in relief.

'Why have you put your desk behind your door?' he asks.

'Uh… privacy?'

He blushes, as though he's only just remembered I'm a teenage girl. He probably has. 'Of course, sorry. I just wanted to say goodnight *beta*. And how much I'm looking forward to celebrating your birthday properly tomorrow. I've booked us a table at Sakonis.'

'Great!' I try to block out images of demons bursting into our family dinner, plates of chilli paneer flying through the air as they attack me. Happy birthday Kali.

'Is everything alright Kali? You disappeared quite quickly at Radha's party. And you barely spoke a word at dinner tonight...'

I wish I could tell my dad. But he would never understand. And I don't want to worry him. 'Everything's fine, thanks Dad! But... there is something I was wondering. For our RE homework, we need to write about the goddess Kali. Do you... know anyone else who had that name? In our family maybe?'

He laughs. 'Oh no! It's not very common these days to name your daughters Kali. They used to do it more in the olden days, I imagine.'

'So, um, why did you?'

'It was your mum's idea. She always loved the name. I'm sure she thought it would bring you lots of luck!'

Clearly, she thought wrong.

'Night *beta*.'

He leaves and closes the door behind him. I rush to shove the desk behind the door again, although if my dad was able to push past, it's doubtful that it will stop a demon. But I need to do *something*.

And then my phone beeps. It's from K!

'Meet me tomorrow morning. I'll send my location first thing. Don't be late.'

Chapter 6

I frown critically at my reflection. I've tried on fifteen different outfits, but I've ended up wearing the same blue jeans and white tank top I always wear. With an oversized khaki shirt as a jacket, because I saw Rihanna wearing one on our last non-uniform day. Although I bet hers didn't come from her dad's wardrobe. It's embarrassing it has taken me 45 minutes to come up with this ensemble, but it's hard to know what to wear on a first meeting with someone who is at least nine times cooler than me. I give my reflection one last appraisal, pulling my hair up into a slick high-ponytail, and stick some kohl eyeliner on. Then I panic it's too much and wipe it off. I glance back at my reflection and sigh. I now have black smudges around my eyes, my hair is less Ariana Grande and more Miss Trunchbull, and my dad's shirt is making my body look like a rectangle. But it's as good as I'm going to get.

I shove my phone and keys into my cross-body bag,

then chuck in a few pens as well. You never know. I head downstairs quietly, hoping to slip out before anybody asks me any questions. But I'm not even halfway down the stairs when–

'Kali? Is that you?' My mum.

'Hee-eyy!' And Radha. Great.

I reluctantly head into the living room where my mum and Radha are curled up on the sofa together, cradling giant mugs of chai, with a platter of biscuits on the coffee table. They're Radha's favourites. Cardamom, buttery things that Mum only makes when she's over. I prefer chocolate. Not that anyone asked.

'You look cute,' observes Radha, even though she looks undeniably cuter than I do, in her soft, cream jumpsuit, with her hair piled up in a messy-but-chic bun on top of her head. 'Where are you going?'

'Just out.'

My mum holds a hand up. 'Wait. Where is 'out?' Who with? And what time will you be back?'

It was so much easier when I could simply answer, 'Tanya.' Her name was an acceptable response for every single one of my mum's questions. But, seeing as she's currently 3,000km away, that's not an option. 'Um, I'm meeting some friends?'

'Friends? *What* friends?'

I know my mum's not trying to shame me, but that feels kind of harsh. 'Just… friends from school.'

'Boys?' She sits up straight, crossing her arms, pulling her mauve cardigan tight around her. 'Who are they? And where are you going?'

I sigh with frustration. I bet K doesn't have to deal with this; her mum has let her pierce her septum. I glance at the clock. I'm going to be late if I don't hurry. I try to think of some names I could give my mum, so she'll leave me alone – and then I have a brainwave that doesn't even involve lying! Well, only half a lie. 'There's actually a big archery competition happening at school today. So… I'm meeting some people there to watch them compete.'

'Archery!' My mum's perfectly threaded eyebrows rise. But, as I knew it would, the mention of school has calmed her down. And if she bothers to double-check, it's all true. I just won't be there. 'I didn't know you liked archery.'

'It's really in right now,' I tell her confidently, because it must be if Joe and Rihanna are doing it.

'Well, I hope getting good grades is 'in' as well!' says my mum.

Radha giggles politely at my mum's bad joke. 'Enjoy archery. And see you tonight at dinner.'

'She's coming too?!' It bursts out of my mouth before I realise how it sounds. 'Um, I mean, I didn't know you were coming!'

My mum tuts. 'Of course she is, Kali. She's family!'

★★★

I'm here. Standing in a quiet corner of the park, surrounded by trees. It's the exact location that K sent me. I walked so fast that I'm now five minutes early and I've got sweat patches on my shirt. I can't decide whether to take it off and ruin my look or keep it on and try not to move my arms. I'm halfway through taking it off when I hear my name. I shove it back on – let's be honest, my look is more of a priority right now – and turn around.

She's there. K. She's even cooler in person. She has really short hair with long bits at the front – her hair actually looks a bit like Joe King's – and a row of silver piercings decorating her ears, as well as the silver ring on her septum that I saw on her profile pic. She's quite petite, definitely shorter than me, but she looks *way* stronger. Her arms are enormous! I can tell they're pure muscle even with her leather jacket on. She's wearing a black tank top beneath it, black combats and black Nikes. But the most striking thing about her is her huge brown eyes. I didn't know it was possible for brown eyes to be so mesmerising, but hers are almost mahogany! I've never seen a shade of brown like it.

Then I realise I'm staring into her eyes in silence like a total creep. I smile, trying to look normal. 'Hi! I'm Kali.'

'I know,' she says seriously, now staring into *my* eyes. It's disconcerting. Especially because I bet she's not thinking about the different shades of brown in my eyes, mainly because they're black and completely boring. What *is* she thinking?

'So, um, do I just call you K?' I ask.

'Yes.' She accompanies her answer with a perfunctory nod.

'Cool,' I say, trying to think of what to say next.

'Were you followed? Is there anyone here?'

'I… don't think so?' K is giving off serious CIA vibes right now.

'And are you on your period?'

I choke on air, coughing loudly. I did *not* see that question coming. Unless – oh my god. I suddenly crane my neck back, trying to look at the back of my jeans. The blood must be showing. I knew Radha's tampons would let me down. 'Oh no! I mean, yes I have it now. Has it leaked?!'

She shakes her head impatiently. 'No. It's fine. But that means we need to be careful. Mine finished a couple of days ago. If we're going to team up, we'll need to get in sync. I reckon spending every day together will do it.'

'I'm sorry, what?!' I stare at her like she's insane. Although my heart did quicken at the thought of us spending every day together.

She stares back at me like *I'm* insane. And then something softens in her face. 'When did it happen for you?' I don't know what she's referring to and it must be obvious because she clarifies. 'When did you turn 16? And get your period?'

'Uh, two days ago? How did you know they happened at the same time?'

She lets out a low whistle. 'Oh wow, you're new. Really new.'

'What about you?' I ask. Even though if I'm honest, I'm not exactly sure what it is I'm asking her.

'September. I'm a Virgo.'

'I'm a Gemini. Are we... compatible? To be

friends?' I know I'm being way too needy right now. But I haven't had a real friend for an entire year, and I really, really miss having one. Not to mention how cool it would be to have a friend like K. Tanya was great and everything, but there's no way she would have been able to pull off a septum piercing.

'It all depends on your moon and your rising,' she replies earnestly. I make a mental note to Google mine as soon as I get home. 'I'm glad you found me, Kali.'

I smile cautiously. 'Me too. But could you maybe, like, explain? What's happening? And if you also get the... uh...' I don't know if I should say it, but then a spark of recklessness alights inside me. Or maybe it's just impatience. 'Demons.'

Her face tightens. Then she nods. 'I'll tell you everything. But first, I need sustenance.' She reaches behind her for a backpack I hadn't noticed her wearing. Black, of course. I'm apprehensive as she rummages around – at this point, I wouldn't be surprised if she pulled out anything from a gun to a vial of blood. But I relax as she produces a packet of high-protein cereal bars.

'My mum buys me those for my packed lunch!' I say, before I realise how young I sound. 'They're... good.'

'I know. They have the highest protein content of all the bars out there. I eat 15 a day.'

My mouth drops open. '15?!?'

K grins at me for the first time. She looks like a totally different person when she smiles – her whole face is radiant and her eyes are dancing with light. 'I need the energy. You will too. So, are you ready to find out everything?'

I look into her eyes, knowing that my life will never be the same again if I say yes. But then I remember that my life has *already* changed. The bloodstained bedsheets at the bottom of the bin are proof of that. I don't have a choice. I gulp nervously and nod.

'I'm ready.'

Chapter 7

'No.' I shake my head. 'I'm sorry, but no. This isn't true. Or it is but they've got the wrong person. I'm not the Kali they're looking for. I'm just a normal 16-year-old!' I pause. 'Okay, a less-than-normal 16-year-old. But the point is, I'm not the right person!'

'I'm sorry Kali, but you are. And you don't have a choice. The demons are coming for us, so you need to get ready. There's no time for denial.'

I stare at K helplessly, still reeling from everything she's just told me. That my theory was right and Raktabija and his clones *are* after me. They're after both of us. They're after any Indian girls with the name Kali.

'But I have nothing to *do* with the goddess Kali,' I protest. 'It's only a name!'

'Names are powerful. In the ancient world, they believed that energies are passed through names. It means we both have a bit of the goddess Kali inside of us. Her energy anyway.'

My mind flashes back to the terrifying print-out Mrs Patel gave us of Kali, with her three eyes and big red tongue. Do I really want her doomsday energy inside me?

'There's nothing you can do to avoid it,' says K, as though she knows what I'm thinking. 'Trust me, I've tried. This is the way it is. The demons come after us, and we're destined to kill them. It will only end when we've killed them all. Or they've killed us.'

I look up hopefully. 'Maybe we can kill them all! How many are there?'

'Right now, around 5,000.'

I let out an involuntary whimper. I was expecting her answer to be in double-digits, not four figures! 'What? How do you know?'

'There's a WhatsApp group,' explains K. 'With us Kalis on there. Right now, there are only four of us, internationally. We lost a Kali in Delhi last year. Demons, of course.'

I reach out to steady myself on the tree, as K keeps going. 'It's good to have you though. New blood is always welcome.' I'm not sure how I feel about being called new blood, but K continues, oblivious. 'This has been going on for centuries. The difference is that, with tech, we can find each other now. We're the only two Kalis in the UK – there's Dottoressa Kali in Italy, Model Kali in New York, and Tech Kali in San Francisco. She's the one in charge of research. She's been using data to figure out how many demons there are and to track them. We're trying to find their lairs so we can attack them en masse. There was a group Kali trip last year to South America to kill a bunch of demon clones hiding out in a cave in Colombia, but… I couldn't join. My mother.'

She says the last two words so darkly that I nod sympathetically. 'There's no way my mum would let me travel alone either.'

K shakes her head. 'It wasn't that. She needed me to go to an awards ceremony with her because apparently it wouldn't look good to not have any family there when she won.' She scowls. 'I missed out on helping take down 200 demons!'

'I'm sorry?'

'Thanks. Anyway, I'll add you to the WhatsApp group. Introduce you to everyone. We're the youngest by far. Model Kali's only 27 but Tech Kali's in her thirties and Dottoressa's even older. They'll be thrilled I've found someone local. It means I can stay by you for the next few days until your bleeding stops.'

'My period? Why?!'

'Oh, I forgot you don't know that bit yet. That's how the demons hunt us. Our blood.'

I stare at her, aghast.

'They can sniff us out when we're menstruating,' she continues, matter-of-factly. 'It's why Kali-ma, the goddess, made sure her descendants – that's us – don't get our periods till 16. So we have time to get strong and grow up before the demon killing starts.'

'That's good of her,' I say sarcastically.

'I know,' replies K seriously. 'We're lucky, too, that the demons' abilities aren't perfect. Sometimes it takes them a while to sniff us out, especially when they're brand-new and have just been cloned. Also, they need to have full strength to do it, so I highly recommend weakening them if they're after you. But that's how they find us. When we're not bleeding, they can't find us at all.'

I blink. 'But… they found me at my house on the first day of my period. Won't they know to just go there again another time, even if they can't, uh, smell me?'

K shakes her head cheerily. 'Nope. That's the best thing about the demons. They're seriously stupid. They're decent fighters, I'll give them that, but they don't have intellect like we do. They rely on scent to find us. Their noses are much more powerful than their eyes. And their brains. They're easily confused – it's like fighting a very simple animal rather than a human.'

'Right. Great.' My voice is faint. This is a lot. But it makes sense. The demons wouldn't have smelled me behind the wheelie bin because they were brand-new clones. And they were too stupid to look.

'Give it a few days, and you'll be free of them again,' says K. 'By the time you're ovulating, you'll be ready to join me and hunt them.'

'Hunt them?!'

'Of course! We're descendants of Kali-ma. We're not going to sit back and hide from these creepy blood-sniffing demon clones. We're demon *slayers*,' she declares. 'I normally give myself a few days off when I'm PMS-ing because it's important to rest to maximise potential. But when I'm ovulating, I'm in peak form, so that's when I go after them. That's why I said we should sync up our cycles: so we can team up and protect each other when we're perioding, then team up and hunt together when we're not!' K looks genuinely pleased with her solution. When I don't say anything, she frowns. 'Kali? Don't you agree?'

I swallow nervously. 'Look. I'm not sure I'm cut out to be a demon slayer. Maybe I can just survive these five days each month–'

'It could be a week,' interrupts K. 'Depends on your cycle.'

I pray inwardly to anyone who's listening – Kali-ma? – that I have a very, very short cycle. 'Okay. But I think I'll just try and survive on my bleeding days, and then, like, *not* hunt demons the other days. I mean, I don't have time. I have school. And frien– well, you know, stuff to do. I'm on level 10 Minecraft.' Her face is settling in the same expression she had when she spoke about her mum not letting her go to Colombia. 'Look, it's not because I don't *want* to help. But I won't be any good at it. I almost failed PE, and that's not a subject you can even really fail.'

The darkness on her face clears. 'You haven't discovered your power yet!'

'Power?' I echo.

'Yes! We all get one. From Kali-ma. Mine is super strength.' She flexes her extraordinary biceps, making her soft leather jacket stretch at the seams. It must be good quality because it doesn't come close to ripping.

'Okay, it's very cool you got a power,' I admit.

'But I didn't!' I show her my biceps as proof; they barely move when I flex them. 'I can't do demon hunting. Maybe I'll be better at demon hiding?'

She rolls her eyes impatiently. 'You got your period two days ago, correct?' I nod. 'And you've been attacked by four demons since then? You said you killed two, and then ran away from two.' I nod again. 'And you think you've somehow slayed two *demons* and survived another two, all without having a single power?'

I think back to the fountain pen incident. And the keys. Wait. 'I... guess I was able to hit them both directly in the eye. Does that mean...?'

'Super aim!' Her eyes sparkle with excitement. 'You're the first Kali I've come across with that power. This is perfect! You can get them all in the eyes. Well, eye, singular.'

'But I have really bad aim,' I say, thinking back to when Hayley refused to partner with me in tennis because I couldn't do a rally over two. 'At least, I used to. Do you think it's changed?'

'Try,' she suggests, handing me a protein bar. She points to a tree with a hole in its trunk. 'Throw the bar into the trunk.'

'That's miles away! I'll never get it in there.'

'Unless you have a superpower… Go on.'

I have nothing to lose so I reluctantly take the cereal bar from her outstretched hand. I know this is going to be just as humiliating as those tennis lessons. The demon killing incidents were obviously pure fluke – it was probably some kind of life and death instinct taking over. It won't work now I'm chucking food into a tree. But K gently nudges me, and I take a deep breath. I raise my left arm, ready to launch the bar. I exhale loudly, throwing the bar as far as I can, knowing it will land on the ground.

Except it doesn't.

It lands *straight* in the hole.

'Oh my god. Oh my god, I did it!!'

A small smile lights up K's face. 'Told you. Right. We're going to need a training regime. And we're going to need to spend a *lot* of time together, so our menstrual cycles sync up ASAP. I'll need you to put in all your period details on an app too. I'll send you a link, so we can see each other's.'

I hesitate, unsure what to say. As much as I wanted a new friend, this is all moving very fast. Syncing up cycles sounds intimate. And I don't know how I feel about a training regime. But before I can express my doubts, I hear a crunching sound in the distance. I spin around quickly to see a snarling one-eyed red demon running right towards us.

Chapter 8

It turns out that demon killing is a whole different experience with K. When the demon first appears, I stand gawping in terror. Until K, who is metres away from it, turns back and shouts at me: 'Tarp! From my backpack! Now!'

I jump into action and start fumbling around in her backpack. I pull out a huge plastic sheet, trying to spread it evenly on the ground, hoping that's what she intended for me to do. I can't believe K's been carrying it around all day – the girl is prepared. I can hear grunting from the distance, and I desperately want to watch her kick this demon's ass, because if anyone's going to do it in style, it's K. But I know that if I don't complete the one task she's given me, she'll be majorly unimpressed. And something in me really wants to impress K.

I've finally got the tarp spread out when I hear her grunt loudly. I look up and my jaw drops. She's got the demon's head under her arm in a headlock and she's dragging it over to the tarp. It's snarling away, kicking out, but K has it held so tight it can't escape.

I feel useless just watching so I reach around in vain for something sharp to aim at its eye, eventually finding a large twig. I snap it in half to make it extra pointy, and I'm about to launch it towards the demon when K shouts: 'Not yet! Wait 'til it's on the tarp!'

Chastised, I watch her drag the demon onto the tarp, yanking it by the neck as it tries to twist away, practically frothing at the mouth. When K is standing in the centre of the tarp, I head over with the twig in my hand, wielding it like a spear.

'Okay, be careful,' warns K. 'We don't want any blood to touch the ground.'

I nod grimly. K has one knee pressed down on the demon's torso and the other on its thighs. It can't move, and she's holding its arms tight. I stand by the demon's head, trying not to gag. I didn't really notice before but there's an awful smell of gone-off meat emanating from the demon, and this angle – me looking directly down at it – is really not doing its face any favours. It turns its enormous eye onto me, looking more repulsive than ever, and snarls.

I shudder, then look at K, who nods impatiently. 'Go on!' She pushes down harder on the demon as it twists in terror. 'Stick. Eye. Now.'

I obey. I grab the stick with both hands and plunge it down as hard as I can into the demon's eye. I swallow the urge to retch as the stick pierces through the eye's membrane and goes all the way into— well, I guess demon brain. There's a horrid squelching sound but I can barely hear it over the demon's cries of pain.

'ARGHHHH!!!'

It writhes around, and blood starts to spurt from its eye. Damn. I quickly try to shield the head with my body. My clothes catch most of the blood – my best outfit is officially ruined – before it occurs to me to just rip my khaki shirt off and use it to plug the demon's eye socket. It works, and the blood stops spurting everywhere, but it's too late: a droplet of blood has already landed on the ground. I turn my head slowly to face K, knowing she's not going to be pleased.

She sighs. 'I'll deal with the new one. You just… make sure no more of this one's blood gets anywhere. It will disappear in a sec.'

I stare at the dying demon in front of me, wriggling and writhing madly on the tarp. I swear it's deliberately trying to spray its blood everywhere before it goes. But within seconds, it freezes. Finally, it's dead. In a minute or so, its body will vanish forever. Thank god. Or maybe I should say, thank Kali-ma.

'Hi-yaaaa!!!'

I jerk my head up to see that the new demon is here – and it's already getting karate chopped by K. She has some serious martial arts skills. I've never seen someone fight like she does. Okay, I've never actually seen anybody fight in real life before, but that's not the point. K has got *style*.

She looks at me over her shoulder as she kicks the demon hard. It yelps and I almost feel sorry for it. 'Has the first one gone yet?'

I look down. There's no trace of the demon. 'Yes! We're good!'

'Okay, get off the tarp!' she calls out, punching the demon in the stomach with her right fist. It doubles over in pain. She kicks it in the groin, and it crumples to the ground, howling. I can't stop staring at her; she's hypnotising. 'I need it. But be careful–'

'Of the blood, I know,' I finish. I quickly check myself for fresh blood. I'm clear. I step off the tarp, leaving my ruined shirt there. I've barely touched the ground when K is right there, squeezing the demon with her arms. She chucks it onto the tarp, then instantly starts rolling the plastic around it. Is she going to suffocate it to death? That's genius!

But once the demon is trussed up like a sausage roll, and all I can hear are muffled grunts, K picks it and hugs it tight. Like it's a long-lost relative she hasn't seen for years. Only it's good thing it's not actually her relative, because she hugs it so tight that there's a loud CRRRRRAACK, and I realise with horror that she's managed to break every single bone in the demon's body. It's safe to say this demon is officially no more.

She dumps the demon roll onto the ground, and wipes her brow with her leather sleeve, seemingly unaware of just how cool she looks right now. 'There,' she says, giving me one of her rare grins. 'Two down. Four thousand, nine hundred and ninety-eight to go.'

***

It isn't easy to concentrate on dinner. Not when I can't stop thinking about K. I still can't believe we get to hang out. And we're *really* hanging out. K's made a schedule for us – apparently it's a Virgo thing – where

63

we're going to meet every day after school in the park for training sessions. And on weekends.

'Kali?' My mum frowns at me. 'Radha asked you a question.'

'She did?'

Radha tuts. She's made an effort for my birthday dinner, wearing big gold hoops and a pink shirt paired with white jeans. Quelle surprise: she's more dressed up than me, the one we're meant to be celebrating. But I have at least showered and changed after the impromptu demon fight; I'm now in a plain black top and black jeans, inspired by K. My mum told me I looked 'funereal' when I walked downstairs which wasn't exactly the look I was going for. But it does feel appropriate after the amount of demon deaths I've seen lately.

'How was the archery competition?' asks Radha.

I resist the urge to make a face — why does she always ask the exact questions I don't want to answer? 'Uh… yeah, fun!'

'Who won?' asks my dad. 'One of your friends?'

'Uh huh,' I nod, grateful that the vagueness of his question means this is true. Although it would be more accurate to say 'classmates'.

'Nice,' says Radha. 'It's good you're making more friends.'

I grin as I think about my one new friend — and then I have another brainwave. Archery doesn't need to be a one-off excuse I can use with my parents; it can be long-term! It's exactly what I need to explain why I'm suddenly going from having absolutely zero plans to permanently hanging with K. I know I could just tell my parents I have a new friend called K — although they're going to freak when they see her piercings — but there's no way they'll let me hang out with her every single day when I 'should be studying instead.' But they *do* understand the importance of extracurriculars, especially in the run up to university applications.

So, I smile sweetly and tell them, 'I've actually decided to take up archery too. It means I'll be training after school every day. And most weekends.'

My mum chokes on the dahi wada she's eating. My dad's chunk of chilli paneer slides right off his fork onto his lap. Meanwhile Radha's glass of nimbu pani lands so heavily on the table that it splashes onto her plate.

'Is it really that surprising?' I ask, still inwardly thrilled at my quick thinking. This is the best lie ever; I can pretend to be doing archery every day and my parents will never know that I don't even know how to hold a bow!

'Um, it's just… you've never really shown an interest in sports, *beta*,' says my mum tactfully.

'Yeah, are you going to be any good?' asks Radha, less tactfully.

Judging by my new superpower, I actually might be. Not that I'd ever give it a go. School activities are not my thing – especially not ones that involve people like Joe and Rihanna. 'Maybe,' I say noncommittally. 'With practice.'

'Well done!' says my father proudly. 'Good on you for believing in yourself Kali. And for trying something new.'

My mum looks uncertain. 'Can't you try something less dangerous? What about netball?'

I hide a smirk. If Mum thinks archery is dangerous, what would she say about my *real* extracurricular?

'Yeah. We'll have to come and watch you compete,' says Radha. 'When's the next competition? I'll put it in my diary.'

My eyes widen. 'What?! You don't have to come! It'll be boring. I mean, you'd hate it.'

'No, Radha's right,' says my dad authoritatively. 'We need to support you! It's not every day you take up a new hobby.'

What am I going to do?! I can't actually do archery –

it's what the popular people do. Imagine if Doomsday turns up, with her bow and arrow? No thanks. I'll never live down the humiliation.

But then I think of K with her martial arts skills. She would be *so* impressed if I pulled out a bow and arrow to kill demons from miles off. And I like the idea of K looking at me with the same awe I felt when she was killing demons. Not to mention how good it will feel to impress Joe if I get endless bullseyes.

Maybe… just maybe… this could be the one school activity I actually excel in. But I'll never know unless I try.

I take a deep breath, then lift my chin decisively. 'When I'm ready to compete, I'll let you all know. I'm signing up on Monday.'

Chapter 9

It turns out archery is hard. Like, *really* hard. I am not scoring endless bullseyes or 'golds' as the teacher, Phil, calls them. I'm not even hitting the target board. Because, as it turns out, even my superpower can't help me if I can't actually get the arrow to launch off the bow in a straight line. After half an hour of trying, I'm no closer.

'Kali, you're still pinging your fingers,' says Phil in exasperation. We're allowed to call him Phil because he's not a proper teacher; he just comes in at lunch to lead archery club. 'I told you to gently let go of the string. Don't ping it.'

I sigh in frustration and try again. I hold the bow up in my right hand, using my left-hand to slide the arrow into place (the fact that I'm left-handed is also against me; Phil paled when I told him because it makes it harder for him to teach me. And he hardly has any decent left-handed equipment, which is why I'm using a finger tab that smells like feet). I lift the bow with my right arm, keeping it straight, and then get my left arm ready to launch the arrow, pulling my elbow back and lining up my fingers with my jaw. Just like Phil taught me.

Before I even manage to release the arrow, he's shaking his head at me. 'Lower the right shoulder. Lift the left elbow. Higher Kali! And then, pull back, and *gently* let go. Don't p–'

It's too late. I must have pinged. Because the arrow flies off high into the air, before landing on the floor, a couple of metres from the target.

I hear a sympathetic cluck behind me. Rihanna. 'I'm sorry,' she says, in the tone you normally use when someone's died. I didn't realise how seriously everyone here takes archery – I thought we'd laugh when we messed up, but nope. It turns out that the only appropriate reaction when someone repeatedly misses the target is to express your condolences. 'You'll get better. Hopefully.'

And then Joe scores a perfect gold, his muscles rippling as he lifts his bow up in the air in celebration. I sigh involuntarily; he's hot *and* talented.

'Nice Joe!' says Phil approvingly. 'See Kali? That's how

you do it.'

I nod glumly. Any hopes I had of impressing Joe with my superpower are officially crushed.

'You'll get there, Doomsday,' says Joe. I get shivers in my spine as his hazel eyes look into mine. 'I only got one gold the first time. Now I get a minimum of six every session!'

That is an unhelpful comment – I haven't even managed to hit the board yet, let alone 'only' get one gold. But then Joe winks at me and my lower body practically melts with desire. I give him what I hope is a confident, sexy smile, though I still can't bring myself to reply to him with words. I'm too scared I'll say something stupid.

'Right, that's it for today,' says Phil. 'Keep it up. Lunchtime practice is on all week. Beginners' sessions are on the schedule in the hallway. And remember, the nationals are on in two months.'

'Just after the Summer Dance!' says Hayley. I turn with a start. I swear she wasn't in the gym hall a second ago. She smiles sweetly at Joe and slides underneath his arm, so he's holding her tight. I feel my heart plummet as I realise, they're back together. Of course they are. Hayley's perfect for Joe, with her long blonde hair, high cheekbones, and triumphant smile. How could I have ever thought I had a chance?

It's a good thing that today has proven I should never do archery again. Even with a superpower, I'm not cut out for this. I'll have to make up something else for my parents – nothing is worth this level of social humiliation. And at least now I don't need to watch Hayley being a perfect girlfriend, supporting Joe at every practice session.

'Kali,' says Phil. 'You need extra practice. So, I expect to see you at all the lunchtime sessions, okay?'

I flush as everyone turns to look at me. I didn't think I'd have to quit *publicly* – my plan was to not say anything and never come back. 'Um, I just… I'm not sure…'

Rihanna raises an eyebrow. 'You're giving up *already*?'

'Doomsday's not quitting, are you?' says Joe.

I remember the wink he gave me moments earlier, and my throat catches. I know it's ridiculous because he's clearly with Hayley, but I can't resist Joe. And he wants me to stay. So, somehow, I find myself smiling brightly and actually speaking. 'Course not! See you all tomorrow!'

'Sick, Doomsday!' says Joe. 'Channel your namesake!'

My smile fades. If only he knew.

My heart quickens as I get to the park where I agreed to meet K. I'm nervous — her realising how unfit I am will probably be even more humiliating than archery was — but I'm also excited. She's the most interesting person I've ever met, and I want to know more about her. And somehow, she wants to know more about me too! Or at least, she wants to know more about my period. She's been texting me all day, asking questions about my cycle, and enquiring whether any demons have found me yet. They haven't. My personal theory is that it's hard for them to find me at school when I'm surrounded by so many hormones and periods, but I haven't mentioned it to K in case it's laughably wrong.

She's added me to the Kali WhatsApp group, but I haven't done much more than just say hi to everyone and heart all the 'Welcome Kali!!' messages. Well, and stalk the other Kalis. I clicked on all their profile pictures to try and get an idea of who they are, and I even googled some of them. I don't know what I was expecting, but they all seem so… normal. Tech Kali went to Harvard! And Model Kali is the one whose Insta I'd seen when I was looking for K! She's more famous than I realised at the time – I can't fully believe she's a Kali like us. While Dottoressa Kali is married to a gorgeous woman called Lucia and has *children*. I'm relieved they're not some kind of crazy cult; they're just unlucky enough to be named Kali.

'Kali!' K jumps out of a bush, and I practically have a heart attack.

'Oh my god, you terrified me!' I breathe deeply to calm my nerves.

'You need to learn to react quickly when something jumps out at you,' she says seriously. 'Not freak out.'

'The training's already started? We haven't even said hi.'

'Oh. Hi?'

I sigh. 'Hi. I'll put my stuff down and we can start.'

'We can chat first if you want?' She bites her lip and looks nervous. I notice she's wearing shorts and a black vest top today, under her signature black leather jacket. Her legs are just as muscly as her arms – no wonder she can dropkick a demon in two seconds flat. 'Sorry, I've never trained with someone else before. I'm used to doing it all on my own.'

Something melts inside of me. 'It must've been so hard for you when it all first started. I can't imagine doing this without you.'

Her jaw tightens. 'Yeah, not everyone could understand.' I'm about to ask more, but she moves on. 'I figured it out quickly though. I already knew all about the story of Kali-ma and Raktabija. I've been obsessed with Kali for years; I had her posters on my wall.'

'You did?! But she's so weird and ugly.'

K's eyes flash with anger. 'This is the goddess we're named after. The most powerful goddess out there! How can you call her weird and ugly?'

'Uh... because she's the goddess of death and doomsday. That's a lot. And you can't deny she is a bit scary looking. With her bloody tongue. And bulging three eyes. Besides,' I add, 'you're the one who changed your name.'

'I chose to go by K when I was five years old and all the white teachers kept calling me 'Callie' instead of pronouncing it properly: 'Khaa-lee',' she says, her eyes flashing. 'Even the ones that managed to say it right would spell it as 'Karly.'' She shakes her head, then looks right at me. 'I worship Kali. She's the strongest goddess there is. And who cares what she looks like? So, she doesn't have the fair skin and basic beauty of someone like the goddess Radha; those are dumb societal beauty standards anyway. Why can't three eyes and a big tongue be seen as beautiful?'

I'm taken aback. I've never thought of societal beauty standards applying to gods before. 'I guess you're right… Especially on the Radha thing. My cousin is named after her, and she's *super* basic. All she ever talks about is her wedding, which is going to be some huge traditional Indian thing even though she's not religious.'

'I respect that,' says K, totally surprising me. 'I'm proud of our culture, heritage and all our traditions.' She pulls her leather jacket off to reveal her arms. Beautiful henna tattoos circle all around her wrists and forearms.

'Wow!' I lean towards them, mesmerized by the intricate patterns. 'Are those real tattoos? Or just henna?'

'They're real, not mehndi.'

'That's so cool,' I blurt out, unable to help myself. 'You're so lucky your parents let you do that. My mum would have a nervous breakdown if I got a tattoo. She'd never let me in the house again.'

A flash of something unreadable appears on K's face. 'I don't have a dad. But yeah, my mum is… chill. She came with me to get them done. Anyway, are we going to train or what? I've brought dumbbells so you can build up your muscle strength.' She pulls out two massive weights from her bag.

'You've been carrying those around with you all day?!'

She raises an eyebrow at me. 'Super strength, remember? They weigh nothing to me. You need to find a way to use your power too, Kali.'

'I have!' I say proudly. 'I did my first ever archery class today.'

Her eyes light up. 'Great! How did it go?'

The smile drops off my face. 'Um… it's a process. I'll get there. The teacher believes in me. I hope?'

Her brow furrows in confusion. 'How can it be a process when you literally have super aim?'

'The technique is pretty complicated.'

Her face suggests she wouldn't find it so complicated. And she probably wouldn't. But hand-eye coordination has never been my thing.

'Okay, well, I guess keep it up,' she says eventually, before dropping her gaze. 'Also, um, I'm sorry to say this. But I've been thinking that until you develop your power, perhaps you should just assist me when it comes to the demon-hunting. So, I'll kill the demons and you do the clean-up. Sorting out the tarp and so on.'

I nod happily. 'Sounds good to me!'

She meets my gaze, shocked. 'You're sure? You're okay with not doing the actual killing?'

'I'll be fine,' I assure her. 'And if I'm honest, I think I prefer the sound of demon-cleaner-upper rather than demon-slayer. It feels more… accessible.'

She shakes her head. 'We really are different. But it's okay. I know you have a demon-slayer inside you somewhere.'

'I'm not so sure ab–' I'm interrupted by a demon launching itself straight at my face.

Chapter 10

The demon's claw scratches against my cheek, but before it can dig deep, K beats it down to the ground with a single blow of her fist. She shouts 'tarp!' as she starts trussing with the demon, but I don't need to be told. I'm already scrambling in her backpack, pulling it out. I've barely spread it out onto the ground when K tumbles onto the tarp with her arms wrapped around the demon. She looks furious, as she squeezes it tight, punching and kicking.

'Um, should I get off?' I ask.

'Yes!'

I scramble off and watch in awe as K wraps her hand around the demon's throat. I don't understand what she's doing until she starts tightening her grip. She's strangling it! The demon is gasping for air, but K is relentless. She squeezes tighter and tighter as the demon chokes, its body thrashing around. But K keeps going. It's like something out of a horror movie.

Until its body finally falls limp.

'Oh my god,' I manage. 'That was… hardcore.'

She stands up, shrugging foliage off her. 'I've got a few ways of killing them. I like to mix it up. And strangling is pretty good in terms of blood management. Although they can sometimes shed a few drops in the fight.'

'Right,' I say. My fingers unconsciously touch the side of my face and I wince. The demon scratched it.

'Blood!' K freezes at the sight. 'Be careful!'

'Don't worry, it's just mine.'

Her face relaxes for a split second, then it sets in fury. 'I can't believe it hurt you. These demons! They're…'

'The actual worst?'

She lets out a rare bark of laughter. Her laugh is unexpectedly deep, but it suits her. 'Yeah. The actual worst.'

Just then the demon disappears into thin air. We both grin triumphantly at each other and high-five. This whole demon-killing thing really is giving me a positive sense of achievement. Even more than I get from Minecraft.

'I'll fold the tarp up again,' I offer. 'As the official demon-cleaner-upper.'

'I'll help. Take a break from demon-slaying duties.'

We work in silence, wiping down any blood with the wipes from her bag and folding up the tarp, before disposing of the wipes in a refuse bag that she also carries around with her. I guess I'm going to have to get my own backpack full of cleaning supplies – but I draw the line at dumbbells. I'm not the one with super strength.

'It's nice having someone to do this with,' says K, as we collapse after our clean-up.

'A hundred per cent,' I agree. 'I'd die doing this alone. Literally.'

'You'll get the hang of it. It just takes time.'

'We'll see,' I say doubtfully. I lean back against the tree trunk and look at K, hesitating. 'You know earlier, you said not everyone understood about all this. Who do you mean? Did you... tell people about it?'

K closes her eyes briefly as she joins me in leaning back against the tree. 'Once. But not people. Person.'

'Who?'

'Lola,' says K briefly. 'My girlfriend at the time. And, well... she couldn't handle it. Especially when... anyway. Yeah. We broke up.' She crosses her arms and looks away from me.

'I'm sorry,' I say, even though there's so much more

I want to ask. I didn't know K dated girls. Does she date boys too? Can I ask her how she identifies? But all these questions are faded by one overriding thought – K's already had a girlfriend. A proper *relationship*. I haven't even had my first kiss.

'That must've been… hard,' I venture. I've never done relationship chat with anyone before. Tanya once kissed a boy at her cousin's christening, but they never spoke again afterwards. I don't know *anything* about relationships, let alone break-ups.

'It was.'

'Had you… been together long?'

'A year.'

'That's ages!'

K shifts uncomfortably and I'm sensitive enough to realise she's still not over it. I decide to be brave and share something too – it's only fair after she has. And, at the very least, it might distract her from her sadness. 'I've… never dated anyone at all.'

'It's better that way,' says K glumly. 'No pain.'

'Yes, but my crush barely knows I exist! Actually, that's not true. He does. He calls me Doomsday.'

K is silent, then, 'That's a cool nickname. He must like you.'

I can't help but laugh. 'Only you would think calling someone Doomsday is a compliment – I hate it. And he doesn't like me. He likes Hayley. Blonde, popular Hayley.'

'Well then, he's an idiot,' says K, crossing her arms and standing up. 'Come on. Time for training.'

'Wait – we just killed a demon! Doesn't that count?'

'No. Come on, grab the dumbbells. I want 50 reps for each bicep.' She looks at my face and relents. 'Okay, we can start with 20. Let's go!'

***

I was hoping to slip into the house unnoticed, but my mum and Radha are standing in the hallway, blocking my way to my room. I thought doctors were meant to work long hours, but evidently not, because Radha is always here.

'How was school *beta*?' asks my mum. 'What's that?! You're hurt!'

I forgot about the demon scratch on my cheek. I glance at my reflection in the mirror and I'm relieved to see it hasn't gone green or anything; I just have two long claw marks on the side of my face.

'Did someone attack you?!' asks Radha. 'With their nails?'

'Um… it was… archery?' This hobby is really turning out to be the excuse that keeps on giving.

'I knew this sport would be dangerous!' cries my mum. 'I told you to be careful!'

'How did *that* happen at archery?' asks Radha.

I want to snap at her, but then I remember K's comment about the goddess Radha being basic and instead, I swallow a smirk. 'Just, you know, sharp arrows. My bad. Anyway, what's for dinner?'

'Pav bhaji,' replies my mum. 'I've left the ketchup and cheese out so you can turn them into English-style burgers.'

'You're the best, thanks Mum!'

'So how was archery?' asks Radha, following me into the kitchen. 'Apart from the war wounds.'

'Uh, fine! I mean, I'm not amazing. Yet. But I'll get there with practise.' I'm hoping the more I say this, the more it will come true.

'Yes, but don't neglect your schoolwork,' warns my mum, heating up the vegetable filling for my Indian burger. 'Grades have to come before hobbies.'

'I know, I know.'

'I think it's cool you have a hobby though,' says Radha. 'Have you made any friends yet?'

'I have, actually,' I say, pleased to be finally telling the truth. 'One in particular. She's really cool.'

'Oh, thank god!' My mum clasps her hands into a prayer position. I look at her, wounded, and she has the decency to blush. 'I just want you to have some friends, *beta*. It's not normal to spend all this time alone with your video games.'

I actually haven't played a single game since before my birthday. Seeing as my life has essentially turned into a video game since I got my period, there hasn't been much need.

'Sooo, who is this new cool friend?' asks Radha. 'And what is it that makes her so cool?'

I can't help but to smile as I think of K strangling the demon earlier today. But I can't share that. So instead, I tell them the other stuff. 'She's... kind of intense. And quite serious. She reminds me a bit of Tanya, in the way she talks, and because she's so direct. But the things she talks about are totally different. She's so *interesting*. And she makes me laugh without even realising she's doing it. I like the way she looks too. As in, her look. She has great style.'

'Serious is good,' nods my mum approvingly. Obviously, that's the one bit she picks up on. 'She's in your class?'

'Same year, but she goes to the private school in town. We met through archery.' Honestly, best excuse *ever*.

'She sounds cool,' says Radha, and I nod in agreement, pleased. 'I think she'll be good for you.' Ugh, and now she's ruined it by being patronising.

'What's her name?' asks my mum. 'Is she white? Or—'

'She's Indian,' I say, and my mum's face lights up with incandescent joy. She's never seen me have a single brown friend before, though, in my defence, that is because my school is 99% white. 'She's called K.'

'Oh Kali! I'm so happy for you,' says my mum in delight. 'Though it is unusual she's called Kay.'

'It's just the letter K. It's a nickname.' For some reason, I don't want them to know it's short for Kali.

My mum looks disconcerted but decides to let this slide. 'Well, you'll have to bring her round for dinner next week. I'll make bhel! And matar paneer.'

'I'll come too!' says Radha, clearly immune to the 'PLEASE STOP TALKING' energy I'm giving off. 'I can help save you if your mum and dad ask too many awkward questions.'

'It's too soon,' I protest, my mind flashing with worst-case scenarios of my mum criticising K's tattoos,

85

Radha giving her a lecture on the medical dangers of piercings, and my dad freaking her out with his relentless optimism and hugs. 'Let's wait 'til I know her better.'

'Nonsense,' says my mum briskly. 'If you're going to spend this much time with a new friend, we need to meet her. Next week.'

Chapter 11

I'm hovering by my desk, deliberately taking ages to pack up, so I can speak to Mrs Patel alone. I've wanted to ever since I worked out that she knew something about the demons, but Mrs Patel has been off sick the last few days. Only now she's finally back.

'Doomsday – you coming to archery at lunch?'

It's Joe. My eyes light up, then fade when I see Hayley standing right behind him, glaring.

'Um, yes,' I manage.

'Hey, what happened to your face?' he asks, looking at my scratches. 'Did you get in a fight?'

'Uh… it's complicated.'

Hayley sneers, and pulls Joe away, whispering in his ear. He laughs loudly and I feel stupid. I know she's said something mean about me. Classic Hayley – to say it behind my back, but not even acknowledge me to my face. I like to think it's not personal and that she'd do the same to any girl Joe speaks to, but it still hurts.

I look around and realise the room is empty, other than Mrs Patel who is gathering up the handouts people left behind. We did Buddha today – a much more peaceful lesson than the Kali one. Mrs Patel sees me standing there, and I swear she deliberately speeds up her tidying.

'Hey Mrs Patel.'

'Oh, hi Kali. It's nice to see you getting involved in some extracurriculars. I heard Joe mentioning archery.'

'Yeah, new hobby.'

I walk up closer to her desk, and she smiles nervously at me.

'I'd better rush off – essays to mark!'

'Can I quickly ask, you know you told me to meet other Kalis? How did you know that would be helpful?'

'I thought it would be good for you to meet other people going through the same things as you,' she says carefully. 'Similar experiences and all.'

'Okay, but how did you know what those experiences *were*? And that they were so 'unusual'?'

Mrs Patel looks at me with a pained expression as she slings her tote bag over her shoulder. 'Kali, I'm sorry, I can't help you anymore. Please, let's not talk about this again.'

I stare at her in confusion. 'But—'

'Did you find another Kali?' she interrupts.

I nod. 'Yes, but—'

Her face clears with relief. 'Perfect! Then she can help more than I can. Good luck.'

With that, Mrs Patel walks out of the classroom, leaving me *seriously* lost. I don't know how much she knows, but she definitely knows something. And for some reason, she doesn't want me to know what.

***

'Bad luck, Doomsday,' says Joe sympathetically, while Rihanna tuts in disappointment. My arrow *keeps* failing to go anywhere near the target. This time it hit the curtain at the back. The previous four times, it didn't even reach the curtain.

'You need to practise your technique,' says Phil, wiping his forehead in exasperation. 'Did you buy the stretchy band I recommended?'

I shake my head. I'm so busy training with K every night, let alone trying to do my homework and not fail school, that it slipped my mind to buy a yoga band to practise my technique. Besides, it's not like it could help. I'm clearly terrible at this. Like I am with most things. I should have known that even a superpower wouldn't be able to improve my sports skills.

Phil looks at me like I've told him I kill demons in my spare time. 'Kali. You need to practise. Or you'll never improve.'

'I've got a spare band you can use,' offers Rihanna. 'I don't need it anymore.' She rummages around in her bag and pulls out a hot pink stretchy band. 'Here.'

'Uh, thanks Rihanna. That's really nice of you.'

She shrugs. 'I get loads of golds. As I said, I don't need it.'

I start doing the exercises Phil taught me before. I'm relieved K isn't here to see me demoted from bow and arrow to resistance band.

'You've got to lift your elbow higher,' says Joe, coming up behind me. He gently lifts up my left elbow, and my heart starts thumping in excitement so loudly I'm worried he'll hear it. Because he's touching me. He's actually *touching* me! The hottest boy in Year 11 has his hand on my arm. I can smell him. He smells of… Head & Shoulders. Mixed with the minty scent of chewing gum. It's the most beautiful thing I've ever smelled. I turn my head to smile at him with gratitude, but instead I choke.

Hayley.

She's standing behind us and the expression on her face is so terrifying that I lose control of the band and it pings out of my hand, launching in the direction of my gaze. Right at Hayley.

She splutters as it narrowly misses her face. If she already looked pissed off, I don't even know how to describe the way she looks now.

'I'm so sorry,' I cry out. 'Really sorry. I'm... not so great at this.'

'You don't say,' she replies coolly. 'No wonder Phil doesn't trust you with an actual bow and arrow. You'd end up in juvie for manslaughter.' She smiles satisfied as I flush, then turns to Joe. 'Babe – I got you bao buns for lunch. Let's go.'

Joe looks at me apologetically. 'Sorry, uh, maybe–'

But Hayley cuts him off. 'Joe! You don't want cold bao, do you? Come on!'

★★★

I collapse panting onto the ground. K's training regime is killing me. But I can feel it's working – today I could do 20 reps without pausing, and I even managed to do

91

a few reps with the 10kg weight. That was categorically *not* an option when we first started out.

'So, you're in the second week of your cycle now?' K asks.

I look up. She's standing over me, her petite but strong body firmly blocking the sun. 'Nobody has ever been this interested in my body before. Not even Dr Gupta.'

She rolls her eyes impatiently. 'Okay, but what does the app say?'

'That I'm no longer bleeding, and soon I'll be ovulating.'

She nods, processing. 'Okay, good. We're only a couple of days out of sync. We should line up by our next periods. I'd normally suggest we use our upcoming ovulation to hunt demons, but I think we should maybe focus on training for now.'

I squint up at her. I'm covered in sweat, even though we've only been here for 45 minutes, but she looks like she's just gone for a casual stroll. Even her hair is falling perfectly over her smooth forehead. 'Yes *please*. Training over demon-slaying anytime.'

She offers me a hand and pulls me up to my feet before I even try to use my own muscles. I keep forgetting how strong she is.

'Thanks. Oh also, there was something I wanted to ask you.'

'Something else about Mrs Patel? I've asked Tech Kali to look into her. See if there's anything to be worried about. But it sounds to me like it's just a coincidence.'

'Maybe,' I say, even though I'm convinced Mrs Patel knows much more than she's letting on. 'But I actually wanted to ask you something else...' I take a deep breath, before the words gush out of my mouth way too fast. 'My mum wants you to come round for dinner next week. I know you probably have better things to do, which is totally fine. This would be seriously boring. You'd have to meet my annoying cousin Radha, my dad would ask you loads of questions about your favourite subjects at school, and mum would overfeed you. But she is a good cook. And we could aways eat quickly and then just go to my room afterwards to hang. I mean, if you want. You don't have to say yes.' I finish my speech and look at K nervously. But she doesn't look embarrassed by how uncool this invitation is. She looks... excited?!

'Great!' she says happily. 'I'd love to come. Thanks so much.'

'Great?' I repeat. 'You know this is a family dinner.'

'It sounds nice. Should I bring something? Like, a present?'

'You're 16. Nobody expects gifts. Just… compliment the food and my mum will love you.'

She nods seriously. 'Anything else? Is there a dress code?'

I laugh. 'No, it's only at home.' Then I pause. 'But if you wear a short-sleeved top, my mum will probably give you a lecture on your tattoos. So, apologies in advance.'

'Okay! I can't wait.'

The weirdest thing of all is, she looks like she actually *means* it.

Chapter 12

I gaze intently at my reflection in the mirror. I need to raise my left elbow a bit more, lower my left hand and *gently* let go, rather than ping. I relax my fingers – and the stretchy band pings right into my reflection's face.

I sigh and pick the band up, ready to try again. I can't remember the last time I put so much effort into practising something, but with archery, I *want* to do well. I want to prove I can do this. I'm not sure exactly who I'm proving it to; Joe, Rihanna, K, my parents, Radha? Probably all of them. But I think it's also about doing it for myself.

I've never really been good at anything before. I'm terrible at sports. I shrivel up with nerves if I ever have to get on a stage, so drama and performing are out. I can't sing. I don't have any rhythm, so my musical talents are non-existent. I can't draw. And I'm not even that smart, which is awkward because I'm Asian and I like video games, so everyone expects me to be a Maths genius.

But if I *do* manage to get some kind of proficiency in archery, then it's proof I am capable of having a skill, and I might even discover more as I get older. I can already imagine my mum's reaction: 'Where's archery going to get you?! That's not a career! Better to focus on your studies.' But it's different for her. She's always busy doing things with the Indian community, and our extended family. Fitting in is effortless for her, but it's not for me.

I've never felt like I have much in common with my cousins even though we're similar ages. Sometimes I think it's because they all go to similar schools, filled with loads of Indian people like them, while my parents sent me to South Bridge – the whitest school in the county. But deep down, I worry it's more than that. I don't feel that similar to my cousins. I don't laugh at the same jokes as them, I don't care about my nails, and I've hardly watched any of the Bollywood movies they're obsessed with.

I don't fit in at school either – I'm the outsider there too. I might like the same TV shows and games as people there, but I stand out in other ways. I'll never forget Hayley making fun of my black leg hair in PE before I learnt to shave my legs, or Jack howling with laughter when I pronounced 'pigeon' the way it was spelled. I didn't know you said it as 'pidgun' because my parents said it the wrong way too – they only came to England as teenagers, so they still have Indian accents and pronounce things differently.

It means I'm always having to hide parts of myself. With my cousins, I try to be more like them. And at school, I try to be less brown – monitoring the way I speak, the food I eat, and what I share about my life, editing out anything Indian like Diwali. It's the only way to get through life without feeling like a freak. I've always wished I had a place where I belong, just the way I am, but I've never found one. And I don't know if I ever will.

'Kali!' The door flies open, and my mum is standing right there. 'Come downstairs, your friend's here.'

'Oh my god, K's here already?!' I drop the yoga band and quickly double-check my reflection, this time focusing on my appearance. Jeans, strappy top and a flannel shirt from my dad's wardrobe to replace the khaki one that died along with the last demon.

'I don't know why you have to wear your father's clothes,' sighs my mum. She's wearing a floral blouse with white trousers, clearly chosen by Radha.

'It's so masculine.'

'It's called fashion,' I retort, even though I'm not fully sure this is true. Everything I know about fashion, I learn from whatever Hayley and Rihanna are wearing. And the occasional reel Tanya sends my way.

My mum raises an eyebrow in evident disagreement, but she has the grace to stay silent. I release my ponytail, so my long hair falls down in loose waves. 'Better,' says my mum approvingly, which makes me want to scrunch it all back up again. 'Hurry up, I want to meet your friend.'

'You haven't met her yet?!'

'I was upstairs when the doorbell rang. Your dad answered it.'

Oh no. I race out of my room, thundering down the stairs, so I can rescue K – serious, earnest K – from my overly enthusiastic dad. He's probably tried to hug her, and K definitely looks like the kind of person who has spatial boundaries.

'I've told you not to run like that!' calls out my mum. 'You sound like an elephant.'

I get to the hallway, breathless. K is standing there alone, wearing a black shiny top with black trousers and her leather jacket. She's holding a bunch of flowers, and she looks… nervous.

'Hey,' I smile. It's sweet to see her fidgeting nervously with the bouquet. I've never seen her look anything less than totally confident – even when our lives were in serious danger.

'Hey back,' she says, waving the flowers. 'I brought these for your mum.'

'She's going to love you. Where's my dad? Was he, um, okay?'

K's face breaks into an open smile. 'He's so great. He's gone to make us… mockitos?'

I sigh. 'Alcohol-free mojitos. They're his speciality. It'll take him 20 minutes to make them – even though they're basically lemonade with fresh mint leaves.'

K laughs, her face relaxed, open and pretty. That's when my mum appears. I feel a burst of pride as I introduce her to my mum. 'Mum, this is K. K, this is–'

'You must be Sunita Auntie,' says K, handing her the tulips. 'These are for you.'

My mum looks like she's about to cry with delight. 'Oh! They're beautiful! And you called me auntie!'

K looks worried. 'Is that not okay?'

'It's perfect!' assures my mum. 'Here, let me take your jacket.' She shoots me an admonishing look. 'Kali, you need to learn to be a better hostess. Have you even offered K a drink?'

'Dad's on the mockitos.'

K takes off her jacket and I realise her top is short-sleeved. I close my eyes tightly, hoping my mum isn't judgy.

But to my total surprise, my mum's face lights up. 'Is that mehndi?! How beautiful! I've never seen such an intricate design before.'

K nods. 'Thank you. It's… permanent.'

'Permanent?!' Now my mum's face looks more like I expected it too. But after a pause, where I hold my breath, she nods decisively. 'I think it's beautiful you're celebrating your culture and heritage. Kali, you could learn a lot from K.'

'Does that mean I can get a tattoo too?' I ask, even though I'm not sure I'd ever be brave enough.

'Of course not,' snaps my mum, and I secretly feel relief. 'Now, come on K.' She ushers her towards the dining table at the back of the living room. 'I've made a selection of starters and matar paneer and dhal for our mains. I hope you like some of those dishes?'

'They are all my absolute favourites,' declares K, officially winning my mum over for life.

***

'That was delicious, thank you Sunita Auntie,' says K, finishing her third plate of paneer.

'It's amazing you can eat so much and still keep your figure,' remarks Radha. I glare at her – doesn't she know it's not okay to comment on people's bodies? She blinks at me in confusion, and I decide to let it go; it's not worth drawing more attention to her comment. Especially when K doesn't seem to have noticed.

'You're welcome, *beta*,' beams my mum. 'We're so happy Kali has made a friend.'

'Mum!!'

'I mean, an Indian friend,' amends my mum. 'There aren't many Indian girls in her year at her school.'

'There *are* no Indian girls in my year at my school,' I correct. 'Only me.'

'It's the opposite in my school,' says K. 'It's Indian central. But there's nobody there I have as much in common with as Kali.'

We share a secret grin.

'Like archery!' says my dad. 'I can't wait to see Kali compete. Will you be competing as well, K?'

'Uh… no,' says K. I've already filled her in on 'how

101

we met'. 'I'm actually more into martial arts and I don't have enough time for both.'

'What kind?' asks my dad. 'I love martial arts movies!'

'I do a bit of everything. Jiu-jitsu. Tae Kwon Do. But also kick-boxing.'

'And your family don't mind you doing such dangerous sports?' asks my mum.

I cringe at her question, but K smiles. 'No, my mum doesn't mind. And it's only us two. My dad left when we were young. My parents were never married.'

'Oh, your poor mum!' My mum's face falls in sympathy. 'That must be so hard for her to do it all alone.'

'Yeah, hard for *her*,' says K in a weird voice. She shakes her head. 'I mean, yes. But she's had boyfriends. She's got one now. And she loves her job – she works in events and she's always busy, at some new party or whatever.'

'Ohmygod, maybe she can give me advice on my wedding!' says Radha eagerly. 'I'd love to speak to somebody who actually works in events.'

'Sure,' says K neutrally. 'She knows everyone, and she loves helping – when it comes to parties.'

'Amazing!!' Radha looks overjoyed. 'Does she have Instagram?'

K takes Radha's phone and types in her mum's name. 'She has a lot of followers, but you can say you know me.'

Radha's eyes practically pop out of her head when she looks at her phone. 'Your mum is DEEPA PADWANI?! She's the most in-demand event planner ever! Oh my god. I can't message her. She's too important. Or can I? Shall I?!'

K shrugs. 'She won't mind. Especially if you're a fan.' I get the feeling Radha's reaction is not unusual for her.

My mum puts her glasses on to peer at Radha's phone, oohing and aahing at the glamour of K's mum's Insta. My dad takes advantage of the temporary break to turn to K. 'So, what belt have you got to with your martial arts?'

'Triple black.'

My dad's mouth drops open. 'No! Kali did you hear that?! Your friend is a martial arts EXPERT!'

K winks at me. 'I'm actually trying to teach Kali the basics. I was thinking we could spend the next few weekends doing it – would you mind that Sanjeev Uncle? Maybe one weekend she could stay over at mine?'

A warmth spreads over me; I haven't had a sleepover since Tanya left. And I'd get to see K's house. Her room. Meet her insanely cool mum. Then the warmth turns cold. What if K realises how uncool *I* am?!

My dad fizzes with excitement at the thought of his daughter learning martial arts. 'Oh, that would be wonderful! Wouldn't it Kali? Imagine, my daughter, a black belt!' K grins at me, and I suddenly relax. This isn't a normal friendship; we're both Kalis. Our connection goes way beyond coolness.

'Sounds like you'll be pretty busy, Kali,' remarks Radha, looking at me over the top of her phone. 'What with archery *and* martial arts. Things are changing quite a lot for you, aren't they?'

'Tell me about it…'

***

K gazes around my room, and I'm abruptly embarrassed by it all. The video games, the Ms Marvel poster, the piles of fantasy fiction next to my bed – seeing it through K's eyes, it all looks so juvenile.

But she turns to me with a wide smile. 'I like your room. It's very you.'

'Oh, thanks.' I leap onto my bed and quickly hide my stuffed frog behind the pillow. 'What's yours like?'

'You'll see it soon.' She sits down next to me, and

I shuffle up to make space. 'When you come over for our–'

'Training weekend?' I offer.

She nods. 'We'll need to work fast. Did you see the WhatsApp chat?'

'Yes, but I didn't fully get it?' There were a lot of military abbreviations, and I gave up trying to Google them all.

'Tech Kali has intel that there are a bunch of demons right here in the UK. And she thinks they are only an hour away from us.'

I swallow nervously. 'How does she know?'

'It's some kind of new software she's developing with heat-tech and satellites. The demons have a way higher body temperature than we do, so they show up as extra bright on heat-tech. Or something like that. The point is she can find them, which means, we can kill them!'

'You don't have to sound so happy about it.'

'You don't have to sound so miserable about it. This is basically our purpose on earth. To slay demons.'

I sigh loudly, lifting my pillow to my face and groaning into it. 'Can't I just go back to when my only purpose was trying to get through school without anybody noticing me?' I put the pillow down quickly, covering up Froggy.

K raises an eyebrow, but she's generous enough to not bring up the Frogster (he has many nicknames, all deviating from his original name: Frog). 'Demon slaying sounds like a way better purpose than trying not to be noticed.'

'Not for someone who can't slay demons...'

'Hey, you have a superpower! You've got this.'

There's a long silence, then finally, I confess. 'Archery still isn't going well. I can't even hit the *target*, let alone the gold. The superpower can't help unless I get the technique right. And I'm struggling.'

'Maybe I can help you?'

'I'm beyond help.'

'Isn't that a bit dramatic? It's just learning how to use a bow and arrow.'

'I know what to do. It's more that I can't *let go*. Apparently, that isn't something that can be taught.'

K frowns. 'Show me.'

Reluctantly, I get up, reaching for my stretchy band. K may as well see how terrible I am, so she'll stop suggesting we go hunt demons.

'Okay, so this is the technique. My arms are in the

exact right place. I mean, they could be a bit stronger, but I feel like the weights are helping with that.'

'And the letting go bit?'

I turn to face K, with my left fingers grazing my face. 'I just need to *gently* let go and release my fingers. But I keep controlling it too much and then it pings, and the arrow does *not* do what it's meant to.'

K nods thoughtfully. 'The key to letting go is acceptance.'

'You do know this is archery not therapy?'

K tuts impatiently. 'It's all the same thing. If you can learn to let go emotionally, you can definitely do it physically. It's like, okay, when Lola broke up with me.' She holds up a hand to silence me before I can ask even one of the hundred questions racing through my mind. 'I'm not going into more detail than that. But the point is… I didn't want to let go. I wanted to cling onto the reality where she still loved me and wanted to be with me.'

'How did you do it?' I ask tentatively. 'Let go?'

'It took a while,' she admits. 'Mainly because I was distracted by demons trying to kill me every time I got my period.'

'Knowing you're about to be attacked by demons must add a whole new layer to PMS.'

107

'That'll be us next week, according to the app.' My eyes widen, but K keeps going. 'Anyway, after a while, I realised that grasping onto the idea of her still loving me was more painful than it would be to let go. So, every time I experienced a thought like that, I just breathed. Really deeply. And with every exhale, I let go. Sometimes I'd even say, 'I accept Lola isn't for me.''

'You did affirmations and yogic breathing? That's so… TikTok of you.'

K shoots me a look. 'They've gone mainstream for a reason, and the reason is they work. Come on.' She stands up and puts the band back into my hands. 'Do the pose again.'

Reluctantly, I obey. When I'm 'ready to shoot', she comes up behind me. I can feel her breath tickling the small of my neck. I shiver as she gently puts her hand on top of mine and instructs me to breathe. 'Gently. Deeply. And now say, 'I let this arrow go.''

Her face is so close to mine I can't focus. It's distracting.

'Just say it,' she repeats, her hand still touching mine.

I take a deep breath, inhaling K's soft, musky scent. I like it. 'Fine. I… let this arrow go.'

'Okay, now on your next exhale, say it again inside

your head, and just let go. Don't think about it. Don't control it. Don't even try and do it right. Just. Let. Go. I'll let go at the same time.'

So I do.

And to my surprise, the band gently releases as mine and K's hands let go.

'It worked!! It didn't ping.'

K smiles triumphantly. 'See? You've just got stop trying to control things. We learn it in martial arts too. Only when you release your expectations can you release your kick with maximum impact. I guess it works with arrows too.'

Chapter 13

I'm ready. I've got this. I hold the bow taut, my left hand lightly holding the string. I whisper K's mantra to myself: 'I let this arrow go.' I inhale deeply and then let it all out with a long exhale, gently releasing my fingers as I do so.

'OH MY GOD!' Rihanna shrieks loudly. 'Kali hit the board!!'

Everyone turns to stare. Joe grins, high-fiving me. 'Nice, Doomsday!'

I blush as our palms meet. But I'm distracted by Phil approaching me. He looks like he's about to cry. When he speaks, his voice is thick with emotion. 'What did I tell you Kali? You can do it. You have this in you.'

I look up at him, surprised at this level of reaction. Then I realise that my arrow is right in the middle of the target. I didn't just hit the board – I hit *gold!!*

'How did you do that?!' asks Rihanna. 'What changed?'

'I… just practised with the band you lent me. And, um, I've been working on letting go. Like, with my breath? Also, affirmations…'

Rihanna nods in understanding. 'Breathwork is seriously good for sports. Most elite teams credit it for their success. But I've not used affirmations for archery before – how do you do that?'

Before I can reply, Joe comes over. 'Sick shot D. Can you do it again?'

Everyone looks at me expectantly. I have no idea. Can I?! But Phil nods encouragingly. 'Go on, Kali. You've still got two arrows left.'

I take a deep breath and nod. I set everything up, and then close my eyes and breathe. As my breath steadies, I open my left eye, exhale out my expectations and my mantra; 'I let this arrow go.' I can't control whether it hits gold, or whether Joe ever asks me out. All I can do is be present and let go. So, I do. And… my arrow hits gold again!

Everyone cheers and it feels amazing! I can't believe it's taken me so long to start doing team sports – nobody ever cheers like this when I go up a level when I'm gaming.

'One more,' says Rihanna, as I set up to shoot again.

111

'Come on, Kali! Use your breath and you might even beat Joe.'

I glance at him, and he winks at me. Oh my god. It's the sexiest thing *ever* when he does that, his one hazel eye looking at me, while the other slowly closes shut. I force myself to steady my breathing, but my insides have melted. I fancy Joe *so* badly – and when he looks at me like that, I forget that I'm boring Kali Kadia, and I feel like I have an actual chance with him.

I try to exhale my mantra like before, and the arrow flies off towards the target. Only this time it doesn't land on the gold. Or any of the circles. It lands on the outer edge of the cork board. It looks like I'm back to failing at archery.

'Bad luck,' says Joe sympathetically. 'But two out of three is still sick, Doomsday.'

'Totally,' agrees Rihanna. 'Let's celebrate with sushi? And you can explain the affirmations to me on the way.'

'Uh...' I have packed lunch with me. Mum's homemade dhal and rice. But I do also have the credit card she gave me for exceptional circumstances... And Rihanna asking me to have lunch with her is *definitely* an exceptional circumstance. 'Sure!'

***

'What is *she* doing here?' asks Hayley, gripping her bento box with her lilac acrylics as she joins our table.

Rihanna shrugs. 'We had archery and then came to get lunch.'

'Doomsday got two golds!' adds Joe, and I can't help smiling at him.

'Don't you get like five every time babe?' Hayley sits by his side, possessively placing a hand onto his forearm. 'Two doesn't sound so impressive.'

I stay silent. Hayley is way better at being mean than I am – there's no point in me trying to beat her. But to my surprise, Rihanna stands up for me.

'It's pretty impressive for a beginner. Anyway, she was just telling us about her cousin's big Indian wedding. Apparently, there are like four whole days of events.'

'Uh, yeah!' I pipe up. 'She's got a big event planner helping her.' Large Instagram followings are things that Rihanna and Hayley care about, so I show them K's mum's profile.

'Oh my god, I already follow her!' cries Rihanna. 'She posts about the coolest events – like weddings with elephants down the aisles, and live Bollywood bands.'

113

I look at her in pleased surprise. It had never occurred to me that people could find an Indian wedding *cool*.

'I think it sounds tacky,' says Hayley, confirming my suspicions. 'I'd rather have a classy church wedding, wearing a white dress and coming in on a carriage. Not an elephant draped in bright colours. That's not aligned with my colour scheme aspirations.'

I know this is classic Hayley, and I shouldn't have expected anything else, but my stomach sinks. Of course, my culture is too much for her taste.

'An elephant sounds sick!' says Joe. 'And four weddings means four days of partying!'

'Uh, I'm pretty sure Radha's not having elephants,' I clarify. 'And it's not exactly four weddings.'

'So, what is it?' asks Rihanna. 'Go on, I want to know! It sounds fascinating!'

I'm wary of boring her, so I rush through it quickly. 'There's the mehndi night, where the women get their henna done. Then there's the sangeet, with dancing and food. That's like the pre-wedding event. And then the actual wedding – which is like, three hours long and super boring. Then the reception party later that evening!'

Rihanna's eyes light up. 'It sounds so cool! I've always

wanted to go to an Indian wedding. All the clothes and food and colour.'

'I suppose it is fun,' I concede. 'Except for when the old people pinch your cheeks and ask overly personal questions about your love life.' I cringe as soon as I've said this. Why did I mention my love life in front of Joe?! It's not like I *have* one.

'I think I could handle them!' says Rihanna.

'You know what, you definitely could,' I reply.

'Oh my god, do you mean that I can come?!' cries Rihanna. 'That would be incredible!! I mean, I get we probably couldn't come to the wedding, but it would be so cool to come to any of the other events!'

I stare, wide-eyed. I didn't mean she could *come* to one. She's my school friend – and I'm still using the word 'friend' lightly. I can't bring her to Radha's wedding, to meet all my relatives and the Indian community.

But Rihanna looks so excited I don't know her to let her down. And Radha probably wouldn't mind *too* much if I brought her to the sangeet. I'll find a way to convince her; flattery normally works.

'Um, yeah, I'm sure you could come to the sangeet!'

'Sick!' says Joe. 'I'm down! Jack will be too!'

'Me too,' says Hayley quickly, fluttering her lashes at Joe.

My heart plummets. I might have been able to get a plus-one to the sangeet, but a plus-four?! And one of them being Hayley Parker?! This is a *nightmare*. She already makes fun of my accent and food – bringing her to Radha's sangeet will give her ammo for the rest of my life!

As if she knows what I'm thinking, Hayley narrows her eyes at me. 'Is there a problem Doomsday? Are you taking back your invite?'

I have no choice but to shake my head. 'Nope! You… can all come! There'll be food, and a party vibe. We do this special dancing. It's called garba, where you dance in circles and–'

'Synchronised dancing?' Hayley raises an eyebrow, and my words die in my mouth. Why did I think it would be a good idea to elaborate on Indian traditions to Hayley? She stands up and looks pointedly at Joe. 'Bubble tea before Maths?'

'You know it!' Joe gets up to follow her, and they walk off, leaving Rihanna and I alone.

I exhale slowly, trying to process the fact I've inadvertently invited the four most popular people in my year to Radha's sangeet. And Hayley already hates every single thing about it.

'Sorry about Hayley,' apologises Rihanna. 'I think the sangeet sounds fun! I can't wait!'

I give her a small smile, deciding to put this all to the back of my mind. I'll deal with it later. Instead, I ask the question that's been on my mind for days. 'Hey, um, are Hayley and Joe officially back together?'

Rihanna snorts. 'She wishes! I mean, not yet. But Hayley always gets what Hayley wants, so... watch this space.'

I sigh in understanding. 'I know what you mean. My cousin Radha's like that. She's perfect in every single way. And everything always works out for her exactly as she wants it to. Every time.'

'Sounds like someone I know,' says Rihanna drily. 'Is it just me or do you ever get exhausted by it?'

'All the time! It drives me crazy.'

'Me too,' admits Rihanna, and I shiver because I know we're not talking about Radha anymore. Rihanna is *confiding* in me about Hayley driving her mad. I don't know what to say back, but it's okay, because Rihanna just smiles. 'Thanks Kali. It's good to be able to talk about this.'

'Of course! Wait... you called me Kali.'

'That is your name.'

'The others all call me Doomsday.'

Rihanna raises an eyebrow. 'You *want* me to call you Doomsday?'

I laugh. 'Kali works.'

'I think it's cool you're named after Kali anyway. You know her name literally means 'the black one'?' I shake my head wordlessly. 'She's one of the only Hindu goddesses with dark skin. And the gods were all nasty to her about it. This one time, Shiva referred to his wife Parvati as Kali, like as a compliment, and she was so pissed with him that she did some magic skin lightening thing, and then became known as the 'golden one'. I mean, that's colourism right there.'

'How do you *know* all this?'

'The essay Ms Patel made us do. I was kind of into it, because... I can relate.'

'But you're beautiful!' I say, only realising how fangirl that sounds once it's out of my mouth. But it's true.

Rihanna grins. 'Thanks. But not everyone thinks so.'

'Who?!'

'It's not just one person. It's racism. Colourism. The usual. I get it all the time because I'm Black and dark-skinned.'

I don't speak for a while, then I share something I'd never told anyone before. Not even Tanya. 'I... relate to that. My skin is way darker than my cousin Radha's, and I know everyone thinks I'm less pretty for it.'

Rihanna shakes her head in understanding. 'The world, my friend, is super messed up. It's why I like Kali so much. She's the goddess who doesn't give a crap what anyone thinks. She's pure power.'

For some reason, this makes me instantly feel better. I smile, thinking of someone else who would love this chat. 'My friend, K, loves Kali too. She's Indian like me. And she thinks that Kali is one of the most powerful goddesses out there because she doesn't conform to beauty standards. And that she's judged for it.'

'K sounds like a total queen,' declares Rihanna. 'And she's right. Kali was the least popular goddess for years, until the 17th century when they gave her a makeover.'

'Wait – what?!'

'Yeah, Hindu scholars stopped drawing her as pure black with the red eyes and tongue and stuff. And instead, they made her sexy and curvy and gave her pale blue skin. *Then* the whole country got on board with worshipping her as the Divine Mother, and the goddess of destruction and creation.'

'Oh my god! They basically bleached her skin!'

This is completely changing everything I thought I knew about Kali. I almost feel sorry for her, being judged so horribly on her appearance.

'I know, right. But at least she's seen for her true self again these days. Though I don't know why they always need to depict her as either stereotypically hot or ugly. Can't they just let her be herself? I mean, that's why I got so into her. She refuses to conform to this whole 'put me in a box' thing, and she isn't one thing or the other. She's *undefinable*.' Rihanna closes her eyes for a second, and her face relaxes in bliss.

'It does sound good. Who needs labels?'

Rihanna's eyes flash open. 'Exactly! I'm so glad you get it, Kali. You know, lately, I've been thinking...'

'About?'

There's a long pause, then Rihanna says, 'So in this one Kali legend, a bunch of priests tried to sacrifice an animal for her, thinking she'd love it. But Kali got annoyed and ate all the priests instead.'

'*That's* what you've been thinking about?'

'The message behind it, not the eating people. The priests were making assumptions on who she was and what she wanted. Like everyone does to me, I mean, to girls all the time. But how do they know who Kali truly is? Only she knows. And actually, she's so much more than just one thing. She's everything *all at once*. She defies people's attempts to tame her or domesticate her – and always has done.'

'Okay, I seriously hope you at least got a 7 for this essay,' I say, officially impressed. 'Because you are a Kali expert.'

'I got a 9. And Ms Patel wants me to do my GCSE coursework on her. I feel like Kali would be proud.'

'Well, *this* Kali definitely is.'

Chapter 14

A LOT has been happening lately. I have officially survived not one but *two* periods. Which is a big deal for anyone, let alone a girl who is hunted by demons every time her womb lining sheds. But K and I managed to get through it together. We finally synced up our periods and she barely left my side the entire time we were bleeding. We even convinced my mum to let her stay at mine because Deepa Auntie was away for work and 'otherwise K would be all alone at home eating microwave meals.' It meant K and I had five full days together, eating my mum's best curries, staying up late chatting after school, and slaying demons.

We managed to bring my demon kill count up to 14 (demon-clean-ups totally count). K's training regime clearly paid off because only four of them were clones that we – okay, I – created. But the best part was that I feel so much closer to her now. She still hasn't exactly shared much about her life, but I do know she frowns when she's thinking, she loves arthouse movies but *hates* glossy teen movies, and she snores gently when she sleeps. I also saw her kill nine more demons in various different ways – two demon rolls, one strangling, three drop kicks and three head bashes – which is actually quite an intimate way to get to know someone. I'm pretty sure she got to know me better too, through my cleaning up skills.

Things are school are also kind of… great. Not with Hayley, obviously. She keeps making subtly rude comments about my packed Indian food at lunch, because yes, I do now eat lunch at the popular table every day, and I can't afford to always get sushi with them; but her comments don't bother me the way they used to. How can it when Joe King always asks for my leftovers *and* compliments me in archery? The other day, he even suggested we do an extra training session together! We haven't actually done it yet, and I'm not sure we ever will because he seems to have forgotten, but the fact that he asked is *everything*.

Then there's Ri, because I call Rihanna 'Ri' now. We've been hanging out loads after archery, and we even message each other in the evenings. Just fun memes and random comments about school, but it's still major. The other day, she even asked what I'm wearing to the Summer Dance. Considering I've never been to a single school dance before – Tanya and I skipped them all, pretending we didn't believe in mainstream capitalist conformity, when the truth was we were both just terrified – I wasn't planning on going to this one either. But when Ri assumed I was, I realised that this time, I actually *want* to go.

Everything's so different from how it used to be. I don't want to just get through the school day without anyone noticing me anymore. I like the fact that I have friends to have lunch with now. And when I walk down the corridor, people *acknowledge* me. I mean, sometimes it's just a nod. But when I'm with Ri, sometimes they say 'hey'. It makes me feel like a celebrity. I wish I'd known earlier that having a skill would have changed my entire life. I would have tried harder in cross country. Or Chess Club. Or any extracurricular ever.

But I never would have been able to do it without my superpower. That, combined with a lot of training and practice, means I'm now the second-best in the archery club. Joe is first and Ri is third, but she seems genuinely happy for me. Obviously, Hayley hates it.

She's the only one who doesn't cheer when I get gold. She just rolls her eyes and mutters comments about 'beginner's luck', then massages Joe's trapezium so he's ready to beat me. It's because of her and Joe that my score still isn't flawless. Even though I have super aim, whenever they distract me – Hayley, with her muttered comments, and Joe, with his beauty – I miss gold.

Still, in the words of Phil, I have 'progressed beyond anyone's wildest expectations.' Which I'm taking as a compliment. Especially because he accompanied this statement with the best news ever. News I cannot *wait* to tell my family!

***

'Mum?' I call out as soon as I open the front door, panting. I raced home so fast you would have thought there was a demon after me. 'Hello?!'

'We're in here, *beta*,' she calls from the kitchen.

I chuck my bag onto the hallway table, even though I'm meant to neatly hang it on a hook, mentally preparing myself after the 'we' that means Radha's here, *again*.

'Guess what?' I announce proudly as I walk into

125

the kitchen. As predicted, Mum and Radha are sitting at the island with mugs of chai and the requisite cardamom biscuits.

Mum raises her eyebrows at me over the top of the chic tortoiseshell glasses Radha picked out for her. 'You look happy.'

I lift my chin high. 'I am. Because my archery coach wants to put me forward for not one, not two, but THREE events in the competition!'

Radha and my mum don't look particularly impressed by this.

'It's a big deal!' I protest. 'The school has to pay for each event we enter, so not everyone is up for three events! It means he thinks I'm one of the top students! And I could win golds.'

'Lovely,' says my mum. 'Well done *beta*. Will it help you get into Oxbridge like your cousin?'

'She can definitely write it on her application form,' says Radha authoritatively. 'Unis love when people care about sports. And archery is niche enough to catch their eye.'

'Fantastic!' My mum's voice is warmer now.

I shake my head. This is all so typical. Nobody even asked me if I want to go to university, let alone

Oxbridge, but here they are, planning my future without my permission. I can feel my energy deflating.

'So, when is it?' asks Radha, rummaging around her soft leather bag for her phone. 'I'll put it in my diary now. Things are getting busy with the wedding – I don't know *why* I thought it was a good idea to plan four events.'

'Because you wanted to do it the proper way!' My mum reassuringly rests her hand on top of Radha's. 'And I can't wait for all your events!'

'What about mine?' I mutter.

'Go on then,' says Radha impatiently. 'When is it? Just don't say Saturday—'

'Saturday 30th July.'

There is silence. My mum's eyes flitter around nervously. Radha's face crumples in pity. 'Oh Kali, that's the day of the sangeet.'

I swallow my disappointment. 'Of course, it is.' I turn to my mum. 'Does that mean you can't come and watch me? Maybe Dad can come for a bit?'

My mum looks confused. 'Kali, *beta*, it's Radha's sangeet. *You* need to be there. You can't go to your competition.'

My mouth drops open in shock. 'What? Why?! She has four wedding events!! I can't miss one for

127

my competition?'

'The sangeet night is one of the most important ones,' says Radha. 'You can't miss it – you're family!'

'It's in the night? That's perfect!' I say in relief. 'The competition's in the afternoon.'

'So is the sangeet,' says Radha.

'But you just called it the sangeet night!'

'Kali, you know all our events start early,' admonishes her mum. 'And we have the rituals to do beforehand in the afternoon, then you'll need to get ready. There's no time for your competition.'

'But I've spent weeks training for it!' I wail.

'Kali!' hisses my mum. 'Leave it! You can't go to your competition. This is much more important.'

'Sorry Kali,' says Radha. 'But you'll have loads of fun, I promise! And… I was going to ask you to do something special the next day at my wedding.' I shrug, resigned. 'It's to do the samayu ceremony!' I stare blankly and Radha's forced to explain. 'It means you greet Kevil's family on the day of the actual wedding. It's kind of a big deal because you represent the bride's side welcoming the whole groom's family to the venue.'

'And you get to have the nariyal on your head,' beams my mum. 'You'll look so beautiful! Everyone will be

128

looking at you.'

'What's a nariyal, and why do *I* have to do it?'

'The bride's younger sister or cousin always does it,' says Radha. 'It's a big honour.'

'You'll look so beautiful in your sari,' adds my mum, a dreamy expression on her face. 'You'll be carrying the nariyal and everyone will be watching. My own daughter.'

'Can someone tell me what a nariyal is?!'

Radha rolls her eyes. 'A coconut!'

'Wait, you want me to wear a saree and put an actual coconut on my head?! That's insane. I'll look crazy! And I'll trip up. Or drop the coconut.'

'Only if you want to offend Kevil's family for life,' says Radha coolly.

'But why do *I* have to do this?! Mum would be so much better at it than me.'

My mum's eyes widen in shock. 'I can't! I'm married!'

That's when it hits me. 'Oh my god. Is this some kind of traditional thing only virgins can do?! It is, isn't it?'

'Don't talk like that,' admonishes my mum. 'It's not about, you know. It's just for maidens.'

'Maidens?!' I'm about to launch into a feminist lecture when my phone vibrates. It's K.

129

Hey, do you want to come to mine tonight instead of meeting at the usual spot?

A rush of excitement hits me. I've been dying to go to K's house, but every time I've suggested it, K's had a reason why I can't come over. We've ended up hanging at mine instead, because my family loves her and it's easier to convince my parents to let me have K over rather than to go to hers. But now, finally, she's asked me over. This is a big deal.

Oh, and it probably makes sense to stay over, so bring stuff to sleepover.

A big deal is an understatement. This is everything I've been waiting for.

'Mum, can I stay at K's tonight?'

She frowns. 'Isn't it a little last-minute?'

'But it's a Friday night, please! It's not like we had plans.'

'Well, I came over,' says Radha.

'I want to tell K about the, um, coconut thing,' I say hastily. If I have to do this weird virgin tradition, I may as well get something out of it. 'And she has Indian outfits I could borrow for the wedding!'

Radha starts laughing like I've made the joke of the year. 'You'll need brand new stuff, Kali! You can't wear hand-me-downs for my wedding.'

But my mum's face relaxes. She's never seen me so enthusiastic about anything Indian before (unless it's edible). 'Oh, go on then.'

'Thanks Mum!' I say. Then I turn to Radha with a big smile plastered on my face, because this is the *perfect* moment to ask for another favour. 'As I'm playing such a big role in the wedding, can I have some friends come to your sangeet night?'

'Oh fine, K can come. Your new bestie.'

It hadn't even occurred to me to invite K. I try to imagine her at the sangeet, hanging out with Ri, Joe, Hayley and Jack. But my imagination refuses to go there. It doesn't work. She's from a different part of my life to my school friends. It would be weird if they mixed.

'I actually wanted to bring my school friends. From archery.'

Radha's perfectly arched eyebrows shoot up. 'Friends plural?! Are they Indian?'

I shake my head. 'No. Why?'

'Because that means they'll turn up in crop tops with their underwear showing, a scarf wrapped around like a saree, and bindis all over their cheekbones like it's a festival,' rants Radha.

To be fair, I can see Hayley doing that. 'I'll make sure

they don't.'

'How many?' asks my mum.

'Four.' I feel like now is not the time to mention that two of them are boys.

She glares at me. 'Kali, that's too much! You can't ask Radha these things!'

I deliberately open my eyes in wide innocence. 'But Radha's family! That's why I'm missing the competition for her!'

Radha has no choice but to relent. 'Oh, alright then. But you should invite K too – what's another person if you're already bringing four plus-ones?'

I hesitate. What if my friends don't *like* K? I think she's insanely cool – but she is very different to them, with her tattoos and her direct way of speaking. Hayley would hate her piercings and hair. Besides, K probably wouldn't like them either. There's no point risking it, so I come up with another solution instead. 'Why don't I just bring K to another event instead?'

'The mehndi night?' asks Radha. 'I suppose so.'

My mum beams. 'I'll ask the caterers to do a samosa chaat! It's her favourite.'

132

Chapter 15

I double check the address on my phone. This is it. K's house. I gaze up in awe at the huge Georgian mansion. I somehow can't reconcile it with the K I know, but it does explain why her leather jacket is designer. If I wasn't already intimidated by her, this house would definitely do it. I glance at the navy Porsche in the driveaway and dry swallow. I reach to press the buzzer, but before I get there, the door opens.

It's K. She looks normal – tiny black crop top with wide-legged cargo trousers – though now I can see how they both have that understated quality only super-expensive clothes have.

'I saw you on the camera,' she says. 'You're early.'

'Only five minutes.'

'Just… come in, quick.' She ushers me into the hallway, and I don't even try to hide my gawping. This is the fanciest place I've ever seen, with its chintz wallpaper and glittering chandelier, *and* I've been to The Ritz in

London (I only snuck in to use the bathroom, but still).

I exhale loudly. 'K, this place is *amazing*.'

She grabs my arm impatiently. 'Yes, I know. Come on, let's go upstairs before—'

'Darling!' I whirl around to see K's mum in the flesh. She's wearing leather leggings with a sparkly grey mesh top over a black... bra? Oh my god, I can see her bra. 'Who's your friend?'

K sighs reluctantly. 'Mum, this is Kali. Kali, this is my mum. She's just heading out.'

'Hi Deepa Auntie,' I say, trying to emulate K's behaviour at my house. But Deepa Auntie doesn't react like my mum did. Instead, she recoils.

'Oh no! I'm not *old*! There's no need to call me Auntie. Just Deepa is fine. Deeps even. That's what everyone calls me.' She beams, and I see where K gets her smile from. Then her eyes widen, her long lashes parting. 'Wait K, did you say she's called Kali? Oh my god! Another one! Isn't that sweet! Look at you both, with the same name. You're such a cute couple, I'm obsessed!'

I choke, about to correct her, but K gets there first. 'Mum!' Her eyes are flashing angrily. 'Kali isn't my girlfriend. She's just my friend. Can you not?'

134

Deepa – I'm not calling her Deeps – puts a hand over her mouth, smiling mischievously. 'Oops! My bad! Okay well, I'm going out. Order whatever you want. I'll be back late, so enjoy having the house to yourselves! Ciao chicas.' She grabs a soft wrap from the coat stand as well as a giant fuchsia handbag, blowing kisses at us before leaving.

I stare at K in silence. I have no words.

'Yep,' she says heavily. 'That's my mum. I was hoping you wouldn't have to meet her.' She turns to start walking up the stairs.

I don't move. 'But K, she's so... cool. And young. And glamorous. And she lets you order in and have the house to yourself?! I mean, this *mansion*?'

K squirms at my questions, pausing on the spiral suitcase that looks like it's straight out of a movie set. 'I know it's a lot. We didn't always have a house like this. We lived in a one-bedroom flat 'til I was five. Then Mum's business took off.'

'You're *so* lucky!' I follow K up towards a giant landing that is officially bigger than my family's living room. There's a soft chintz armchair, a little antique table piled high with copies of Vogue, an enormous doll's house, and a chaise longue that looks like it's come out of one of the Vogues. Even Hayley would be impressed by this! 'I can't believe she gives you so much freedom. I'd die for a mum like yours.'

'It's not all it's cracked up to be.'

I collapse onto the chaise longue and pose like I'm Marie Antoinette. 'Well, I'm into it!' K suppresses a smile. 'Oh, also! It's Radha's mehndi night next week and I wondered if you want to come?'

K looks genuinely touched. 'Yes! I'd love to. That's so kind of your family to let me. Wait, they do know you've asked me, right?!'

'It was their idea. My mum said to tell you the caterers are doing a samosa chaat for you.'

'That's so nice of her! I'll message her to thank her. And Radha.'

'You have their numbers?'

K looks at me like I'm crazy. 'Obviously. I took them when I came over for dinner so I could thank them for everything.'

I really need to work on my manners. It didn't even *occur* to me to thank Deepa for having me. 'No wonder my mum loves you. They won't even need to use any mehndi on you; you already come prepared.'

'I'm a cheap date.' Then she blushes. 'I mean, uh…

136

come on.' She's off down the hallway, and I reluctantly slide off the chaise longue to follow her to her room.

I blink, dazed as I walk in. Everything is purple. All of it. The bed. The curtains. The carpet.

'Oh my god. It's so…'

'Purple. My favourite colour when I was 10. Mum got carried away. But at least it's *dark* purple, not lilac.'

I nod, dazed, trying to take it all in. The giant four-poster bed. The TV on the wall. The walk-in wardrobe. The en-suite bathroom with a claw-foot tub. And the gleaming bow and arrows on the bed. 'Wait, what's that?!'

K bounds onto the bed and brandishes the bow proudly. 'Surprise!'

I clamber up to join her – this bed is seriously high up – and stare at the bow. It looks exactly like the one I use at school. Hera. And this one has a label that also says… Hera.

'K, is this my bow from school?!'

K nods happily. 'I wanted to celebrate all the golds you're getting, so I stole her for you!'

'What?! K, you can't do that! Phil will, I mean… but… why?!'

'I just told you – as a celebration. But also, because you're ready to put everything into practice!'

My blood runs cold. 'You want me to do archery in the real world? On the demons?!'

'Of course. That's why you've been training, right?'

I think guiltily of my recent training sessions – trying to flirt with Joe, giggling with Ri the whole time, and basking in Phil's praise. I'd completely forgotten that one day my target wouldn't be a gold but a demon eye. 'So, um, I guess we wait 'til we get our periods?

K shakes her head and holds out her phone. She's got an app out and unfortunately, it's not Deliveroo. 'The period app says they won't come for another 13 days. But this weekend, we're both ovulating. Which makes it the perfect time to go hunting for demons.'

'Are you sure? Can't we wait? Please?'

'No, this is important Kali.'

'Please?' I plead beseechingly.

K relents. 'Fine. Tonight we can practise. But tomorrow morning? We're off demon slaying.'

***

The practice session is like nothing we've ever done before. We're in K's garden, and I'm holding my arrow out as far away from my body as possible. It stinks of

138

paraffin and all I want to do is throw it in the stream that runs through K's garden. Because yes, her garden has a private stream. But instead, K comes forward with her lighter.

'Ready?'

I glance at her. Her brow is clear, eyes expectant, and her expression suggests that launching a flamed arrow across her garden into the stream is a normal Friday night activity for her. It probably is.

'Get the bow ready,' she commands. 'Then I'll light it for you at the last minute.'

I gulp, nodding. This was obviously not my idea. K told me about it when we were in her room eating the pizzas she'd ordered to soften the blow. Apparently, she'd come up with the idea as soon as she heard about my superpower. She knew I could kill demons from afar with my archery skills, but it would mean blood spurting everywhere. So she conceived the frankly perilous idea of setting the arrows on fire, so they'd burn up the demon blood before it touched the ground. It turns out she's set demons on fire before, so she knows their blood is flammable.

What we don't know is whether I'll be able to *fire* the flamed arrows. It's not like I have a perfect

139

track record when it comes to non-flamed arrows, especially when Joe and Hayley are around, so this could go either way.

'Okay, I'm lighting it!' I force myself to concentrate as she brings the open flame of her lighter to the paraffin-drenched cloth tied around the tip of the arrow. The second it sets alight, I close my eyes, quickly exhale with my adapted mantra – 'I release this burning arrow' – and then… release.

'Yes!! You did it!!'

I open my eyes to see the arrow sizzling away in the centre of the stream. It worked. And my hands are burn-free.

'Let's go again. And this time, aim for the frog statue in the stream. You might want to keep your eyes open too.'

I squint. 'But that's tiny! I can barely see it from here!'

'Exactly. Let's go!'

I reluctantly lift my bow to my shoulder. This is really not what I'd expected when K invited me round for a sleepover. 'Can we watch a movie afterwards? A Pixar maybe?'

'If you hit the frog five times in a row, we can even watch one of those gross teen movies you like.'

My eyes light up. 'Really? Even if there's

a heteronormative plot from the 00s?'

'Fine. But in that case, you need to hit the frog 10 times.'

I sigh. 'Pixar it is.'

Chapter 16

Normally, I spend Saturday mornings lazing in bed. Not at K's house. She set her alarm for 6am so we could sneak out and get to the demons nice and early. She was up late messaging in the Kali WhatsApp group, gathering info on exactly where the demons are located (deep in the woods somewhere; Tech Kali sent the coordinates) and discussing strategy. She tried to tell me about it, but I was engrossed in the Pixar movie. Now I'm standing in the forest, with a bow and paraffin arrows, regretting my decision.

I turn to K. 'It feels like this is all happening a bit fast... I only launched my first fire arrow last night, and now you want me to join a demon massacre?'

K hesitates. 'I know. But you did hit the frog nine times in a row.'

'And then on the tenth time, I set fire to a tree.' Luckily, K had the hose ready, so we took the fire out before it spread. But there's now one seriously scorched plum tree in her garden.

She scrunches up her face. 'Kali, I wouldn't ask if I didn't think you could do it.'

I sigh, looking around. We're at the top of a hill, hidden by thick trees, so we're out of sight from the demons. But we can still see them. They're a couple of yards away, grouped together in a copse at the edge of the forest. 'I guess I don't really have a choice.'

K beams. 'That's the spirit!' She gets back to prepping the arrows while I take her high-tech binoculars to spy on the demons.

They're standing in a group together and seem to be having a very animated conversation. I didn't know demons could chill like that. I always thought they were more like wild predators, but it seems not. 'I wonder what they're chatting about,' I muse aloud. 'Are they discussing our period cycles? Waiting to sniff us out? Or are they trying to figure out who's on cooking duty and who's washing up?'

K snorts. 'They don't *talk*, Kali. They're like beasts. They hunt. They grunt. End of. You've seen how dumb they are.'

'Well, right now, they're totally hanging out. It looks like their general discussion has turned into

143

a bit of a debate. There's one in the middle talking, like he's trying to convince the others about something. Maybe they'll even do a vote soon.'

K frowns. 'What?'

I hand her the binoculars. 'Look. It's the one with… oh wait, they're all identical. How are we meant to distinguish between them?'

K squints through the binoculars, her breath tightening. 'You're right… They're… communicating. But I don't understand. They don't *do* this.'

'Maybe you've just never *seen* them do it before? Because normally they're hunting us, but right now we've caught them unawares?'

K looks uncertain. 'I don't know… The demons act on instinct, they don't do discussions. They're more like animals. This doesn't feel right.'

'I agree. It's probably best if we go home and watch movies in bed. Whilst eating everything in your kitchen.' I looked in Deepa's kitchen cupboards last night – they're full of the entire M&S snack aisle and I can't wait to dive in.

'Definitely not! There are at least 20 demons over there. We can't let them go. They'll only come and try to kill us when we have our periods.'

'Ugh, fine. Guess we're going to go crash their demon hang.'

'Yes,' says K in evident relief. 'So, ideally, you'd want to be shooting all 20 arrows in about two minutes. That's if every single arrow hits its target. But as you're new to the fire bit, I'm guessing you'll need a bit more time. Can you get them all in five minutes?'

I stare at her like she's insane, then I speak slowly. 'No, I cannot. It takes me at *least* a minute per arrow, and that's when they're not on fire!'

She sighs. 'You need to work on your speed. There's no denying that. But in the meantime, I've got a back-up plan to help you.' She opens her bag to show me a bunch of brown parcels. 'Fireworks. I got the biggest, most powerful ones!'

'Fireworks?!'

'Yep,' she says proudly. 'I can launch them into the middle of the demons, so we'll take down a few at once, then you can get the rest with the arrows.'

Oh god. This is actually happening. We're about to attack a group of demons. I wonder if there's a better word for a gathering of demons – Flock? Harem? Crapload?

I face K in fear. 'What if I'm too slow? What if...

I'm not ready?'

Her big brown eyes blink at me. 'Kali, you can do this. I believe in you. I know you've never done it so fast before, and these arrows are on fire. But you can still do this. I know you can. And I'm right here to help you.'

K doesn't lie. And if she really believes I can do it, then maybe – just maybe – I can.

'I suppose the fact that the arrows are on fire should help me shoot them faster. My main motive is to avoid a burnt hand.'

K laughs. 'I love how you bring humour into everything you do. Even when it's a life-or-death situation. It's one of my favourite things about you.'

My instinct is to make another joke, but K's last sentence stops me. 'One of' – that means she has other favourite things about me. I feel the warmth of her comment wrap around me. K thinks I'm funny *and* she has other favourite things about me. If that isn't enough validation to get me through a demon massacre, I don't know what is.

I nod decisively. 'Okay. Let's do this. Bow and arrow at the ready.'

K's lithe body springs into action. 'Great. I'll launch

a few fireworks alongside you, and then I can help you spot the demons to fire at.' She turns to face me, her eyes shining with excitement. 'I can be demon spotter! Or demon locator?'

'Or maybe we can discuss the exact vocabulary later, and just focus on the demons for now?' I suggest.

'Good call,' agrees K. 'Okay. I'm getting the fireworks ready. You're okay to light your first few arrows alone?'

I nod, taking a deep breath. I need to get my bow in place, set my arrow on fire, then aim it at a crapload of demons. I bet even Phil would struggle with this. But he doesn't have a superpower. Nor does he have K by his side, ready to launch supplementary fireworks.

'I'm ready,' says K. 'You?'

'Yep. Three…' I light the tip of the arrow on fire. 'Two…' I quickly put the arrow into place. 'One…' I exhale, let my fingers go, and– 'Fire!'

I hear a roar in the distance as my arrow hits a demon and then, a second later, there's a loud explosion as K's firework explodes in the middle of their gathering. I squint through the smoke in the trees and catch sight of another demon, racing towards us. I go into autopilot mode, setting another arrow on fire as though I've been doing this for years, and fire it right at the demon's eye.

'Yes Kali!' K punches the air as my arrow hits the demon and it explodes into flames. She grabs the binoculars. 'There are a few left at the back, so I'll do another firework. You can catch the ones coming towards us, right?'

'Hell yes!' I feel adrenaline coursing through my veins, energised from our success. I start lighting arrows and launching them as K helps me. She uses the binoculars to call out exactly where the demons are, and I fire off my arrows deftly, hitting every single demon I aim at. They don't make it anywhere near us because I get them all beforehand, knocking them down as they run up the hill towards us.

If Joe King was impressed by Doomsday scoring golds at school, this would literally blow his mind. Just like I blew the head off the last demon coming towards us.

I don't know how long it goes on for – probably a lot longer than the five minutes K was hoping for – because it's all a blur. But when the demons are finally gone, and we've checked there are no new clones in sight, K turns to face me. Her eyes are shining in the moonlight and she's glowing. I can't tell if it's the moonlight, a high from the demon massacre, or just because she's ovulating. But either way, she looks amazing. 'I think that for your first ever demon-slaying mission, you can call that a major victory.'

'It wasn't just me. We couldn't have done it without your fireworks.'

K touches my arm. 'Kali. This was all you. Yes, I got a handful. But you're the one who made sure there wasn't a single demon left. You're the one who hunted them down.'

A shiver runs through my body, and I let out the deep breath I'd been holding back. I look down at Hera and my remaining arrows, feeling a rush of pride. I didn't just hide from the demons or clean up after them – I *slayed* them. And the weirdest part is that I loved every second.

Chapter 17

'Kali, wait up!' Ri calls for me as I leave the archery hall. 'Have you done something different? You look amazing today!'

I glance at my reflection in the glass doors. I'm wearing my normal uniform, with my hair loose, and my favourite trainers. Same as always. But I *do* look different. The way I'm standing makes me look taller, and my skin is glowing just like K's was on Saturday. 'Uh, maybe it's because I'm ovulating?'

'Nice! For some reason I always get spots when I'm ovulating…' She shrugs. 'Anyway. I wanted to say well done. You are killing it in archery! Joe's definitely jealous you're beating him.'

'But he still got a higher score than me,' I point out. We did a practice competition to prepare for the real one – the one I won't be going to because of Radha's sangeet.

'Yeah, but you got way more golds than him!

You *only* got golds. Apart from the two times you missed the target…'

The first time, Joe winked at me and it threw me off my game. The second time, Hayley made a comment about my shooting stance. Apparently, I look like the Hunchback of Notre Dame when I'm squinting at the target.

'Also, you need to remember you're doing it bare bow,' continues Ri. 'And Joe's using the sight. So, you're technically doing the way harder version.'

I smile to myself as I remember how cute Joe looks when he carefully attaches the ruler to his bow, squinting to make sure it's lined up with the gold, his tongue poking out of the side of his mouth as he concentrates. It's adorable.

'To be honest, the sight just confuses me,' I admit. 'There are even more instructions to remember for it. Bare bow seems easier.' Especially when you have a superpower.

'Yeah, which is why you're going to be on *fire* at the competition! I can't wait to see you beat all the boys.'

'I won't,' I tell her, my voice as glum as I feel. 'It's Radha's sangeet that day.'

'No!' Ri gasps. 'The one we're coming to?'

I nod. 'You can all still come in the evening. But I have to be there early. We're doing a special ceremony at home first. It sucks.'

'But surely, you're allowed to take a few hours off for the biggest archery competition in the country? Especially when you've got such a strong chance of winning?'

'That's what I said! But apparently not.'

'That is beyond annoying!'

'I know!'

'What are you both so annoyed about?' Joe breezes past, putting his arms around our shoulders. I feel my breath speed up at the sudden physical touch. 'The fact I beat you both?'

Ri slides his arm off her and rolls her eyes. 'Sure, Joe. I can't sleep at night because all I think about is you beating me by five points.'

'I knew it,' grins Joe.

I wish I could join in their easy chat but every time Joe's there, I freeze, so all I do is smile awkwardly.

'What's up, Doomsday?' he asks. 'Other than getting nine golds in a row 'til you randomly go rogue.'

Uh, yeah, because of him and his ex throwing me off my game. 'Nothing. Just… trying to keep progressing!' Why am I being so formal?!

Luckily, Ri speaks for me. 'Yeah, Kali's killing it, but she can't come to the competition. It's her cousin's sangeet. That's what we're annoyed about. She won't get the chance to beat you.'

Joe turns to me with genuine dismay written across his face. 'What?! That's not fair! You have to compete!'

'I want to, but I can't.'

'I'm sure your cousin will let you when she knows what a big deal it is. Maybe I can speak to her for you?'

My eyes widen in terror at the thought. I can't think of anything worse!

Ri scoffs. 'Yeah, if you want them to force Kali off the team forever, that's a great idea. Anyway, I've got to go – my mum's making curry goat for dinner. See you tomorrow!'

We wave bye, and then suddenly, it's just me and Joe King. Alone. My throat goes dry.

'So, um, where's Hayley?' I croak.

He shrugs. 'Shopping or something. I don't know why she comes to archery when she clearly doesn't care about it.'

'Doesn't she come to support you?'

'And post about it on her socials,' says Joe darkly. 'Whatever. Anyway.' He bites his lip. 'So, uh, do you

153

have plans for the Summer Dance?'

'The Summer Dance?' I echo back. He can't mean…
No, obviously he can't. As if I'd even think that!

'Yeah, like, do you have a date?' A shadow of uncertainty
falls across his face, and it makes my stomach tingle.
I've never seen him look vulnerable before.

I manage to shake my head no.

'So… shall we go together?'

I just gawp at him in response.

He fidgets awkwardly. 'I mean, if you want?'

This time I manage to nod. 'Um, yes! I mean,
sure. Cool.'

Joe grins. 'Sick! It's a shame it's before the competition
or we could wear our gold medals.'

I smile weakly. 'Yeah… So, um, sorry to check, but do
you mean you don't *already* have a date for the dance?'
I know I shouldn't bring her up again, but I can't help
it. 'Not… Hayley?'

He frowns, irritated. 'No. We're not together, even
though she acts like it. And I asked you, didn't I?'

'Yes.' My voice is faint. 'And, sorry, can I clarify – you
asked me, because…?'

'Because you're really good at archery, you're kind of
cool and, you know…' I really don't know. 'You're cute.'

My mouth drops open. Joe King thinks I'm cute – and he's not even joking.

★★★

I've been desperate to tell K everything about my chat with Joe – I'm still reeling from the fact it even happened – but when I finally break it to her, right in the middle of our training session that evening, I don't get the reaction I was hoping for. Maybe I should have waited until we'd finished training. She's always marginally less serious once the work's over.

She nods in response. 'Cool.'

'Uh, K, this is way better than cool! This is the boy I've fancied for as long as I can remember. He is the hottest guy in the entire year. And he's asked *me* out!'

K puts down the weights and looks at me in that piercing, intense way she has. 'Okay, he validates you and he's hot. But what do you *like* about him?'

'Loads! He's really fun! And insanely confident.' I sigh longingly. 'I wish I had his confidence levels.'

'So, he has qualities you wish you had?'

'Definitely. He makes everyone laugh too. Another quality I wish I had.'

'You make *me* laugh,' points out K. 'And, sorry, just to check – we are talking about the guy who calls you Doomsday, a nickname you hate?'

'It's grown on me!'

She shrugs. 'So long as you're happy.'

I put my water bottle down and face her. 'Clearly, you're not. Why are you so anti-Joe?'

She bites her lip, suddenly looking younger than her 16-and-three-quarter years. 'Sorry. I'm probably projecting.'

'Projecting what?!'

It's K's turn to sigh. 'Nothing. Ignore me. So long as you feel good around Joe then I'm happy for you.' My face is blank. 'You know… connected, light, excited, playful and safe. The five most important things to feel in a relationship.'

I've never thought of how I *feel* around Joe; I've been more focused on how he feels around me. But I definitely feel excited around him – it's insanely exciting that he's into me. We connect over archery. And the rush of hormones makes me feel light. I don't feel playful with him, not the way I do with Ri or K, but that's probably because he's a boy. *He's* definitely playful, which is the most important thing. And I do also feel a little anxious, which stops me from feeling safe, but that's only because I want to come across well. It's not Joe's fault – it's mine.

'I think I do,' I reply uncertainly. 'But what are you projecting, K? Is it about your ex? Lola?'

Her face clouds over. 'We need to get back to training. 20 more push-ups.'

'Will you tell me if I add in 20 burpees?'

She shakes her head but gives me a small smile. The mood has lightened again. 'When is this dance anyway? Just so I know you won't be free for demon hunting.'

'In two weeks!'

She checks her phone and frowns. 'Kali, we'll have our periods then.'

The blood falls from my face. 'You're kidding me. I cannot have a demon ruin my date with Joe King.'

'It might be better to cancel. They'll be hunting us.'

I feel like crying. I should have known this would be too good to be true. Being friends with Ri, getting asked out by Joe... obviously it's all going to end in total misery because I'm Kali Kadia and my life is cursed by demons. Literal and metaphorical.

K's face softens. 'I suppose we could make it work.

We can hunt the day before, so we reduce demon numbers. Weaken them before the dance. Then they'll probably leave us alone for a day or two while they regroup. I can even patrol outside if you want.'

'You'd really do that for me?'

'It's not that big a deal. I patrol demons all the time. Doing it outside your school will just be... a change of scenery.'

'Thank you!' I rush up and squeeze her tight in a hug. 'You are the absolute best! Now I just need to find something to wear.'

'I probably have something in my wardrobe. My mum loves buying me dresses I never wear.'

'Are you serious?!'

K nods. 'Sure.'

I squeeze her even tighter, and then lean back so I can gaze into her eyes. 'K, I am so, so glad Mrs Patel told me to find you. Even if it means we have to slay demons, it's totally worth it.'

K blushes, and it's the sweetest thing ever. 'Me too. Come over whenever for the dress.' Then she straightens up. 'But I'll still take those 20 burpees.'

Chapter 18

I feel my heart thud in trepidation as I walk through the school gate. I'm terrified to see Joe again. I still can't believe he was serious when he asked me out yesterday. Part of me believes he's going to rescind the date invitation, because it was all just a big prank, like in those sexist teen movies I love and K hates. What if Hayley orchestrated the whole thing?!

I halt in the middle of the corridor – that would BREAK me. But then I remember this is Joe King. I've spent enough time with him lately to know that when he makes a joke, he needs instant gratification. There's no way he'd make a joke that would only give him validating laughter in *two weeks' time*.

This calms me down and I'm breathing normally when I walk into Maths. But I know I'm still being weird, only giving Ri a wave instead of going over to talk to her like I ordinarily would. When Joe walks in, I pretend I haven't seen him and keep my head firmly engrossed in my textbook. I get through the entire lesson pretty much the same way, focusing more on Maths than I have in my entire life. When the lesson ends, I run out, straight to Chemistry. They're in a different group to me so I'm safe for another hour. Until the bell rings for lunch, and it's time for archery.

'There you are!' Ri jumps up behind me, grinning as her long braids swing round her face. 'I haven't spoken to you all day. How was your evening?'

'Good thanks! I hung with my friend K – the one who's also into the goddess Kali? We, uh… practised martial arts together.'

'That's *so* cool,' says Ri, and it looks like she really means it. 'I wish I had a friend who was into the same kinds of things as me.'

'Um, Hayley?!'

'Yeah, of course, she's my ride or die,' says Ri quickly. 'But… she's not exactly into archery or sports. Or the same music as me. Or even the same fashion. We're quite different.'

This is news to me. I'm trying to think of the best way to reply when Hayley chooses that precise moment to come up behind us.

'Hey girl!' She puts her arm around Ri, and gently

pulls one of her braids. Ri winces. 'How's the archery going? Hope you're beating Kali!' She smiles at me sweetly. 'All in the name of friendly competition, of course!'

'Kali's actually pretty good,' says Ri. 'A natural.'

I flush, pleased. 'I never would have improved if you hadn't helped me out. With the stretchy band and the tips. Your technique is amazing, Ri.'

Ri looks delighted, but Hayley is clearly bored. 'Right,' she yawns. 'Where's Joe?'

I flush deeper. 'I don't know. Why would I know?'

Ri gives me a weird look. 'He's… inside already. It's his turn to set up.'

Hayley flounces into the hall, leaving Ri and I trailing in her wake.

Ri pauses. 'Kali, you won't say anything, will you? About what I said about, um, friendships?'

'Of course not!'

Ri's face relaxes. 'Okay, good. Also… is there something going on between you and Joe?' I know my face gives it away before I even speak. 'I knew it! You were so obvious just then!'

'He asked me to go to the dance with him.'

Ri's eyes widen. 'Oh my god. Hayley is going to

kill you.'

'She might… not.' But I don't really believe what I'm saying. 'Joe said they're not together,' I add in a feeble last-ditch attempt to convince both of us this will all be fine.

'Officially, but since when does Hayley care about the details?! In her head, he's hers. And now he's asked you to the dance.' Ri looks at me hopefully. 'Unless, you said no? And nobody will ever need to know?'

I bite my lip and stay silent.

'I thought not. I've seen the way you look at him in archery. Do you *really* like him?'

I squeeze my eyes shut, nodding slowly. 'I have for ages.'

'Well,' she sighs. 'This is going to be an eventful archery session. Let's try and keep anything sharp away from Hayls.'

***

Archery is eventful from the get-go. Joe was in charge of setting up. And for once he decided to do the full inventory check. Which means Phil found out Hera was missing. I (accurately) denied having anything to do with her disappearance, but it still didn't go down well.

Phil ranted and raved about the rising cost of equipment, and then shoved the last left-handed bow at me. Diana. This bow might be named after the famous ancient hunting goddess, but unfortunately, she's almost as old, and it shows. I'm so anxious that I only score two golds, while Ri gets five and Joe gets six. Phil isn't impressed. The only one who's happy with my performance is Hayley, because it means I'm now at the bottom and Joe is at the top.

I have two more arrows left to improve my score. I force myself to focus on my breathing and my mantra. But as I'm exhaling, Hayley turns to Jess – one of her groupies – and they cackle loudly. It throws me off my game and I miss the target altogether. It's not the loudness of their laughter; it's that I know it's aimed at me. When I go to shoot again, Hayley does the same thing. Another laugh – except this time it's a low snigger so nobody can accuse her of deliberately sabotaging my shooting. But I still hear it, and it throws me off. I'm out.

Ri frowns at me, and I shrug helplessly. She comes to the line to shoot her last arrow and scores a gold, meaning her and Joe are tied in first place. I cheer loudly for her, and Hayley shoots me a dirty look.

She comes up to congratulate Joe, hugging him. I feel a wave of jealousy run through my body. *I should be the one hugging him – why is it always her?*

'I'm so lucky I get to go to the Summer Dance with the best archer in school as my date, and the other best archer as my best mate,' says Hayley smugly.

Ri's eyes widen and Joe looks at the ground. He doesn't say anything, and I stare at him, a lump in my throat. Oh god, what if *this* is the prank – the moment that's being live-streamed to the whole school? I quickly scan the room for a camera, but my paranoias are unjustified. There's nothing there. Just me and my humiliation. I look at Joe again, and this time he raises his head. Our eyes meet. The desperation in my eyes must be obvious because Joe squirms uncomfortably, then turns to Hayley. He glances at me again, as if hoping I'll say it for him.

But I don't. And then he finally does it. 'Hayls, I'm going to the dance with Doomsday.'

'WHAT?!' Hayley's mouth drops open. She gapes at me, and then at Joe, like some kind of stunned puffer fish. 'I'm sorry, did you just say you're taking *her* to the dance?'

Joe nods and comes to stand next to me. He takes my

hand in his. It's clammy but I don't care. He's holding *my* hand in front of Hayley. After he just told her he's taking me to the Summer Dance. This is quite possibly the best moment of my entire life.

'Yeah, sorry,' he says, and my heart races. This is the most romantic thing ever. Never in my wildest dreams did I imagine Joe would stand up for ME against HAYLEY. I feel so special right now – and it's all down to Joe.

'What, is this some kind of Make A Wish foundation thing? Is this her last ever dance?' Hayley jerks her head at me as she says 'her'. I guess the best moment of my life was pretty short-lived.

Joe frowns. 'What foundation?'

'She thinks I'm terminally ill, and you feel sorry for me,' I whisper in Joe's ear.

The look Hayley gives me as she sees me so close to Joe's face makes my blood run cold.

'Oh,' says Joe. 'You're not, are you?'

I shake my head, wondering if the intensity of the situation has gone to his head. It wasn't that complicated an insult.

But in that exact moment, Hayley starts giggling, her peals of laughter ringing around us. 'Oh my god, your faces! I was kidding, obviously. As if I care. That's cute you're going as friends. Archery buddies.'

I wait for Joe to correct her – that he likes me as more than a friend. But he just looks relieved.

'In fact, we can all go together!' announces Hayley. 'I'll book a limo for all of us! My treat, obvs. And I'll stock it up with snacks and drinks.'

The wide grin on Joe's face already suggests he's about to agree. But my stomach still sinks when he does. 'Sick! Thanks, Hayls! We can all do an afterparty at mine too – my parents are going to Barbados that week.'

'Afterparty – woo!!!' Hayley does a cute little twirl and high-fives Joe before smirking at me.

And with that, my dreams of a solo date with Joe King are officially destroyed.

Chapter 19

I stare hungrily at K's wardrobe. She has more dresses than I've seen in my entire life and each one is more beautiful than the last. I turn to her, not bothering to hide the awe on my face. 'K. I am dying of jealousy right now.'

She shrugs, embarrassed. 'Don't. You can have whatever you want.'

'*Borrow* whatever I want,' I correct. 'Some of these are super expensive. I can't take them!'

'Well, borrow long-term. It's not like I'll ever wear any of them – except this.' She takes out a short black leather dress. I can already see how good she'd look in it. 'The others are just my mum trying to make me into someone I'm not.'

I nod slowly, thinking of all the times my mum has tried to force me into Radha's castoffs. Not only have none of them suited me, but most of them don't even *fit* me properly because Radha is two sizes smaller than me, meaning her wardrobe is not great for my self-esteem. But K's is. We have different body shapes – she's short and muscly, while I'm taller and categorically less muscly. But it seems to balance out because as long as I don't pick a super short dress, they're the same size I wear.

'So… can I try them all on now?!' I burst out, no longer able to play it cool. 'Like a movie montage!'

She raises an eyebrow. 'Do you need a playlist too?'

'Yes!!! Can we take photos of them all too?'

'I was kidding.'

I blush, realising how uncool I am right now.

But then K laughs. 'Oh, fine. You know, I feel like such a girl with you, Kali. I never normally do stuff like this.'

'Uh, yeah, because you're too busy slaying demons.'

'450 to date,' says K. 'Not that I'm counting.'

My jaw falls open, and I almost drop the red chiffon dress in my hand. 'Wow. Well, in that case, you really *do* deserve a break. And I think trying on all your dresses is the answer. You're going to do it with me, right? A movie montage only works if we both do it.'

She hesitates. 'I guess I could try on some Indian outfits for Radha's mehndi night? You could help me pick one?'

I clasp my hand to my heart. 'I cannot think of anything I'd like to do more.'

She opens another cupboard door and I let out an actual scream. It's like Aladdin's cave stuffed with the jewelled, bedazzled fabrics of her Indian outfits. I finger the silk, net, chiffon. and cotton, knowing these are *way* more expensive than mine.

'I cannot *wait* to see you in these,' I tell K, meaning every single word. 'Music?'

She taps her phone and high-energy Bollywood pop music blares out of her speakers. 'Let's do this.'

***

We both stare silently at my reflection in the mirror. I didn't know I could look like this. I'm wearing an electric blue satin dress. It's really simple – tight, short and one-shouldered. But the colour looks amazing against my skin, and with my hair tied up in a messy bun (an unintentional look I just discovered along with the insight that trying on dresses is quite a sweaty activity), I look like a whole new person. The kind of person Joe King would take to the Summer Dance.

'You look…' K coughs. 'Good.'

I grin happily. 'K, I love it, thank you so much. I feel *amazing*.'

K smiles shyly. 'You… look it too.'

'Joe's going to *love* it! And I can't wait to show Rihanna.' K looks down, fidgeting with the emerald-green lehenga she's wearing. 'Wait, don't take that off!' I protest. 'You look amazing in it!'

'I don't know if it's very me,' she says uncertainly. 'It's not—'

'Black,' I finish. 'But it's not exactly neon yellow. It's subtle. And honestly…' I look at her properly, taking in the green velvet crop top that shows off her glowing, brown skin, and the tight muscles of her abdomen, while the crushed silk skirt, patterned with white dots, flows out around her legs. She looks *hot*.

'What?' asks K uncomfortably.

I swallow, realise I'm staring at her. I turn my reddening face away from her, reaching for my phone. 'You… look so good we need a selfie!'

She squirms away, but I force her to stay still, and we both pose for the camera. I make a face at the last second, and K bursts out laughing. That's how I capture us. Me sticking my tongue out and scrunching

170

my eyebrows, while K's face is lit up with laughter. I love it.

But K grabs my phone, her brow furrowed.

'Don't delete it!'

'It's not that,' she says. 'It's the Kali WhatsApp group. It's blowing up.'

We scan the messages quickly. It looks like the Kalis are freaking out that the demons are plotting something. Tech Kali has found a new demon lair, only a few miles from the last spot K and I attacked. So far, so normal in the demon world. But what's different is there is a major hive of activity around this new location. Tech Kali thinks it's not just a group of demons hanging in a forest like normal – she thinks they're *building* something.

'I'm calling them,' says K decisively. 'It makes no sense. Demons can't build.'

Within seconds, all the Kalis have answered the call, filling the small screen with boxes of faces. I step back to watch in excitement. I haven't been on a group call with the Kalis before, and it feels like something out of a spy movie. Especially when K starts speaking. 'What's the situation?'

'I don't really know,' admits Tech Kali. 'But there

is more heat than I've ever seen before at this new location. There must be a record number of demons congregating in this lair. And it looks like they're building something else... I've noticed them carrying supplies in and out.'

'I didn't think they were smart enough to do that,' frowns Model Kali. She's insanely beautiful – even whilst frowning – and I'm momentarily distracted by her face. 'Since when did they learn to do stuff like that?'

'They might be evolving,' suggests Dottoressa Kali. 'To become smarter and improve their living conditions.'

'We've never seen that before,' says K. 'Are they capable of evolving when they're clones?'

'They could be planning something against us,' says Model Kali.

Tech Kali doesn't look convinced. 'They don't *plan* – they act. And clones can't evolve. They're carbon copies.'

'Unless something's changed,' says Dottoressa. 'If they've gained some kind of extra power.'

'Kali and I saw them talking the other day,' says K. 'Not their typical grunting animal stuff. But some kind of debate. They almost seemed *human*.'

I nod. 'Is that not... normal?'

'Absolutely not,' says Tech Kali firmly. 'Raktabija

could do that. He's beyond powerful. But he was killed by Kali-Ma. It's just unfortunate one of his clones got left behind and now we have to deal with these multiplying ants.'

I wouldn't exactly compare these bloodthirsty demons to harmless ants, but I stay quiet.

'Besides,' continues Tech Kali. 'The clones don't have intellect. They're not like humans.'

'Unless they're changing,' points out Model Kali. 'Or evolving, like Dottoressa said.'

'But can that happen?' asks K. 'Is it possible?'

'I don't know,' admits Dottoressa. 'We've not exactly ever had the chance to research demons in the science world. I don't think it's likely, but… anything's possible.'

'It's a good thing that K and New Kali are nearby to keep an eye on things,' remarks Model Kali. That's my epithet for now – New Kali. I would have preferred something more personal, but at least it's not Worst Kali.

K nods. 'Definitely. Whatever's going on with these demons, the solution is simple. We're going to have to take them down.'

'Wait, what?' I laugh nervously. 'Not *alone*, surely? Not with so many of them there? I mean, these might be super demons!'

'We'll join you,' says Tech Kali. 'But we'll need time. A couple of weeks. So we can research more about what we're going into. We don't want to rush into things without knowing what we're facing.'

'It'll be like South America all over again,' grins Model Kali. 'A massacre.'

K's eyes shine at the thought. 'We'll find out more intel in the meantime. And stalk the area.'

'But be careful,' warns Dottoressa Kali. 'Don't go too close. We don't want them to know we've found their hideout.'

K nods. 'Okay. Speak soon everyone.' And with that, the call's over and all the faces have disappeared from the screen.

'Wow,' I say. 'That was… intense.' I suddenly realise I'm still wearing the blue dress, which feels very much at odds with the current situation. I turn away from K, stripping it off, pulling on my oversized T-shirt and lycra shorts instead.

'Something's definitely up,' says K, determinedly not looking at me change. 'I knew it when we saw the demons talking like that the other day. I think they're planning something against us.'

'But Tech Kali said they're just clones; they don't

have the capacity.' I turn to face her, dressed again. 'It's probably nothing major.'

K bites her lip anxiously. 'Kali. Don't get upset. But… I don't know if it's a good idea for you to go to the dance.'

'What?!' I stare at her in dismay. 'But we've planned it! I've got the dress! We agreed it was okay!'

'I know, but with everything that's going on with the demons – I don't have a good feeling about this.'

'I'm not going to cancel my date because of your gut feeling!' I cross my arms. 'It's only one night. And the demons could get us any time.'

'Only when we're bleeding. And you know the dance is the first night of our periods. That makes it high-risk.'

'Well, what if our periods come a day late?'

'They're more likely to come a day early.'

I scowl. 'Don't act like you know my body better than I do.'

'I'm just saying I've been doing this longer than you have.'

'K, it's one night! This is a big deal to me. If something happens, I'll leave the dance. But I'm not cancelling. I'm going with Joe.'

K scoffs. 'Of course you are, *Doomsday*.'

My mouth drops open. 'I can't believe you just said that.'

K has the decency to blush. 'What? It's fine when he says it, but not me?'

I shake my head angrily. 'You're just jealous, K.'

'I am not! What am I meant to be jealous of? Some guy who won't ever use your name — a name that's incredibly beautiful *and* powerful?'

'No, you're jealous of me,' I shoot back. 'Because I'm going to a dance. With a date. And friends. While you don't have a date *or* friends, from what I can see.'

There is silence. I instantly know I've gone too far. K turns away from me and I feel a pang in my chest. Oh no. Please can she not be crying. I've never seen K cry before, and I *really* don't want to be the reason behind her tears.

'K, I didn't mean that. I'm sorry. I know you were with Lola, and—'

She interrupts me, her face puce with rage as she whirls back round. 'You have *no* right to say her name. You know nothing about my life, Kali. All I've done is try to help you. But if you don't want my help, fine. Whatever. You deal with these demons solo.'

My stomach twinges. The thought of fighting demons without K is not something I ever want to face. But I push that thought down. 'I know nothing about you because you don't share! You're a closed book, K. It's impossible to get to know you. At least *I* open up.'

'Yeah, about how much you like Joe and Rihanna. Do you know that's all you've spoken about the last few times we've hung out? You don't even ask about me anymore. And I know you've invited them all to the sangeet, not me. Radha told me when we were messaging.'

I swallow a lump of guilt. But I haven't done anything wrong – I'm allowed to have more than one friend. 'So? I've invited you to the mehndi night!'

'But not the sangeet, with all your school friends. I'm not stupid. I know you don't want them to meet me. Because you're embarrassed of me.'

'That's not true,' I protest. 'It's just... you're all so different. I thought it would be easier this way.'

'Easier for *you*,' says K. 'How do you think I felt when Radha told me that?'

I'm going to kill Radha. 'Well, maybe I wanted to keep you separate because I thought you'd judge *them*! Look how you reacted to me telling you about Joe!'

'Only because I care about you! Not that it's reciprocated. Whatever, Kali. Maybe it's best if you go.'

'Oh, I already am!'

'Good,' says K, throwing the dress at me. 'Don't forget this. You'll need it for your dance.'

'I don't need anything from you!' I turn angrily, grabbing my bag. I can feel tears stinging my eyes but there's no way I'm letting K see that. I open the door and crash into K's mum.

'Kali, darling!' She beams at me. 'I wanted to ask if either of you want some snacks. Cookies and things. Isn't that motherly of me?'

'Congratulations Mum,' snaps K. 'But we're in the middle of something.'

If I ever spoke to my mum like that, she'd kill me. But Deepa Auntie – I've tried, but I can't just call her Deepa – breezes into her daughter's room like nothing happened. 'You look lovely in that lehenga darling, but you might be a bit overdressed for dinner?' Then she picks up the blue dress from the floor. 'Oh, this! I always thought you'd look unbelievable in it, K!'

K's voice is tight with rage. 'Kali's borrowing it. For her dance!'

'No, I'm not–' I object.

'But you must!' Deepa Auntie rushes to give me the dress. 'You'd look stunning in it. Oh, I'm so happy you and K are togeth– uh, friends. Now I get to buy you clothes too!'

K's eyebrows practically knit together in fury. 'You can't buy her clothes! Just… no.'

'Uh, I'd better go…'

Deepa Auntie thrusts the dress into my hands. 'At least take this, darling!'

I let her give it to me. I know I should refuse on principle, but I really can't resist this dress. 'Okay, thanks. Uh, bye.'

K lifts a hand coolly. Her expression is unreadable.

I walk out of the room, a wave of emotions bubbling up inside of me. I can't deal with any of them, so I shove them down, and storm out of K's ridiculous mansion, head held high. I don't need her. I can do this solo.

Chapter 20

'Kali, *beta*?' My mum's head peers round my door. 'Are you changed yet?'

Unfortunately, I am. I'm wearing a lime green lehenga decorated with tiny sparkling gemstones. The result? I look like a neon Christmas tree.

My mum beams at the sight. 'My grown-up girl! You look beautiful!'

That's a lie. I scowl in response. 'Isn't there anything else I can wear? It's very… *green*.'

'I told you to come and choose one yourself for the mehndi night, but no, you were busy with K and archery and who knows what,' admonishes my mum. 'So, Radha and I picked one out for you. She specifically chose this for you.'

Of course, she did. Yet another way she's ruining my life.

'Anyway,' continues my mum, rearranging my chundri. 'What time is K coming?'

K *isn't* coming. Or if she is, she hasn't told me. Because we haven't spoken since our fight. The only reason I know she's still alive is because she shared a video on her TikTok (karate chopping a plank of wood in half). I shared one too – me scoring a succession of golds in archery – in case she also wanted confirmation I was alive.

'Kali?!' My mum waves at me impatiently.

'Um, she's actually not coming. She's… busy.'

My mum's eyebrows shoot up. 'Busy?! But she was so excited about tonight! We were texting about it last week.'

I really don't know how I feel about the fact that K and my mum message. But I do feel a twinge of guilt. K was really looking forward to tonight. Maybe I should apologise? I shouldn't have said what I did about her not having friends, and it must have hurt when she found out she wasn't invited to the sangeet.

But she's never been excited for me about Joe – it wasn't even what she said that day, it's everything she *hasn't* said. Friends are meant to be happy for each other when one of them gets a date – not just scowl and tell them it's too dangerous to go! K owes me an apology too, and I don't see why I should make the first move.

'Her mum needs her for something,' I lie. 'But I have another friend coming instead. Rihanna.'

'What?! Does Radha know?'

I shake my head. Right now, no part of me cares about Radha's feelings – it's not like she cares about mine. 'No, but she said I can have a plus one, so what does it matter?'

'She said you could invite *K*,' clarifies my mum. 'We know her. I don't know anything about this Rhiannon.'

'Rihanna. But I call her Ri. We're friends from archery. And she's really nice – you'll like her.'

My mum frowns, but instead of asking about Ri's grade average and what her parents do like she normally would, she brings the conversation back to her BFF. 'Did something happen with K? Is she alright?'

I exhale sharply. 'I don't know! It's not exactly like K opens up to me. She barely tells me anything about her life.'

'Of course not; she's more traditional. She's not like your white friends, telling everybody ever thought they've ever had.'

'Mum! You can't say that!'

'Oh, I didn't mean it in a bad way. I just mean K is

more like us. Because of our culture. Not like Tanya, who is a lovely girl, but did we really need to know about her IBS in such detail?'

She has a point there. I was Tanya's best friend and even *I* didn't need to know about the consistency of her poo after eating chickpeas. 'Well, at least Tanya *shared* with me. K won't even tell me about her ex-girlfriend!'

My mum frowns. 'Ex-*girl*friend?'

I suddenly realise what I've said. But… it's not a secret. K's the most out person I know. And my mum will be fine with it, I'm sure. But I'm still oddly nervous as I spell it out. 'K… goes out with girls. She identifies as a lesbian.'

My mum's eyebrows shoot up, clearly uncomfortable. 'Oh. I didn't know.'

Now *I* feel uncomfortable – and I don't even know why. 'Is that… I mean… what do you think about it?'

My mum starts fiddling with her wedding rings. 'Nothing! K's a lovely girl. I'm just surprised. It's not very common. For an Indian girl to be… that way.'

That way?

My mum clears her throat. 'I'm not saying I *mind* that she's, you know...'

'You can say the word 'lesbian'.'

'I know I can!' My mum's voice is rising. She clears her throat, then speaks carefully. 'It's just this is going to make her life so much harder.'

'But lots of things make life hard!' Like being attacked by demons. 'Like… being the only Indian in your school. Or having your best friend move to Greece. Life isn't easy. And sexuality isn't something people should feel bad about. It's not a big deal!'

My mum looks taken aback. 'I didn't realise you were so passionate about this, Kali.' Neither did I. 'But you don't need to get upset. I won't treat K any differently. Is that why she's not coming tonight?! Oh, I do hope not!'

I shake my head. 'No.'

My mum looks relieved. 'Good.' Then she looks worried again. 'What about this Rihanna? Is she gay too?'

I'm about to say no, then I realise I've never heard Ri talk about liking a guy, ever. Or talk about liking a girl, either. Or… anyone, really. 'I have no idea. Does it matter?'

'Of course not! I don't know why you're so worked up about this. It's not like you're, you know.'

'Yeah, but, I mean, I don't…' I shift awkwardly. I don't have the words to explain why I feel the way I

184

do right now. So, I give up. 'It's fine. Don't worry.'

My mum's face relaxes. 'Good! And you don't need to worry – I'll always be polite to your friends. Even if they tell me all about their IBS!'

I manage a smile.

***

'Kali, this is *unreal*.' Ri stares at my garden in awe. It does look a lot better than normal. For a start, there's a huge white marquee in it, draped with strings of clear fairy lights. There are cushions in dozens of different fabrics scattered on the ground and old strips of colourful sarees hanging from the ceiling. Each corner of the tent has a 'mehndi station' with local artists decorating the hands and feet of all our female relatives. But the best bit? A huge table on the side covered in the silver buffet trays of Indian caterers.

'Let's get food,' I urge. 'There's chilli paneer. And chaat.'

'I have no idea what that means, but I'm down!' Ri grabs a recycled plastic plate and follows me into the queue. 'I'm so glad your mum had a spare Indian top for me to wear. I would have felt so stupid if I'd had to stay in my shirt.'

185

'You look really good in it,' I tell her, taking a step back to admire her properly. She's wearing a chiffon indigo kurta over her jeans with a sparkly blue bindhi. 'Better than me in this green thing.'

She grins. 'I don't know, I reckon Joe King might like it…'

I blush. 'Stop!'

'Let's take a selfie!' She pulls out her phone and we make faces at the camera, laughing at ourselves onscreen. 'I'm going to tag you. I bet Joe will message you about it.'

I shake my head quickly. 'No! Not in my Indian outfit!'

Ri's brows furrows in confusion. 'What, why not?'

I don't know how to explain it. It's not that I'm embarrassed of my culture, but I'm not exactly keen to show it off either. So, I make a joke instead. 'I don't think Joe's ready to see me dressed like a Christmas tree.'

Ri laughs and my dad bounds over, holding a tray with two glasses on it. 'Girls! I made you both mockitos. But don't tell anyone or they'll all be asking for them.'

'Thanks so much, Mr Kadia,' says Ri. 'That's super nice of you.'

'Call me Uncle Sanj! Everyone does! Have you got food yet? Don't be shy – load your plate up with as much as you can.'

186

'Dad, we're in the food queue right this second. We're on it.'

He grins back at me, and suddenly, I wonder how *he'd* react to K's sexuality. I have a feeling he'd be much more relaxed about it than Mum. But what if I'm wrong and both my parents are weird around people being gay?! Panic rises in me, and I realise I need to know right now. I blurt it out before I have time to rationalise that the buffet queue isn't the best place to have this conversation. 'Dad, K's gay. As in, she dates girls.'

Ri coughs loudly, choking on air. 'Sorry, um, mockito went down the wrong way.'

I face Dad, nervous. But his expression hasn't changed. He's still smiling amiably. 'That's nice. Does she have a girlfriend?'

I let out a breath I didn't realise I'd been holding. 'No, they… broke up last year.'

'I'm sure K was much too good for her!'

I put my plate down and give my dad a hug, squeezing him tight. He pats my head in surprise. 'What's this for, Kali?'

'Nothing. It's just a really good mockito.'

★★★

Ri and I are sitting in the back of the garden together on a low wall, eating our second plates of food, trying and failing to be careful of the drying mehndi on our hands. Mine is already smudged, and Ri's is going the same way.

'Your family is really cool,' she says, in between bites of crispy bhajia. 'You're so lucky.'

I raise my eyebrows. 'I'm sorry. Did you meet Radha?'

Ri laughs. 'Her meltdown when that other guest was wearing the same outfit as her was a bit extra. Especially when Radha looks way better in it.'

'You missed out the fact she's spent the whole evening calling you 'the girl who isn't K.' And lectured us on how we'd smudge our mehndi if we ate afterwards.' I look down at my ruined mehndi and scowl. 'I hate that she's right.'

Ri shrugs. 'It will still look cool. And the rest of your relatives are so friendly. Your dad is amazing.'

I smile proudly. 'He really is, isn't he?

'I loved how chill he was about K's sexuality. There's no way my family would react like that. Black Caribbean families tend to have *opinions* on that kind of thing.'

188

I hesitate. 'My mum wasn't so chill either... I told her earlier and she gave me this whole 'thank god it's not you, because it makes life so much harder to be that way' speech. It was kind of depressing.'

Ri suddenly looks glum, prodding her chilli paneer.

I know it's not my place, but just in case she needs someone to ask, I do it. 'Ri... are you... I mean, how do you identify? In terms of your sexuality?'

Her eyes rise to meet mine, wide with fear.

'You don't have to tell me,' I say quickly. 'I'm sorry. I shouldn't have asked. It doesn't even matter. I like you for you, not for who you like.'

'But that's the problem,' wails Ri. 'I don't like *anyone*!'

'That's okay. I mean, so long as you like me – as a friend.'

She rolls her eyes at me. 'Kali! I'm trying to tell you that... well, I've *never* liked anyone.' She lowers her voice so it's practically a whisper. 'I think... I might be asexual.'

'Oh,' I say. 'I didn't know. Thanks for sharing it with me though. I'm glad you felt comfortable enough to tell me.'

She stares at me like I'm crazy. 'THAT'S your reaction? You don't think I'm weird? Abnormal?!'

I stare at *her* like she's crazy. 'Because you might be

asexual? That's not weird at all! Loads of people are. And you're Rihanna Taylor. You're the coolest girl in our year. You being ace would just want to make everyone wish they were ace.'

'I don't know… I'm Black. I don't know any other Black asexuals. My family wouldn't get it, ever. My older sister is the most sexual person ever, and that's seen as normal. Not what I am. Whatever that is.'

'Normal is overrated,' I say firmly. 'And it doesn't exist. Trust me. I might look normal – actually, I probably don't – but I'm *definitely* not. Nobody is.'

She sighs. 'I know you're right, but this just feels… hard.'

I nod, squeezing her hand. 'I get it, Ri. I'm sorry you haven't been able to talk to anyone about it. But you can talk to me whenever you want. I completely accept you in every way. And I might not be able to relate to the asexuality, but I *totally* relate to feeling different.'

She smiles. 'Thanks Kali. It does feels good to talk about it. You know, it's why I got so into the goddess Kali… She doesn't believe in labels or being defined. I get the feeling that if she was asexual, she'd own it, and would eat anyone who didn't like it.'

I laugh. 'You're right. She's so powerful, isn't she? I always hated being named after her because she's the scary, weird death goddess. But I'm starting to see that she's also *fierce*.'

'She's my favourite goddess ever. I think you're lucky to be named after her.' Then she pauses, fingering the edge of the kurta. 'Also Kali, you promise you won't tell anyone about this, right?'

'Promise. It's between us.'

'Thanks.' The relief is evident on her face. 'I did once try to discuss asexuality with Hayley. Not about me, but in general. It, uh, didn't go well. I don't think she believes in asexuality.'

'I don't think asexuality is something you can believe in. It's just a fact. But... is that why you've been feeling less close to Hayley lately?'

Ri hesitates, then nods. 'I know what she can be like, but we have always got on. She's really loyal and a lot of fun. Except... her comment on asexuality really bothered me. I know she probably would have been nicer if she'd known I was speaking about myself. But I was too nervous to say anything.'

'If she's a real friend, she'll be there for you. But in the meantime, I am. Whenever you need me.'

Ri hugs me and I squeeze her back, grateful for this friend I never thought I'd have.

Chapter 21

Today is the day. It's finally happening. I am going to the Summer Dance with Joe King. And Hayley, Ri, and Jack. But that's not the point. I check my reflection one last time in the mirror – I'm wearing the electric blue dress with my favourite trainers, and I've teased my hair into a messy bun with a few tendrils of hair framing my face at the front. It's not perfect but it's as good as I'm ever going to look.

'Kali?' The door opens. It's Radha. 'Oh my god, you look so cute!'

Even her compliments sound patronising. 'Thanks.'

'Can I take a picture of you?'

I stare at her, confused. 'A selfie of us together?'

'No, just you!'

'But… why?'

She rolls her eyes. 'You're practically my little sister and you're going to prom. It's a big deal.'

'We call it the Summer Dance.'

'Kali, can I just take this picture? It might make a nice profile pic!'

'Fine.' I turn to face her, smiling awkwardly.

Radha snaps a photo of me and beams. 'See? You look amazing!'

She's right… I look better than I've ever looked before. Even my smile somehow looks cute rather than cringe. 'Thanks,' I say begrudgingly. 'It's nice.'

She takes this as an invitation to sit down on my bed, curling her bare legs underneath her. 'So. Do you have a date tonight?'

'No!' My voice sounds strangled. I clear my throat to sound more normal – I really don't want my family to find out I have a date. My mum will probably force me to stay home, or worse, send Radha as a chaperone. 'I mean… I'm just going with some friends.'

She raises an eyebrow. 'And there's no one in this group you like?'

I'm silent.

'Come on Kali, you can tell me! I'm your cousin.'

I never share with Radha. But I also never go to the Summer Dance, let alone with Joe King. These are extenuating circumstances and considering that K and I aren't speaking right now, and Ri has a conflict of

193

interest with Hayley, I haven't been able to discuss this as much as I want to. Reluctantly, I tell her. 'Okay, fine. There is someone.'

Radha squeals. 'I knew it! Tell me more!! Who are they? I know them, don't I?'

'It's Joe King. He's the cutest guy in the whole year and he's asked *me* to go with him!'

Radha looks surprised. 'Oh wow. A guy. Cool. And… you've liked him for a while?'

'For as long as I can remember. He's really funny, and chill, and he's so good at archery.' I blush as I remember him standing up to Hayley for me at archery, holding my hand, saying he was taking *me* to the dance. I had tingles running through my whole body – until Hayley insulted me. 'I just never thought he'd like me back.'

Radha shakes her head. 'Kali, you really need to work on your self-confidence. Why *wouldn't* he like you back? Or anyone else for that matter?'

I brush off her question. As if Radha would get it. She's basically a brown Barbie. Just then, my phone vibrates. It must be from the others saying they're outside.

But it's K. My heart races as I open the message. It's the first time I've heard from her since our fight!

Hey. Be careful tonight. The demons are still up to something

and we don't know what. Also, not sure if we're still in sync,
but my period just arrived. Yours?

That's it?! There's no warmth at all. No apology.
No 'I miss you.' Not even a good luck for the dance
tonight! All K cares about is my period and demons.

'Who is it?' asks Radha. 'Wait, why am I even asking?
The way your face lit up when you opened it means
it's obviously Joe.'

'Just leave it!!' I snap.

Radha's face crumples. She gets up. 'Fine. I just wanted
to wish you luck. I'll send you the photo I took.'

'Thanks,' I say, instantly feeling bad. 'I'm sorry for
shouting. It's just…'

'Don't worry about it. Nerves. Have fun tonight.'

The door closes behind her, leaving me alone. I don't
want to do this, but I know I have to. I slowly hitch
my dress up and pull my knickers down. My stomach
sinks as I see a familiar wet patch glistening on the
fabric. Blood. I don't know what to do. I spent my last
period with K right by my side. Every time a demon
popped up, she was there to kill it for me. What if a
demon shows up at the dance? I don't know if I can
do this alone.

My phone vibrates again. This time it's Joe.

We're outside!!! Come down! This limo is SICK!

I stare at my knickers – and then I grab a tampon from my drawers. I'm not going to let a bit of blood stop me from living my dream.

***

'Let's get this party started!!' Hayley downs a shot and turns the music up, dancing around in her seat. I'd look insane if I started flailing my arms around like her, but she makes it look effortlessly sexy. Her outfit helps. She's wearing a strapless gold dress with floaty bits coming off it, and matching gold heels. With her blonde hair swishing in a long ponytail, she's literally golden, and I feel boring in comparison. I shift uncomfortably, realising that in my rush to leave the house, I didn't put my tampon in properly.

'Are you having fun Doomsday?' Joe leans over, and I get shivers as I inhale the deep woody scent he's used. Until I start coughing; I must have accidentally breathed in too much.

'Oh my god, I love this song!' Ri starts seat-dancing to the Afrobeats song, badly singing along to the rap bit. I can't help but laugh with her. She's not trying to be sexy like Hayley, but she's a million times cooler in

196

her black tuxedo with a lacey bra top beneath, paired with neon trainers. She looks like a celebrity, especially with her narrow rectangular sunglasses.

Joe and Jack are in tuxes. They both look good, but there's not really more to say than that. Let's be honest, female fashion is way more interesting than the male variety.

'Selfie time!' coos Hayley. She pulls out her phone, tapping quickly with her gold nails, and we all pose behind her. I find myself at the edge of the photo, hidden by Hayley's ponytail. I try to angle myself differently, but it's too late. Hayley takes the photo and all you can see is one of my eyes. It's closed.

'Kali, you closed your eyes,' she says accusingly as though it was my fault. 'Also, we're almost at the dance. Are you going to do your hair now?'

'Uh... it's done.'

She quickly covers her mouth with her hand. 'Oh my god, sorry! I didn't realise you'd deliberately styled it like that.'

The others are busy making some kind of cocktail, and don't notice the insult. I'm glad there's nobody to see me flush with embarrassment.

'Where did you get your dress from anyway?' asks Hayley. 'It's gorgeous.'

I feel like I'm walking into a trap, but I don't know how to avoid it. I have no choice but to reply. 'Thanks, I borrowed it from a friend.'

Hayley nods. 'Thought so. It looks way more expensive than your normal stuff.'

And there it is. I turn away from Hayley's smugness and grab a drink from Jack's hands. I don't know what's in it but I down the whole thing.

'Yes Kali! Par-taaaay!' says Jack. He pours more brightly coloured drinks for everyone, handing one to Hayley, who simpers in delight. 'For you, gorgeous.'

My phone vibrates. It's K again.

Have you seen the Kali WhatsApp group? They think the demons are planning something tonight.

Can't she just leave me alone?! It's hard enough dealing with Hayley's subtle put-downs, let alone being reminded of demons every two minutes.

I'm fine, I type back angrily. *Chill.*

She replies instantly.

Do you have your period?

Is she serious?! I'm in a limo on my way to the most important night of the school year and she's still obsessing about my menstruation! There's only one way to get her to leave me alone.

I tap out a lie.

No. So can you just leave me alone? Thanks.

I look at my phone waiting to see if she'll reply – but nothing. Finally. I should probably read the messages in the Kali WhatsApp group… But the demons are always planning something these days. It can wait 'til tomorrow.

Joe taps me on the shoulder. 'Babe, do you want a drink?'

I reach for it thirstily, and down the sugary mixture instantly.

'Uh, we were meant to drink them together,' said Hayley pointedly. 'And cheers first?'

I flush, my head spinning. I shouldn't have drunk so fast. 'Oh. Sorry.'

'I'll pour her another,' says Jack, looking at Hayley as he hands me another drink. It almost spills everywhere as I reach for it.

'Okay, let's do it!' says Ri. 'One, two, three – cheers!!'

We all pour our drinks down our throats, and I can't help laughing as I look around the limo. This is everything I'd ever dreamt my school experience would be – hanging out with boys, going to a dance with Joe King, and having friends like Ri (I still can't count Hayley as a friend) – but I'd never thought it would actually *happen.* I'm literally living my dream.

Chapter 22

I've imagined walking into the dance on Joe King's arm so many times and it always plays out the exact same way. He has his arm through mine, and we push open the double doors of the school gym. Time slows down and there's an iconic song playing in the background. Everyone stops dancing and stares at us in total awe. While Joe looks into my eyes with pure love.

But reality turns out to be very different from my fantasy. When we push open the doors, nobody even notices. They're too busy dancing to some sugary pop song that everyone will have forgotten by next summer, and Joe doesn't look in my eyes *once*. But the biggest difference? While I'm on Joe's right arm, Hayley is hanging off his left arm.

'So… shall I go get us some drinks?' I ask Joe when it becomes clear he isn't going to ask.

'Perfect!' Hayley blows me a fake kiss while still clinging tight to Joe.

I walk away in anger. I'm sick of this battle with Hayley. I only wanted to go to the dance with Joe because I thought he actually liked me – if he wants to be with Hayley, why did he bother asking me? And if he doesn't want to be with her, why doesn't he just tell her to leave us alone? I feel like I've been caught up in their weird game and I hate it.

I'm so absorbed in my thoughts that I don't notice Ri come up behind me. 'Hey Kali. Are you okay?'

The punch I'm pouring spills all over my dress and I groan in frustration. 'Ughhhh. This is not my night.'

Ri grabs a napkin and dries the wet patch. 'It'll come out. Are you okay?'

I shake my head. 'Thanks. It's just… I thought Joe and I would have a chance to really get to know each other tonight. But we've barely had a single conversation without Hayley popping up.'

Ri sighs. 'I wish I could say I'm surprised, but you know Hayley…'

'Unfortunately, I do.'

'Maybe I can help?' she suggests. 'I can tell her I want a best friend dance! I'll get the DJ to put on her favourite song. Then you and Joe can have some alone time.'

My heart lifts with excitement. 'Would you really do

that for me?'

'Sure! That's what friends are for.' She winks at me, then slips into the crowd. Within seconds, the DJ has put on Taylor Swift, and Ri is dragging Hayley into the middle of the dancefloor. They're swallowed up by a mass of sweaty bodies, and finally, I'm free. I waste no time in rushing over to Joe with two glasses of punch.

'Doomsday!' he cries, grabbing my wrist. The punch spills on my dress again – okay K's dress – but this time I don't care because he's twirling me around like we're in a movie.

I protest, laughing. 'I can't dance!'

'Of course, you can – you're already dancing as well as you shoot arrows.'

That isn't true, but I'm too dizzy to mind. I let Joe spin me around, giggling as we dance in circles, leaning into the sensation of letting go. This is the most un-Kali Kadia thing I have ever done, and I don't want it to stop.

Joe pulls me close to him and his breath tickles the nape of my neck. My every cell prickles with exhilaration. 'Did I tell you how pretty you look tonight?'

'I think you did earlier. But it's always good to hear it

twice,' I reply honestly. Then I cringe at myself. I was meant to be flirty and cute – not factual!

But Joe laughs. 'You're so funny. And you're *sick* at archery. You're like, the exact opposite of Hayley.'

Hayley is incredibly stunning, popular, and confident so I'm not sure this is the best compliment. Nor do I really want to hear her name when we're having a moment, but Joe is obviously trying to be nice, so I smile.

'Do you, uh, want to go outside?' he asks. 'Get some air?'

I freeze. I know what this means. 'Do you want to get some air?' is a direct synonym for 'do you want to kiss me?' It happens in every teen movie I've seen. And now it's happening in my actual life.

I force myself to nod. 'Yes. Please. Now?'

Joe grabs my hand, and we sneak out of the hall without Hayley noticing – she's still in the middle of the dancefloor with Ri. I have no idea where we're going, but Joe clearly does, confidently leading me down the hallway into the Maths classroom. I refuse to entertain the thought that he has done this before. Instead, I let myself feel special, chosen, wanted, as he shuts the door behind us.

'Hey,' he whispers.

'Hey,' I whisper back, suddenly terrified. The high I felt earlier has gone and I feel scarily clear-headed. I try to remember everything Tanya and I learnt about kissing from YouTube, but my mind goes blank as Joe steps closer towards me. His face is so symmetrical. He smells of woodiness, of sweat, of boy. Oh my god, I can't believe this is about to happen!

Before I can fully freak out, Joe is right by my face. He looks into my eyes and my heart starts racing at 100 miles an hour. This is the boy I like – and he's about to *kiss* me. I feel overcome with desire, my whole body tingling like mad in anticipation of what's about to happen.

He leans in slowly, and his lips – soft, plump, wet – land on top of mine. This is so momentous that it takes me a solid two seconds before I remember I'm meant to do something too. I try to copy him, moving my lips the way he does. It's harder than I thought it would be.

He slides his tongue into my mouth, and I instantly pull back, semi-repulsed by this wet muscle intruding into my personal space. But this is what real kissing is. So, I gingerly stick my tongue into his mouth, just like he did to me. I have no idea what I'm meant to be doing with it, but Joe groans in delight the second

I touch his tongue with mine, so it can't be that wrong. He slides his tongue over mine, like he's giving it a massage, and I focus intently on imitating him. The YouTube videos lied. They said that as soon as it starts, it will feel natural, and you won't even need to think about it.

But I can't think about anything *but* what I'm doing. I sneakily open my eyes to check how Joe is. I'm terrified he'll think I'm bad at kissing, but his eyes are closed, and he looks fully engrossed in our kiss. It's a relief, and I close my eyes again, desperately trying not to overthink things. Things improve marginally, but I still feel awkward, like my tongue and lips aren't where they're meant to be. We're not moving in sync, and it feels weird. I bet Hayley never has this problem.

Just then I hear a loud sound. The door. I break away from Joe's lips, pretending I haven't noticed a strand of drool linking our mouths together. I turn slowly to see who has caught us. I don't know what would be worse: a teacher or Hayley.

It takes a few seconds for my eyes to register that there's a third option I hadn't even considered and it's a million times worse than either a teacher or Hayley. There's a demon standing there, and it runs straight towards us, with its classic demon cry. 'ARGHHH!!!'

My brain feels sluggish, and I stand there blinking like a total idiot before my muscle memory takes over. I spring into action, grabbing a packet of biros from Mr Arthur's desk. I seamlessly launch one straight at the demon's eye. It pierces it perfectly, causing the demon to collapse to the ground, instantly dead, as drops of its blood scatter onto the floor. I freeze in total horror. What was I thinking?! How could I have forgotten to sort out a tarp situation?! I've made everything worse!

'Kali, what's happening?!' Joe's eyes are wide with pure fear. I know I'm meant to be fully preoccupied by the demon intrusion, but I still notice he's called me Kali not Doomsday. It feels quite nice. But now is not the time to focus on that. I've inadvertently just created four – oh no – *five* more demons.

I grab Joe's hand. 'Run!!'

We race out of the classroom and into the hallway. I have no idea where to go. I need to find a way to kill the demons without their blood getting on the ground. I try to think quickly – the lacrosse fields? No, that's pure ground. The language labs? No, too complicated. The swimming pool? Yes! It is already covered up with tarp – if I get the demons on there and kill them, all the blood will land on the plastic!

I lead Joe straight towards the pool. We're running as fast as we can, but the demons are right behind us. I push open the double doors, beyond grateful that South Bridge's caretaker is so old he constantly forgets to lock everything. Joe and I have just managed to get to the far side of the pool when the demons enter. They crash through the doors, running towards us, their faces snarled and teeth gnashing in anticipation. I gulp, praying my plan works.

And it does. The demons don't run around the side of the pool like Joe and I did – they start racing right across it, on top of the tarp. I get my pens ready to fire them off.

'They're coming for us!' cries Joe, grabbing my arm. I shake him off in annoyance. He's distracted me and it means my first pen misses the demon I was aiming for. I force myself to breath before I fire off the next one. I come back to my mantra: 'let go'. Then I quickly fire off a succession of pens using all my strength, desperately wishing they were fire arrows. But luckily the pens are enough. The demons start collapsing onto the plastic cover, their blood pooling around them.

'Kali, what have you *done*?' Joe doesn't look impressed by the fact that I've just saved our lives. He looks...

grossed out. By me. 'How do you know how to do this? Who are you?!'

I stare at him, lost for words. I can't believe this is how he's reacting to the fact that I just managed to take out six demons. I saved his life – and he's looking at me like *I'm* a demon.

Then I hear a sound behind us. I whirl around to see that two of the demons haven't died. They've lost their eyes but they're still alive, rolling on the pool cover. It's not over.

I fumble for my pens, trying to get ready to fire. I only have two left. I cannot miss.

'Why aren't you answering me?!' asks Joe. 'This is wild!'

I glance at him as I'm getting into position to launch my pen, and I suddenly see myself through Joe's eyes. The girl he brought to the Summer Dance as his date is launching biros at a bunch of one-eyed demons. Demons that appeared as soon as he kissed her. His nickname for me has never been so fitting. I am Doomsday in action, bring doom with me wherever I go.

'ARGGH!'

The demons let out their blood-curdling scream as they manage to get up onto their feet. The loss of their eyes has made them angrier than ever. I prepare to launch the pens with all my strength. But I'm not fully present and I forget the mantra. I'm too busy thinking about what Joe must be thinking. I fire my pen right at the demon's heart – but it doesn't pierce it like I wanted it to. It doesn't even touch the demon's skin. I missed.

'Kali?' This time, Joe's voice is trembling. It's obvious he is terrified, and honestly? Same. The demons are metres away from us. I only have one pen left. I need to save us. But I don't know how. And I can't stop thinking about what a freak I am. An oddity. A weirdo. Just like the goddess I'm named after.

The demons poise themselves, ready to launch themselves at us. I need to at least take one of the demons out so I can hand-fight the other. I fire the last pen at the demons – there's not a second to spare – and it flies right towards them. But it doesn't hit either of them hard enough to kill. All it does is scrape one of the demon's wrists, and then drop to the ground. It's over. I don't have any more left.

The demons open their mouths wide, and make a loud joyful sound, as though they're laughing at my failure. This is it. They're going to kill me. Joe whimpers at my side, and I feel my body flood with guilt. It's not fair he's been dragged into this. He's not a Kali. I am.

This is my battle. Not his.

Without thinking, I step in front of him, blocking him from the demons. 'Come on then. Let's do this. Come at me.' I raise my fists to my head like K taught me. K. God, I wish she was here. But the regret and longing that floods my body is too painful, so I swallow it away. Instead, I turn to Joe and whisper: 'As soon as you can, *run*. I'll keep them away from you.'

His wide eyes register my words, and he nods imperceptibly. I turn back to the demons and breathe as they bend their knees to jump, ready to attack. I can do this. I've got this. I protect my head as they fly through the air towards me – but my fists don't make contact with demon skin. Because they haven't landed by me at all. I whirl around in confusion to see they've jumped straight over me to get to Joe. I scream as they grab his arms.

'NO! Not him. It's me you want! Me! I'm Kali!!'

I race up to them, ready to punch and beat them K-style. But I don't get a chance. Because one of them kicks me hard, and I'm flung on the cold, hard tiles, all the way across the other side of the pool.

'Help!!' cries Joe. 'Help me!'

I get up, ignoring the burning pain in my ribs, and

run towards him and the two demons. But they're getting away from me. I run faster, out of the pool, into the corridor, but by the time I get to the open fire exit doors, standing outside the school, the demons are nowhere to be seen. They've gone. And they've taken my date with them.

Chapter 23

I'm freaking out. I don't know what to do. I'm running around the school looking for Joe – praying for a sign of him or even the demons. He's not in the school car park or the sports fields. He's not in any of the classrooms. The hallway. The bathrooms. The girls *or* the boys.

'Uh, what are you doing coming out of the boys bathroom?' Hayley is standing in the hallway, twirling her hair round her nails, staring at me like I'm insane.

I *feel* insane. I ignore her question, asking my own instead. 'Have you seen Joe?'

She shakes her head, a slow smile spreading across her face. 'Did he ditch you? Sorry Kali, it's probably not personal. Although, he's never ditched *me* at a dance before.'

'I need to find him. Now.'

She smiles sweetly. 'Why don't you freshen up first? You look kind of....' She makes a face at me, then opens the nearby disabled bathroom door and urges me in. 'Here. It's private and you can fix your face.'

'No! I don't need to freshen up; I need to find Joe!'

But Hayley shoves me into the bathroom anyway. She's stronger than I expected. I'm momentarily distracted by my reflection in a huge mirror on the wall (no wonder Hayley loves this bathroom). I have mascara smudged under my eyes, sweat glistening all over me, and my hair is a bird's nest. But this is the least of my worries.

I turn back to Hayley, ready to demand she moves out of my way, but instead she slams the door shut. My blood runs cold. I tug hard on the door handle. But it's locked. 'No, Hayley!! Come on! Let me out!!'

'Sorr-eee. Guess I'll have to find Joe alone.'

I bang on the door. 'Please! You can have Joe – I don't care! Just let me out!! It's urgent!'

But I'm met with silence – the only sound is the distant fading of Hayley's platforms clacking down the corridor. She's gone. And I'm alone. Locked in a toilet, while the demons have my date. I start to hyperventilate. This is a nightmare. They're going to kill Joe. They could be killing him *right now*. Cutting him into pieces and roasting him on a fire. No. I can't think about that! If they wanted to kill him, they would have done it right here. They've taken him alive for a reason. It's a kidnapping. Maybe they want me and the other Kalis as ransom? They'll need Joe alive for that. This thought calms me down. Joe's okay. All I need to do is get out and rescue him.

I pull out my phone and slide my finger across the screen, waiting for it to light up. But it doesn't. Nothing happens. I press the button on the side. Nothing. I press all the buttons in total panic. But it's futile. My phone is dead. And nobody knows I'm here.

I start banging on the door. 'Hello?! Help!! HELLO?!!' Silence.

But I refuse to give up. Somebody has to come through this corridor at some point. Even if they're just coming to find a quiet classroom to make out in like Joe and I did. My stomach tightens at the memory. It already feels like a lifetime ago.

I bang louder. 'Hello?!!!! Anyone!! HELP! PLEASE!'

'Um, hello?' There's a faint female voice in the distance.

'In here!!' I shout back. 'The disabled toilet! I can't get out!'

'I'm coming,' says the voice, getting louder as it comes closer. 'Hang on…' I can hear them fiddling with the lock. It takes forever. And then, finally, the door opens. 'Kali?!' It's Mrs Patel. 'What are you *doing* in here? And why was this locking the door?' She holds up a gold hairband.

'It… doesn't matter. I have to go. They've got Joe.'

She pales, reaching out a hand against the wall to steady her. 'Not…'

'The demons.'

'I don't understand… Why Joe? Why not you?'

I shake my head impatiently. This confirms my suspicions that Mrs Patel knew about the demons all along, but I don't have time for some big chat. I need to get Joe back. 'Who knows? Ransom maybe. A trap. But either way, I need to find them.' I turn to leave but Mrs Patel grabs my arm.

'Kali, wait. How do you feel about Joe?'

'What?!' I stare at her like she's unhinged.

She shakes her head impatiently. 'Forget I'm your teacher. Just… tell me. Do you… feel desire for him? Fancy him, as you kids say?'

I give up. Nothing makes sense right now. I may as well tell Mrs Patel about my crush. I look her in the eyes. 'I've fancied him for four years. And I don't think I've ever felt as much desire for him as I did earlier, just before we kissed.'

She relaxes her grip on my arm, and her eyebrows furrow. 'Maybe… But… How would they know that? Unless… No… I always wondered if they could evolve… One day… I just, oh…'

'What is it?!'

She swallows loudly. 'Kali, I… I might be wrong, but you need to know something. About the goddess Kali. It could help.'

'Anything. Please.'

'Kali is also the goddess of sexuality. Not everyone talks about this much because, well, taboos. But sexuality and desire are incredibly powerful. That's why Kali, as one of the most powerful goddesses in Hinduism, represents them.'

'So?! What does that have to do with the demons taking Joe?!'

Mrs Patel sighs. 'I think… well… there's a legend, but it's unproven. That if Kali puts her desire onto somebody, as in, if she has an object of her affection, that person will also become powerful. Their blood will become imbued with the power of Kali's sexuality.'

I gasp as it hits me. 'Are you saying that if a Kali likes someone, their blood can become more powerful?!

'Possibly.'

Oh my god. The demons want Joe's blood – and it's all because I fancy him. I grab my clutch bag and run.

216

'Kali! Darling!' Deepa Auntie opens the door and beams at me. 'You wore the dress!' Then she hesitates. 'Although, your face… Are you…'

'Too much dancing,' I say lightly. 'Is K here?'

'Upstairs. She's not in the best mood.' Deepa Auntie smiles apologetically. 'I think she probably thought you'd ask her to be your date to the dance.'

I ignore Deepa Auntie – even though her comment has annoyingly lodged itself into my mind – and run up the stairs to find K, my head spinning. Too much time has already been wasted, thanks to Hayley, so I burst open K's door without even knocking. She's sat on her bed with her laptop.

'Kali?!'

I collapse onto her bed, panting, ignoring the dizziness in my head. 'K, I need your help.'

She crosses her arms. 'I thought you didn't need my help. You specifically said 'leave me alone.' So I did.'

'That was before! The demons have got Joe! They took him!!'

To my surprise, K's face doesn't register shock. Instead, she just nods quickly. 'Another one. Okay.'

'What?! Why aren't you freaking out?'

'It's happening worldwide,' she says, typing on her laptop. 'Which you'd know if you were keeping track of the WhatsApp group.'

'My phone died! And if the demons were stealing people's crushes you could have TOLD me instead of just asking about my cycle!'

'That started happening *after* you told me to leave you alone. And it was all in the WhatsApp group anyway.' She looks directly into my eyes, and I flush under the intensity of her gaze. I should have read those messages. 'The demons have got Tech Kali's fiancé. And Model Kali's crush. And Dottorressa's wife has gone. 'The Kalis weren't even there to protect them. The demons found them without the Kalis even being there. It was planned.'

'Oh my god.'

'Is that what happened to you?' asks K.

I squirm. 'Not exactly…' I was with Joe. If I hadn't been so distracted, I could have killed all the demons, and they never would have taken him. But K doesn't need to know that right now. 'I'll explain later. Tell me more.'

K angles her screen to me, so I can see all the messages in the group chat. I scan them in panic, exhaling loudly as I absorb the details of the demon-nappings and all the warnings to BE EXTRA ALERT. 'I can't believe it… This is a nightmare… What do we do?!'

'We come up with a plan to get them back,' says K. 'We just need to figure out what they want with them first.'

'Mrs Patel!' I garble. 'I mean, she told me something.' I try to remember everything she said. 'Uh, so Kali's also the goddess of sexuality, which means when we fancy people, their blood gets extra powerful, and the demons have figured it out.' I take a deep breath, then look into K's eyes. 'I think they want to drink Joe's blood.'

To K's credit, she doesn't freak out. The only sign she's even heard me is that her eyes widen slightly. 'I need to tell the others.'

I nod impatiently, waiting while she conveys the information to them. 'So, what's the plan? How do we get Joe back? And the others?'

'We need to go and scout out this demon lair near us. Check to see if our theory is right and they're holding all the crushes there.'

'And then we break them out?'

'Eventually. But first, we need more intel. And we need to wait for the others to get here. We can't take

219

on this many demons alone.'

I hate that she's right. 'Okay, but can we go now? I need to know that Joe is okay!'

She nods tightly. 'Fine. I'll get the kit and meet you downstairs.'

'In the hallway? Don't we need to hide from your mum?'

'I'll tell her we're going back to your dance. She'll be thrilled.'

My stomach lurches as I remember Deepa Auntie's comment about K wanting to go to the dance with me. I wish she had. Then none of this would have happened.

'Okay. Let's do this.'

Chapter 24

'It's down here,' says K, leading the way through a quiet path. 'Be careful not to make a noise on the twigs.'

I angle my torch onto K's figure, following her every step. 'How do you know?'

'I came to check it out as soon as Tech Kali spotted all the activity going on here last week.'

Of course. I was meant to go with K. But instead, I accused her of having no friends and stormed out of her house. I swallow the memory away. 'Right. What did you find?'

'I've been a couple of times now and Tech Kali is right – it looks like they're building something inside this warehouse. I wasn't sure what, but now I'm assuming it's some kind of system to get the crushes' blood. Other than that, I couldn't see much. None of the demons ever saw me, so they don't know we know about their lair. I put it all in the WhatsApp group days ago.'

I silently curse myself for actively avoiding the group

since my fight with K. I'd silenced the notifications and ignored the growing number of unread messages, all because I was annoyed with her and our demon-slaying lifestyle. But I was an idiot. If I'd kept up to date and been more careful, Joe would still be here.

'Ow!' I trip over something and fall onto the dry ground. I wince, reaching for whatever tripped me up. 'A phone! It's Joe's!'

K puts a finger to her lips to warn me to be silent, gesturing at me to keep the phone safe. I slide it into my pocket and realise we've arrived.

The demon lair is a huge, abandoned warehouse. From the outside, there's no way you'd ever know there were dozens of demons inside, sucking the blood from innocent civilians. It's simply a large, wooden structure, with a few narrow windows way up high. We need to get up there to see inside.

I turn to K, but she's already on it. I follow her as she silently springs up onto a closed rubbish bin on the side of the building, pulling herself up onto a narrow ledge, and crouches down to peer into one of the thin, rectangular windows. She gestures at me to join her. I clamber onto the bin far less gracefully than she did, trying to be as quiet as possible. I'm sweating by the time I reach her side, ready to look into the window. It takes a moment for my vision to adjust to the darkness. But slowly, the scene unfolds.

There are demons *everywhere*. Their skin is glowing red in the moonlight rays. There are more of them than I've ever seen in my life. And they don't look like the crazed predators I'm used to. They're conversing with each other. In different groups. Some of them are carrying things. Others are talking. But most of them are standing around a giant vat. I squint trying to see what's inside, but the angle of the window means it's impossible to tell. I turn my gaze to the other side of the warehouse in frustration. It's so hard to see anything when there are so many demons in the way. Where's Joe?!

And then I see him. He's slumped in a corner, next to three other humans. They're all tied up and it looks like there are thin tubes attached to their arms. We were right; the demons are taking their blood.

I turn to K in dismay, pointing silently to their corner, and she uses the binoculars to get a clearer view. I'm so relieved he's alive. And the others. But how long will that last if all their blood is being drained from their bodies?! Suddenly, the energy inside the lair changes.

The demons start barking at each other in their grunting, angry language. One of them gesticulates wildly – he must be in charge. The others reluctantly obey and make their way over to the humans. I feel my every muscle tense up. If they try to hurt Joe, I'm going to smash this window and jump in. I don't care how badly the odds are stacked in my favour; I can't sit back and let the demons kill my date.

But to my surprise, the demons simply remove the tubes from the humans' arms, then walk away. I exhale deeply as I see Joe rubbing his arm. He looks annoyed, but okay. He says something to the Indian man next to him. That must be Tech Kali's fiancé. And there's a cute white guy with glasses. Model Kali's crush? And a beautiful woman in a suit. Dottoressa's wife. They're all okay.

Just then, another group of demons approach, carrying some kind of package in their hands. My throat constricts with terror. What is it? Weapons? Drugs? I imagine the worst as I grab the binoculars from K and zoom in. The demons are holding boxes. I hold my breath as I wait to see what they pull out. A demon hand reaches in and it comes out with…. a sandwich. My mouth drops in total shock. I squint and realise it's not just any sandwich – it's an M&S sandwich. The boxes are full of M&S meal deals – bottles of water, juices, crisps, and sandwiches.

The demons start throwing the food to the humans who grab it gratefully. I can't stop staring in disbelief. This is the weirdest thing I have ever seen. But it's also undeniable proof the demons are planning on keeping our crushes alive. I breathe out in relief.

K taps my arm. 'Some of the demons are starting to sniff around,' she whispers. 'I have my period. We need to go before they find us.'

Wordlessly, I nod, following her back down the side of the building and into the woods. I have no idea how to feel about what I've just seen. This is *really* not how I expected the night to end.

***

'This is a good thing,' says Tech Kali, her pixelated face nodding up and down. 'They're keeping them alive.'

'It's insane!' cries Model Kali, waving her manicured hands wildly. 'How have these demons figured out what humans need to stay alive?! And how have they managed to rob a goddamn M&S?! They're practically becoming humans themselves!'

'It is scary,' admits Dottoressa. 'We need to completely change the way we think about them. I can only assume something's happened to their DNA over time and they're starting to evolve.'

'I have a feeling that drinking all your crushes' blood is only going to speed up that process,' says K, as blunt as ever.

Model Kali recoils. 'Oh god – poor Liam. He didn't sign up for this. He doesn't even know I fancy him! He's only photographed me for a couple of shoots and now he's been transported across the globe to some grubby building in a grey, cold country with demons sucking his blood.'

'England's actually quite hot right now,' I say. It's my first contribution to this conversation and I'm not surprised when everyone ignores it. Why am I going on about the weather when our crushes have been kidnapped?!

'I'm just grateful they're not hurting them,' says Dottoressa. 'Though I really hope the equipment they're using to take the blood is sterilised.'

I don't have high hopes about that, but now doesn't feel like the time to share them. Instead, I ask the one thing I desperately need to know. 'When are we going to get them out?'

'We can't rush,' says Tech Kali. My face must show exactly what I think of this because her expression softens. 'Look, I want them out as much as all of us do. My fiancé's in there. He's going to be terrified. He doesn't even know that I'm…' She clears her throat. 'The point is we cannot storm in without a plan. My count says there are *thousands* of them in there – it looks like every single demon is congregating in this giant warehouse. And they're not the demons we're used to. This hostage-taking proves it. For whatever reason, they're changing. They're capable of planning and raiding supermarkets to feed their hostages. If they've already been drinking their blood, they could be more powerful than we can even conceive.'

'She's right,' sighs Model Kali. 'I hate it too, but we need to wait until we've come up with a plan that means we can take down 5,000 evolved demons and get four innocent civilians out alive.'

I gulp. That does not sound like a simple feat.

'But K and New Kali, *please* keep checking on them,' says Model Kali. 'Daily, please. I need to know that Liam's okay.'

'Of course,' says K. 'I'll go twice a day. Maybe I can

227

even install cameras? Ones where the footage comes through an app.'

Tech Kali nods. 'Already on it. There's some equipment on its way to your house right now. Once it's installed, we can all be on surveillance duty. Checking 24/7 on the hostages and how they're doing. If anything changes, we implement an urgent rescue mission. Otherwise, we make the most of this time to get as much information as possible, so we know exactly what we're dealing with. Preparation is key.'

'But how long are we going to leave them there?!' I ask. 'You're talking like it's going to be more than a day!'

Dottoressa looks right at me. 'It's the only way. Tech Kali's right. We can't treat these demons like the ones we're used to. They've changed. They're becoming more like… Raktabija.'

There's a moment of tense silence as we all absorb this.

'He's dead,' says Tech Kali firmly. 'Kali-Ma killed him. Nobody's seen him since.'

'Thank god,' mutters Model Kali. 'If he's involved, we're all dead.'

'Okay, but *how long* are we leaving the hostages there?' I repeat. 'People will know Joe's missing! We have school on Monday!'

Tech Kali frowns, calculating. 'Next Saturday? That will give us time to come up with a plan and get as much reinforcement and equipment as possible.'

The others nod reluctantly. I stare at them all in total shock. 'A WEEK?! I'm sorry but you can't leave Joe and the others with the demons for a week! They'll DIE!!'

'It's six days and we'll keep checking on them,' promises K. 'If anything changes, and the demons stop taking care of them, we go in. Right?'

'Hell yeah,' agrees Model Kali. 'The second they hurt a single one of them – or the M&S sandwiches stop coming – we're there. I'm going to fly over ASAP anyway so I can help you all prepare. It'll be easier in person.'

'Me too,' says Dottoressa. 'I'll book my flight now. And don't worry New Kali – Lucia can handle herself. She'll look after Joe too, I know it.'

I sigh, resigned. This is not the plan I would have chosen. But I know I can't take on 5,000 demons alone. I have to trust the others.

'I'll join later in the week,' promises Tech Kali. 'I can do more from here, with my tech set-up. I'll be monitoring *everything*. And in the meantime, we all need to make sure nobody suspects anything about the hostages. This has to be covered up.'

'I'm on it,' says Model Kali. 'I'll tell people Liam and I have gone to England together. Romantic mini break.'

'But you've only worked together twice,' I point out.

'Exactly. Plenty of time for him to fall for me.'

'Lucia's family won't suspect anything, and I'll tell her work she's sick,' says Dottoressa. 'There's no problem there.'

'Ditto on this end with Kiran,' confirms Tech Kali. 'I've got it under control.'

'I do not,' I say emphatically.

'I'll help you Kali,' says K. 'And I'll put the cameras up first thing tomorrow. It's getting late. Check in again tomorrow?'

'Twelve hundred hours EST,' says Tech Kali. 'Over and out.'

The Kalis end the Zoom call and I'm left staring at K's blank laptop screen. 'I can't *believe* this. It doesn't feel real.'

She nods. 'I know. But Tech Kali's right – we can't have this coming out and the police getting involved. Can you pass me Joe's phone?'

'What are you going to do with it? We don't even know his code.'

She taps the screen and within seconds, triumphantly

points it at me. It's unlocked. 'How…'

'I guessed his passcode. It was 1234.'

Of course it was. I take the unlocked phone from K's palm and instantly open up Joe's WhatsApp. I feel marginally guilty I'm taking advantage of his demon-napping to look at his messages, but firstly, it could be useful to help with a cover-up excuse. And secondly, I can't resist.

I go straight to his chat with Hayley. There are endless messages from her, dripping with emojis, while Joe's responses are sparse. I grin with satisfaction as I see how desperate she looks, and how unbothered Joe clearly is. Then I remember why I'm there. I scroll through his other chats, looking for his parents. He's got a recent message thread with 'Pierre French Exchange.' I forgot all about Pierre. He came here once to stay with Joe, and everyone was *obsessed* with him. Mainly because he was hot, French and… well, that's it. His accent was almost as perfect as his eyes. It turns out he and Joe still message all the time, and their recent ones are about organising a trip for Joe to visit Pierre in Paris. They haven't chosen a date yet.

I pause. It isn't the *worst* idea. Everyone would easily accept Joe skipping the last week of school to go to

Paris – it's classic Joe behaviour. He's always going on spontaneous holidays. But normally his parents are the ones organising them. Would they be okay with him going off to France alone, last-minute?

'What are you thinking?' asks K.

'He has a French Exchange,' I say slowly. 'And Joe's rich enough to easily get on a last-minute plane to Paris. Plus, his parents are away in Barbados this week. But – would they let him?'

'If his rich, absent parents are anything like my mum, our problems are solved,' says K. 'Don't worry, I'll handle it.'

My shoulders relax. 'Thanks.'

'It's fine.' She pauses. 'But… there is something else. I, uh, feel like we should probably stay close to each other for the next few days. I know you don't have your period yet, but when it comes, we'll be easily discoverable. And with everything that's happening, I think it makes sense to, uh, put our differences aside. And focus on this. Purely because it's the most effective thing to–'

I interrupt her. 'K, I get it. You're right. Let's do it. Also… I lied. I got my period today too.'

She frowns. 'You *lied*? Kali, this is serious stuff!

It's life and death.'

Guilt solidifies in my stomach. 'K, I know! Okay?! That's why all I want to do is just find a way to get Joe back!'

K nods, curt. 'Fine. Let's just focus on defeating the demons.'

'Thank you.' I truly mean it. 'I still have that spare mattress in my room, if you want to stay? It'll be easier to convince my parents to let you stay at mine rather than for them to let me stay with you the whole time.'

'Okay.'

'And… I've already messaged my mum to say I'm staying at yours tonight, if that's okay? I think she's happy about it – she missed you at the mehndi night.'

A distant look flashes across K's face and I regret bringing up the mehndi night. But before I can say anything else, she nods. 'And your friends?'

'What about them?'

'They don't know anything's up?'

I shake my head silently. When I switched on my phone, I had a few messages from Ri asking where I was, but nothing that suggests she knows my kiss with Joe was interrupted by demons. I'll message her an excuse. 'Everything's fine,' I say, even though life couldn't be further from fine right now.

'Fine,' echoes K. 'It's probably best if you sleep in one of the spare rooms.'

The last time I stayed over, I slept in K's giant bed with her, and we spent hours laughing and chatting until we fell asleep at 3am. Things couldn't be more different now. But I can't let myself think about our friendship issues – or how to fix them. I need to focus all my energy on saving Joe.

Chapter 25

'Where is he?' Hayley corners me in the hallway.

I gulp, my back up against the noticeboard. 'Where's who?'

'Joe, obviously,' she snaps. 'I haven't seen him since the dance, and it's got to be because of you.'

'He's in France. He texted to say Pierre invited him over last minute. Didn't he tell you too?' I know he did. K and I wrote the message. We even put in a heart emoji to appease her.

Hayley scowls. 'Yeah, of course. We speak daily. Unlike you and him.'

'Then, everything's fine!' I try to slip away, but Hayley blocks me.

'No, it's not.' She crosses her arms. 'Joe doesn't just disappear like this. I know him, and this is not normal behaviour. He isn't *organised* enough to book a last-minute trip to Paris. And why hasn't he put anything up on his profile yet?'

I make a mental note to ask K to photoshop something for Joe's socials. I should have expected something like this from Hayley. Everyone else easily accepted the lie – K's messages were so convincing that Joe's own parents told him they were proud of him and transferred £1,000 into his account for his trip! At least that's one bonus for Joe to find when this is all over – but Hayley is not everyone.

'Maybe he's too busy living in the moment to post?' I suggest. The look on Hayley's face tells me she's not buying this. 'Look, I don't know what you want from me! All I know is Joe's having the best time, and he'll be back for the archery competition.'

'He'd better be,' says Hayley archly. 'Because if he's not…' She glares at me, and I realise I'm marginally more scared of her than I am of the demons. 'I'm blaming you.'

With that, Hayley stalks off in her hot pink trainers, leaving me physically and emotionally crumpled against the noticeboard.

***

The rest of the day goes from bad to worse. Phil was so furious about Joe disappearing to France that

I couldn't bear to break it to him that I wouldn't be at the competition either. It's no longer just about the sangeet, it's about Joe. Saturday is the day we're going to rescue the crushes, and I'll have to sneak off from the sangeet, or make up an excuse, or whatever it takes. I don't care. Joe is all I can think about. I was so distracted in practice that I hardly got any golds. But Ri did – she beat her personal best, which appeased Phil. She doesn't know it, but right now, she's South Bridge Secondary's best chance of winning a single event at the competition.

Hayley came to cheer Ri on, though I reckon she was also there to check on me. She's so suspicious she's practically stalking me in the school corridors. I don't know what she thinks I've done with Joe – hidden him in my locker?

And then there's K. She spent last night at my house, sleeping on the mattress in my room, but it was so different to how it used to be. Everything we said was functional, like we were business partners rather than friends. I know we need to talk about the fight. I know I need to apologise. But I'm scared. It could go wrong. We might end up fighting again, or it could remind her of just how rude I'd been. And I can't risk it. I need K right now. There's no way I can get Joe back without her.

'Kali?'

I look up from my locker to see Mrs Patel coming towards me. She's clutching her files to her chest and looks nervous.

'Mrs Patel! They've still got Joe and—'

'Not here!' She glances down the corridor, then gestures for me to follow her. I'm on a free period so most people are in lessons or the library. She finds an empty classroom and closes the door behind us.

'Is Joe alright?' Her face is tense with anxiety. 'I thought the worst when I saw he wasn't here this morning, then I saw the email to the school about his spontaneous French exchange visit, and I presumed you had something to do with it.'

I nod. 'We didn't want anyone to freak out. But he's okay. The demons have him and some of the other Kalis' crushes. They're taking their blood like you thought. But they're also keeping them alive. They've basically raided most of M&S for sustenance supplies.'

She staggers, the colour draining from her face. 'It's worse than I thought. They've got stronger. They're developing.'

It's time for me to find out what Mrs Patel has to do with this. I stand up tall and look her in the eyes.

'Mrs Patel, are you... a Kali too?' I hold her gaze as I wait for the answer with bated breath. I know her name is Durga – it says so on the school website – but she might have changed it. Or Kali could be her middle name. It's the only explanation.

Mrs Patel shakes her head slowly. 'No. I'm not. But... my sister was.'

Oh my god.

And then I realise she used the past tense. 'She... was?'

Mrs Patel takes off her glasses, suddenly looking very young. 'I'm named after Durga, the goddess who is said to be an incarnation of Kali. But my twin sister was named after Kali herself. She died almost twenty years ago. The demons killed her.'

I collapse into the nearest seat. I always knew the demons were dangerous, but to hear they killed Mrs Patel's sister makes that peril even more real. 'I'm so sorry,' I whisper. 'What... happened?'

Mrs Patel wrings her hands together, clearly reluctant to speak. 'I really didn't want to talk about this with you or get involved in any way, but maybe I've been making a mistake. I don't know.'

'Please Mrs Patel. It might help us get Joe back.'

There is a long pause, then she nods. 'It... all began

239

when were 16. I'd had my period for a couple of years already, but Kali hadn't got hers. It was strange because we were identical twins. She was so happy when it finally arrived on our 16th birthday. But then it wasn't long before the first demon showed up too. I was right there. I couldn't believe it when Kali managed to kill it. I'd never seen her do anything remotely athletic, but suddenly she was like an action hero, flying around the room.' Mrs Patel pauses to explain. 'Her superpower was speed.'

'Wow. And… did she know what was happening?'

'We figured it out together. Our parents had told us the legend of Raktabija years ago, so when we realised the demons could clone when their blood hit the ground, we realised it must be Raktabija's clones who were after her. And the fact it was happening to my sister and not me meant it had to be linked to our names; it was the only difference between us. We didn't meet any other Kalis for years. We got by alone. A team. We were always close, but this brought us even closer. I was the brains – I researched the demons as much as I could to help her – and she was the brawn. She must have slayed hundreds of demons.'

'She sounds incredible,' I say softly.

'She was,' agrees Mrs Patel. 'And on top of it all, she had to deal with our parents' disappointment. She chose not to go to university and didn't ever want to get married. She wanted to focus on slaying the demons. Until… the day they got her. She was 26.'

I clutch the edge of the table tightly. That's Radha's age. 'What happened?'

'It was all my fault,' says Mrs Patel, looking past me, out of the window. 'I came up with a plan I thought was genius – a plan that could kill all the demons at once. All we had to do was resurrect the goddess Kali herself so she could defeat them like she did in the legend. But it didn't work. The demons found us while we were trying, and failing, to resurrect her. They attacked me, and Kali had to save me as well as defeat the demons. She died saving my life.' Tears fall down Mrs Patel's face. 'It was all my fault. If only I hadn't come up with that ridiculous plan! Of course, it was never going to work. And then it got my sister killed.'

I want to cry too. This is the saddest story I've ever heard. 'I'm so sorry. But Mrs Patel, it isn't your fault. It's the demons' fault. You were just trying to help.'

She gives me a watery smile. 'That's why I didn't want to speak to you about any of this. My getting

241

involved is what led to Kali's death. So, this time, I wanted to do the opposite, and stay away as much as possible. But I couldn't help trying to get close to you over the years. I knew what was coming for you, you see. And when you turned 16, it brought everything back with my sister.'

'I thought you just wanted to hang out with me because we're the only brown people in the school.'

Mrs Patel laughs loudly. 'Oh, Kali. No. It's… because of this. I'm so sorry it happened to you too. But I'm so glad you know other Kalis. It was completely different for my sister back then, without technology. We only had each other. And I let her down.'

'It wasn't your fault,' I repeat stubbornly. 'It was the demons. Which is why we need to stop them. Once and for all.'

'I wish I could help. But I can't. I'll just make things worse again.'

'What about your old plan? Couldn't we try and resurrect Kali-Ma again? That's how the gods defeated Raktabija. Maybe it's how we can defeat the demons too!'

Mrs Patel shakes her head adamantly. 'No, Kali. It won't work. We tried it. And it got my sister killed.'

'It could be different this time,' I persist. 'And didn't

you say it *almost* worked?'

'Please, just... leave it. I won't be able to live with myself if anything happened to you as well. Promise me you won't ask me how to resurrect Kali again.'

I really don't want to make this promise, but Mrs Patel looks so frail and sad that I know I have to. 'Okay. I promise I won't ask you.'

But I don't promise to not ask the internet. I'll try *anything* to get Joe back.

Chapter 26

I can't believe it's already Thursday night. I don't know how I've got through the last few days. The only thing that helps is knowing I can open the app on my phone to check on Joe via the cameras at any time. And that every evening after school, K and I go over to the warehouse in person to check that nothing's changed.

Model Kali and Dottoressa are here too. They're staying at K's house while her mum's away, and K is at mine. They've joined us on a few reccy missions to the warehouse, and while K and I are at school, they're developing the plan with Tech Kali. So far, it involves a *lot* of fireworks. It's the only way to get rid of so many demons at once.

I think we're ready to go now, but the others are more cautious. They're worried that the demons could be evolved enough to use the hostages to get out – or sacrifice them. We need to make sure we get the hostages out *before* we set the lair on fire with all our fireworks. That's the final bit of the plan we haven't solved yet – how to communicate with the hostages and make sure they know when we're ready to attack so they can escape in time.

Tech Kali is coming over tomorrow morning. She's surprisingly chill about leaving her fiancé in a demon lair, but apparently, she's been working on research that could change everything. Every time we ask her what it is, she's evasive because 'it's best to only share certainties.' I think it has something to do with the blood the demons are taking from our crushes. I hope it will help persuade everyone to go along with my plan to resurrect Kali-Ma but judging from their reactions so far, it seems unlikely. Nobody thinks it's an option – not even K. And I've been going on about it every single evening we've spent together. I'm even doing it now.

'Why don't we just *try*?'

'Sure, let's do it right this second,' says K, her voice dripping with sarcasm. 'What does your website say again? We just drip some of our blood to the ground – I probably have some period blood I can use if you want? – and then what, we chant, stick our tongues out, do a yoga pose, and the goddess herself appears?'

I groan in frustration. 'You know there's more to it than that. But this website really thinks it could work.'

'Sorry but I'm not sure I trust invokinghindugoddesses. com,' says K, squinting at the URL. 'Besides, Mrs Patel's sister tried and failed.'

'But that's because they were doing it alone, and she wasn't even a Kali! Imagine if all of us Kalis did it together with our joint blood and power.'

'I need to check on the Kalis,' says K, reaching for her phone. 'We have a meeting tomorrow to discuss the final part of the plan.'

'But I already have it! This is the best way to take down every single demon and save the hostages. It's how they did it in the original legend.'

'Legend being the optimal word. Kali, we can't just invoke a goddess. This isn't one of your teen movies.'

'They're not *my* teen movies – they're a genre dedicated to our entire generation. And yes, we can.'

K slumps down onto her mattress, the left strap of her black tank top sliding down her shoulder. 'Whatever. You can take it up with Tech Kali in person tomorrow.'

'I will,' I reply, hotly. I start scrolling through more websites, checking I haven't missed any information on how to invoke a goddess. Then I open the camera app to check on Joe for the 400th time that day. Right now, he's in the corner of the lair, sitting on the sleeping bags the demons have procured for them, chatting to Lucia and digging into a tub of M&S mini bites. I sign in relief, for the 400th time that day. I'm always terrified I'll see something awful, but so far, nothing has changed.

Just then the door opens.

'Sunita Auntie!' K bolts upright, smiling at my mum.

'Hi *beta*,' says my mum. Her tone is normal, but her eyebrows furrow as she looks at me and K. Something's wrong. 'I was just thinking that… as your mum is away for so long this time, maybe it makes sense for you to sleep in your own room, K? So you can girls can, um, have some space?'

'But we don't have a spare room,' I point out. 'Why can't K just stay here like she has for the last three nights?'

'She can!' assures my mum. 'You can, *beta*! I just thought perhaps you'd be more comfortable on the sofa bed in the living room?'

'Of course, Auntie,' says K slowly. 'Whatever is best for you. I'm sorry to be an inconvenience.'

My mum flushes. 'You're not, of course not!

Any friend of Kali's is welcome here. And I know your mum has helped Radha out so much with her wedding – you know she's managed to get her the Roseland hotel for the reception! Radha's on cloud nine – apparently, it's very exclusive. We're more than happy to have you stay here, it's just… maybe…'

'I'll come downstairs and help you make up the sofa bed,' says K.

'Oh, don't worry about that *beta*,' trills my mum, her voice light with relief. 'I'll call you when it's done!'

She shuts the door behind her, and K looks at me. 'You told your mum I'm gay?'

I flush harder than my mum did. 'I… yes… but… that can't be it. Why would she wait so many nights before saying anything?!'

'Precisely because it's been so many nights. She's freaking out.'

I'm silent as I wonder if she's right. My mum was unusually weird just now. And she didn't exactly respond well to me revealing K's sexuality.

K shrugs. 'Whatever. I guess she wouldn't let a boy sleep in your room, so probably best not to let a lesbian sleep there either, right?'

'It's not… I don't…' I briefly squeeze my eyes shut,

mortified. When I open them, K has a sad smile on her face.

'It's okay. I still appreciate your parents letting me stay. It's nice for me to see what a normal family looks like.'

I snort. 'Normal?! This family is *not* normal.'

'Trust me, it is. I don't even know my dad. And my mum is…'

'Your mum is *amazing*. She's so chilled out!'

'My mum doesn't care about me,' says K flatly. 'Why else would she let me do whatever I want? How many mums let their 16-year-olds get tattoos? And stay out all night?'

'Of course, she cares! She loves you!'

'If that's the case, then I wish she'd show it sometimes,' says K, looking down at her short, clipped nails.

'Oh, K.' I don't know what to say. I had no idea K felt like this about her mum. But it explains why she likes hanging out with mine so much. Compared to Deepa Auntie, my mum *is* normal. 'I'm sorry.' And then I realise I really am. 'K, I'm sorry for *everything*. I wish I hadn't been so rude to you that day at your house. It wasn't okay of me. And you were right all along. I never should have gone to the dance.'

'I'm sorry too,' says K automatically. 'I should have

understood you needed to go to the dance, and I should have been there, patrolling, like I'd said I would. It's my fault this all happened.'

I shake my head rapidly. 'No. It's not your fault. At all. You don't need to apologise. *I* do. I was wrong, and the stuff I said…. it was cruel. I want you to know I didn't even believe what I said about you not having friends. I was just trying to hurt you.'

'But… it's true. I don't have real friends at school. Everyone thinks I'm weird – the lesbian with tattoos and piercings who only wears black. No wonder you didn't want your friends to meet me.'

'That's not true!' And I realise it isn't. Not anymore anyway. 'It was a me problem, not a you problem. Honestly. I think you're amazing, and who cares what anyone else thinks? Also, if you're weird, then hello, so am I! We both get hunted by literal demons when we're on our periods!'

'Yeah, but I'm weird in a neurodivergent way too,' says K quietly. I'd guessed she wasn't neurotypical a while ago – so many of her mannerisms remind me of Tanya – but she's never specifically said it out loud before, and it makes me want to hug her. 'I'm not like everyone else.'

'So?! You're you, which is even better! You're the

coolest person I've ever met!!' It's breaking my heart to hear K – confident, beautiful, warrior K – talk about herself like this. I slide down onto the mattress next to her, grabbing her hand in desperation. 'K, please. You're a demon slayer. You're a triple black belt. *You're* incredible. You're like nobody else I know. You're so serious, it's adorable. But then your whole face lights up when you smile, and it's like *magic*. You're beautiful. You're so loyal. You're… the best person I know, K. And you're the only person I'd ever want to slay demons with.'

K stares into my eyes, and hers seem to be getting bigger, rounder by the second. I feel hypnotised by them. The layers of brown. The tiny gold specks in the iris that I hadn't ever noticed before. 'Do you really mean all that?' she asks.

The energy between us is so intense I can't speak. I simply nod. I didn't even *know* I felt everything I just said. But I do. It's all true.

'I feel the same way,' says K softly. 'I can't stop thinking about you, Kali. You're so infuriating, and impatient, and stubborn – but you're also the most amazing girl I know. You're completely hilarious; nobody makes me laugh like you do. You're kind. You're so much more special than you think you are. And you're a total contradiction. You're gentle but you're angry. You're timid but you're brave. You only want to be a demon-cleaner-upper – then you kill dozens of demons with blazing arrows. You make no sense. And yet... you make total sense to me.'

My heart is racing. Nobody has ever said anything like this to me in my entire life. I feel like I'm in a romcom. But I can't be. Because it isn't Joe King saying all this to me – it's K.

Her eyes are still fixed on mine. Our hands are still touching. I am so aware of the feel of her skin on mine. It feels electric. I can't breathe properly. And then, suddenly, it's all too much. I can't deal with it. I turn my head by a fraction, so my eyes are no longer staring into hers, and I gently relax my hand. Her fingers slide out of mine, and I feel my breath gradually return to normal.

Then K abruptly says, 'I came to the mehndi night. I was there.'

'What?!' I face her in shock. 'What do you mean?'

'I'd RSVPed yes and I didn't want to let Radha down. I know how important attendance is with events – my mum's drilled it into me. But when I got there I... saw you outside in the garden. And you were there, holding hands with your friend, the beautiful one with the braids. Rihanna.'

'Wait, and *that's* why you left?!'

'I felt there was something between you two. And I didn't want to interrupt.'

I burst out laughing. 'Between me and Ri?! That's hilarious!'

K's face softens into a smile. 'Is it?'

'Of course! Ri is just my friend! The person I like is Joe.'

K nods slowly, the smile falling off her face. 'Joe. Your date. I… yeah. Of course. How did it go? Before the demon-napping.'

I hesitated. I still haven't told anyone about what happened between us. Maybe this is my moment to finally share it with a friend. 'Well… he and I kissed. A proper one. Tongues and all. It was my first real kiss!'

K's face is motionless for too long, then she smiles brightly. 'Wow. Cool. That's… great Kali. I'm happy for you.'

Suddenly, I regret what I said. I shake my head. 'I mean, it wasn't that big a deal. My only focus right now is on getting him back. I mean, freeing him. Freeing all the hostages.'

'Yeah. Same.' She clears her throat, then stands up. 'I'd

better go downstairs. Your mum has probably made the bed up now. And you might not see me in the morning. I'm going to go straight to mine to meet the Kalis.'

'I'll come with you!'

'No, it's fine, I'm taking the day off school, but I know it's harder for you to do that at your school, so you can come find us later in the day.' She grabs her bag, turning to look at me before she walks out of the door. 'Goodnight Kali.'

I feel a wave of inexplicable sadness wash over me. 'Goodnight K. I...' I want to say something else, but I don't know what. So after a long pause, I give up. 'Sleep well.'

K closes the door after her and I lie back on my bed. I don't know what just happened. But I think K and I might have had a moment. A Moment with a capital M.

Chapter 27

Our periods ended last night, and K left first thing before I even woke up. It's been the weirdest period ever – and I do not say that lightly. I'd gotten used to fighting off demons every time I bled, but this time, not a *single* demon attacked any of us Kalis. I suppose it's because they're too busy squeezing the blood out of our crushes. The whole thing gives me shivers. But at least tomorrow is finally the day when we get to save them.

'Kali? Are you going to just sit there on your phone all morning or do you think you might be able to spare a moment to help your only cousin-sister organise her wedding?' Radha's glaring at me and for once, she doesn't look great. She's wearing her thick black glasses, her hair is piled on top of her head in a greasy bun, and her forehead is lined with tension. The stress of the wedding has got to her and she's freaking out.

'I'm busy,' I tell her, turning back to my phone and

taking another bite of toast. Tech Kali has arrived so they're all busy sorting preparations for tomorrow, and I want to be on top of every detail. I've learnt my lesson from the last time I stopped paying attention to the WhatsApp group.

'What can be more important than my wedding?!'

I raise an eyebrow and Radha has the decency to look embarrassed.

'Okay, sorry, it's just this is my wedding weekend and I need to make sure there aren't any disasters. Like your wedding saree.'

'What's wrong with my saree? I mean, other than the fact it's pink and sequinned and my worst nightmare?'

'Kali, I need to know the blouse fits you! Can you just put it on? Please?!'

I sigh, putting my phone down. 'Fine, but I'm taking my chai with me.'

Radha claps gleefully and I reluctantly follow her up the stairs. 'I've laid it all out in your mum's room! Come on!'

I pull off my school shirt and wrestle myself into the pink saree blouse instead. It fits. But that's the only positive thing I can say about it.

'You could try and look a bit happier,' scowls Radha.

'I can't have you in the wedding photos with that expression on your face. Especially not when you're holding the nariyal.'

'Isn't it enough I agreed to do it?'

Radha's eyes widen and I brace myself for her rage. But to my surprise, she just collapses onto the bed. 'I can't do this anymore.'

'I'm sorry Radha. I'll smile for the photos.'

But she shakes her head. 'It's not that. I'm… struggling.'

I don't think I've ever heard Radha say those words before. Not even during her medical exams. I gingerly sit down on the bed next to her. 'What's wrong?'

'I don't know. I've just been feeling really alone with everything lately.'

'Alone?! But what about Kevil? The man who's marrying you so you'll never be alone again? He ADORES you. And Mum? And Dad? Aren't they both at the sangeet venue right now, sorting everything out for tomorrow?'

'Yes, but I can't speak to them about this!' Radha sniffs and I realise she's *crying*.

I don't know what to do. But I have to do something, so I awkwardly reach out and pat her soft mehndi-covered hand. 'I'm sorry. Is it that you miss your mum?'

'Yes, every day. But also, getting married is terrifying! This is, like, a major commitment.' I refrain from pointing out she knew this when she got engaged. Instead, I try to make my face look sympathetic. It works because Radha keeps going. 'I want to marry him; I'm just freaking out. I'm scared I'm signing my life away. I feel like people are already expecting me to stay the way I am forever – and I'm only 26. I'm so jealous of you Kali, you've got your whole life ahead of you.'

My mouth drops open. 'I'm sorry… you're jealous of *me*? You're literally the daughter my parents always wanted. You're perfect. I mean, in their eyes.' If Radha knew I thought she was perfect, she'd never let me forget it.

'Yeah, because I'm pretty and smart and a doctor,' says Radha, reeling her attributes off in a bored voice. 'But that's not all I am! And I feel like nobody even sees the rest. They just box me in. Whereas you… you don't let *anybody* box you in. You like those lame video games, but then you go to the Summer Dance in a limo with the cool kids. You never did any sport, then all of a sudden, you're gifted at archery. You do whatever you want, Kali. I was never brave enough to be so contrary. I always did what everyone expected of me.'

I blink as my perspective of Radha shifts. It never occurred to me she'd have a problem with people seeing her as perfect all the time. But all along she's felt that nobody ever sees the real her because they're too busy focusing on her surface qualities, assuming that's all there is to her.

Which is *exactly* what I've always done.

I swallow guiltily. 'I'm sorry Radha. That sounds hard. Obviously, there's more to you than your looks and your job. But, um, like what specifically? What is that you would have done if you'd been brave enough?'

Radha pulls out her phone hesitantly. 'Promise you won't laugh?'

'Cross my heart, hope to die.' I wince at my choice of words.

'Okay. Well… I write poems.' Radha looks nervous, like she's still expecting me to laugh.

'That's *so* cool! Show me!'

Encouraged, she taps on her phone to pull up her notes. I peer over her shoulder to see a list of names of *Indian goddesses*. 'Wait, you write poems about Indian goddesses?!'

not because I hate it! This is seriously good Radha.'

'You're… not kidding?' she asks cautiously.

'No! I need to read another one. Right now. I'm doing Radha.' I clear my throat before I read.

RADHA

They all define you as Krishna's other half,
Making your love for him your only path,
They hardly ever call you by your own name,
Radha-Krishna is what brought you fame.
But the truth is, you're so much more than this,
You're the incarnation of love, divine bliss.
You've got what everyone's looking for:
True peace, self-love, and so much more.
You're the answer to our earthly pain –
Healing all as we call you by your name.

Radha blushes. 'That one isn't so good. It's hard to write decent poetry when you're too close to the subject.'

'I think it's amazing,' I say honestly. 'It's true, everyone defines Radha by her love for Krishna, because he's such an important god. But she's special in her own right.'

'You know, she represents love itself, especially

261

'They're literally about Indian goddesses. It's the perfect moment.'

Radha shakes her head. 'They're too feminist. Too progressive. Anyway.' She sits up, a mischievous glint in her eyes. 'Talking of feminism, how are *your* friends?'

'Fine. I… don't really see the link?'

'What about K? How is she?'

'Also fine. But I'm still not getting where you're going with this?'

Radha sighs impatiently. 'Kali. I'm not blind. I can see the tension between you two. *All* the tension.'

Surely she can't mean…? My blood runs cold as I scrutinise her face for a sign, but Radha crosses her arms and stares back. I say nothing. I'm not breaking this silence. It goes on for several seconds, and then she cracks as I knew she would.

'Fine, don't open up to me! All I'm trying to say is, I support you on whatever path you choose. Romantically. And otherwise.'

My throat tightens. This is too much. But Radha keeps on going.

'Why don't you just channel Kali-ma? She lets herself be the embodiment of pure nature, not circumscribed by society and rules.'

263

I stare at her in silence. I don't know how to respond. It feels like Radha's saying... but why would she? I like Joe King. He's the person I've kissed. There's nothing going on between me and... anyone else.

'It doesn't matter who you date,' says Radha, forcing her point down. 'Even if your parents are weird about it.'

I still can't reply. I'm frozen.

And then there's a sudden bang and I leap off the bed. But It's not a demon – it's just Radha slamming her hands down. 'You know what,' she says. 'I'm done caring so much! You have to live your life no matter what anyone thinks. Including me. So if you want to skip the sangeet and the ceremonies tomorrow to go to your competition, do it.'

'What?! You can't be serious!! It's important to you!'

'I am. You do you. Dating-wise and life-wise.' She pokes my arm with her finger. 'Stop looking at me like that – it's weirding me out.'

But I can't stop. This is not the Radha I know. Her wedding is the most important thing to her, ever. She's been Bridezilla of the year, and yet she'd let me skip her pre-wedding event for an archery competition?

'Yes, she would,' says Radha archly, and I realise I said that last bit out loud. 'I maybe got a bit carried away with the wedding stuff. But I don't *really* need you there tomorrow, so long as you're at the wedding. And you're right, four events is a lot. I'd rather you chose you. Archery is… your poetry. You need to follow your heart and do what's right for you. Not what your family want. Even if that family is me.'

I close my eyes and breathe deeply, processing it all. This is the nicest thing Radha has ever said to me, hands down. I try to think of something equally as lovely to say back to her. But before I can, she jumps up, clapping her hands, startling me again.

'Right, get out of that pink thing. I want you to wear something you feel comfortable in. How about I lend you something…' She starts rustling through Indian outfits in my mum's wardrobe. 'I brought all my stuff here so your mum could help me choose what to wear. And I think you should wear… this!'

'Radha, it won't fit me,' I protest as she pulls something out. 'It doesn't even matter–' But then I stop mid-sentence. She's holding up a navy lehenga outfit. Dark silk, super simple, with a delicate silver pattern trimming the edges of the square-necked crop top. It's beautiful. And instead of a traditional lehenga skirt, the bottom half is loose palazzo pants.

'It's too big for me, so it'll be perfect for you,' says Radha authoritatively. 'Try it on.'

I do. And she's right. It's the first Indian outfit I've ever felt like myself in. And it's *comfortable*. I could run in this!

'Knew it,' she says triumphantly. 'It's yours – keep it.'

I turn to her, emotional. 'Thanks Radha. For this, but also for… everything. I really appreciate what you said, and–'

Radha interrupts with a shriek, waving her phone around. 'Oh my god, the flowers haven't turned up! I need to go to the venue. I'll see you later, okay? Bye!'

Radha runs out of the room, leaving me in her outfit with a smile on my face. I know she's not running away because the wedding stuff is more important than me – she's running away *because* I'm so important to her. The conversation we just had proves it. For all Radha's confidence, she's as scared of intimacy as the rest of us.

I take a moment looking at my reflection in the mirror. I do look good in this outfit. Powerful. It reminds me of the Kali poem. I scrunch my brows, trying to remember it. It was so good. It almost contained the energy of the goddess, with its energetic, angry chant. I slowly recite it to myself in the mirror, surprised that all the words are coming back to me. It's simultaneously soothing and hellraising. I feel grounded as I recite it – but also ready to kick some demon ass.

Which is appropriate, because in that moment, the bedroom door bursts open. And it's not Radha. It's a demon.

I instantly jump into the warrior position K taught me, ready to fight, even though my mind is whirring with questions. I finished my period yesterday – the demons shouldn't be able to find me! But this demon clearly has. It launches itself right at me, and I fight it away, looking around desperately for a weapon. If I can get it to my room, there's a sheet of tarp I can use. I manage to get the demon out into the hallway, and then I freeze. The demon didn't turn up alone. It brought back-up. 10 extra demons.

I breathe shakily. I don't know how I'm going to fight off 11 demons. I grab Radha's hair straighteners from the console table, wishing they were plugged in. But before I get a chance to switch them on, the demons all race towards me in a coordinated attack. I hit as many as I can with the straighteners – enough to wound, but not to draw blood. They roar loudly in pain and for a moment, I wonder if I can fight them all off. Until one of them takes the straighteners from my hands and snaps them in half. Another demon glares into my eyes and grabs my wrist. The others reach out to do the same thing, all holding me tight so I can't escape. Utter dread spreads through my body. This is it. The end. I'm going to end up like Mrs Patel's sister.

I wish I'd made up with K. Told her how much she means to me. The thought of never seeing her again breaks my heart. Let alone how it will feel to never see my family again. But I refuse to let myself sink into the despair. The thought of K gives me courage. If it was her, she wouldn't cower from the demons. She'd face them like the warrior she is.

So, I raise my head – the only part of my body not restrained by demons – and try to look my murderers in their singular eyes. I'm trembling all over, but I'm brave enough to face the demons like an equal. Like the Kali that I am. A girl born to be a demon-slayer.

I stand strong, waiting for them to strike, for the inevitable blow. But not one demon reaches out to hurt me. Instead, they all nod, synced up like some kind of boyband, and then start running. Fast. With me gripped tightly between them.

That's when I realise what's happening – they're demon-napping me, just like they did to Joe King.

Chapter 28

'Doomsdaaaay? Hellooo?'

I groan, rubbing my head, then flicker my eyes open. There's a blurry face in front of me and it smells kind of bad. I blink, leaning back to escape the smell of stale BO. That's when I see its source.

'Joe?! What... what are you doing here? Oh my god – the demons took us!'

'You're awake!' cries Joe, looking way too happy for someone who's been taken hostage by demons. 'Everyone, this is Kali! But I call her Doomsday. Cool outfit, by the way.'

I sit up dazed, looking around me, and then down at my navy lehenga. I'm in a dark warehouse, laying on a sleeping bag, right next to Joe. The other hostages are scattered around us: Liam, Lucia and Kiran. They wave at me.

'Another Kali,' says Liam. 'Shit. I thought it was weird we're all linked to Kalis. And now... this.'

'What's going on?' asks Lucia anxiously. 'Is my Kali okay?'

I nod. 'She's good. Everyone is. But... are *you* all okay?'

'I mean, it's kind of annoying we're stuck in here,' says Joe. 'There's not exactly much to do. But the food isn't bad. And it's good to see you!'

Have the demon brainwashed the hostages too – or is Joe naturally this nonchalant about being demon-napped?

'We are alright,' says Kiran, his voice quiet. 'They take our blood daily. But it's never too much. I get the sense they want us alive, so they have a source of fresh supply. Not that we know what they're doing with it.'

'I think they might be drinking it,' I say.

Lucia and Kiran look grossed out while Liam is on the verge of fainting. But Joe lights up with excitement. 'Sick! Demons are drinking my blood.'

'So, what's the plan?' asks Lucia. 'How do we get out?'

I automatically reach into my pocket for my phone, but it's not there. Lehengas don't have pockets, which means my phone is still at home. But it doesn't matter. The Kalis know where we are. They already have a plan. And the cameras mean they'll know I'm here too.

'The Kalis are on it,' I say with more confidence than I feel. 'They've got cameras to monitor the situation.

270

They know where we are and what's happening. They're going to come for us tomorrow.'

'Sorry, what exactly *is* happening?' asks Kiran politely. 'And why is my fiancé involved?'

Liam and Joe are as clueless as he is, but Lucia shifts awkwardly and I remember she knows everything. She hasn't told the others though – and I don't know if I can either. Is it really on me to reveal to Kiran that his fiancé is a demon-slayer? And does Liam *really* need to know he's there because Model Kali fancies him and it has made his blood potent? That could put him off ever dating her and I don't want to be the reason behind that. Nor do I particularly want my Summer Dance date to find out I'm a demon slayer.

'Let's let Kali have a moment,' says Lucia, saving me from answering. 'She's been through a lot. Come on.' She gestures for the others to follow her, and I press my palms together in grateful relief.

'You should eat,' says Joe, who has decided Lucia's words don't extend to him. 'It'll help with the headache. Tuna and sweetcorn sandwich? Or a Mexican three bean wrap?' He proffers them out, and I reach for the wrap. 'This is all pretty crazy, isn't it? With the…'

'Demons? Yeah, crazy sums it up.'

271

'What's the deal with them?' I really don't know how to explain the deal to him, especially when my head hurts, and I have to think of a way to get us out of here. But Joe keeps going. 'Why did the demons find you at the dance? Do you, like, know them?'

I wince with shame as I remember his face when he saw me fighting the demons back then. The way he looked at me. The revulsion. Like *I* was a demon... It makes me want to disappear into the ground. But I can't. Because I'm stuck here. With the boy I've spent so long obsessing over.

I stare at Joe in helpless silence, trying to think of a way to explain my way out of this. He watches expectantly, digging into his tuna sandwich as he waits. I don't know what to say. But as the silence continues, the shame starts to fade. Why *do* I feel so embarrassed about happened? Joe doesn't seem to care about how bad he smells – he's even making it worse by munching on tuna! So much has happened that it feels absurd to still care so much about what Joe thinks of me.

That's when I decide to ditch the shame once and for all.

I turn to Joe and tell him the one thing I never thought I would. 'I'm a demon slayer. It's why I'm so good at archery – aim is my superpower. I got it when I turned 16. Along with my period.'

His eyes widen and a chunk of tuna falls out of his mouth. 'Whoaaaah. So you're like, a superhero?'

I can't help but laugh. *That's* the reaction I was so scared of? 'Sure, I'll take that. But please don't tell the others for now – not all of them know the truth and it's not on us to tell them.'

'Scout's honour,' says Joe, crossing his chest. 'I can't believe you fight demons. That's so cool. You're like the goddess you're named after! The one that licks up demon blood.'

I wait for the inevitable shame to come at this comparison but… it doesn't. Instead, I just bite into my wrap. It's surprisingly good. 'Yep,' I reply, my mouth full. 'That's actually why this happens to me. Because I'm named after her. It happens to all Indian girls called Kali.'

'Whoaaaa!'

I take another big bite. I don't know if it's the Mexican three bean or the effect of telling the truth, but I suddenly feel better than I have in weeks. And I don't want it to stop. I swallow my next mouthful, wiping my mouth clean before turning to face Joe properly. 'But I do want to apologise to you about getting caught

up in all this, Joe. The demons only took you because...
well... they realised that the blood of someone that
a Kali fancies is extra powerful.'

He squints in confusion, the seconds ticking by, and
then– 'No way! You fancy me!'

'I mean, we did kiss. And I agreed to go to the dance
with you. Is it that surprising?'

In response, Joe flicks his hair back, and stares intently
at me with his gorgeous hazel eyes. I wait for the familiar
rush of longing to overpower me. But... it doesn't.

'I fancy you too, Doomsday. So how about we, uh,
repeat that kiss?'

He really is beautiful, but I'm not sure I actually *want*
to kiss him, and it's not just because he hasn't showered
since the dance. Our kiss wasn't great. Maybe it's
because I have terrible technique, or maybe we have
zero chemistry. But either way, I don't really feel like
repeating it.

'I'm actually okay for now, thanks,' I reply, surprising
myself more than him.

'Okay.' He shrugs, nonplussed, then– 'Wait. If I'm here
because you fancy me, then how come *you're* here?'

I roll my eyes, ready to explain the obvious, then
I pause. Why *am* I here?! The demons can only sense

us when we're on our periods and I finished mine already. They found me when I wasn't bleeding. And they haven't taken any of the other Kalis. They've only taken me – and our crushes. It doesn't make sense why I'm here.

Unless…

'Oh my god,' I exhale. 'She likes me. For real.'

'Who likes you?' asks Joe, still chomping on his tune.

My heart is thudding with excitement and I have an inappropriate urge to laugh out loud. K Likes me with a capital L. The demons didn't take me because I'm a Kali, but because K *fancies* me! That moment we had last night – it was real.

A rush of warmth spreads through me. I can't believe someone as cool and beautiful and funny and kind as K likes *me*, Kali Kadia. I am *her* crush. Even using the possessive pronoun makes me feel tingly.

Then I pause. Why am I so excited about this? What does that mean? Do I like her back? I know I think she's incredible and when I thought the demons were going to kill me, she's the only person I wanted to see one last time. But I've never liked a girl before. I like Joe King… right?

Joe burps and I scrunch up my face, waving his

gross breath away from me. 'Do I have competition, Doomsday? Who is it? Because I will *take* them down!'

I snort at the thought of Joe trying to take K. She'd have him in a headlock before he'd even put his tuna sweetcorn down. 'It's… my friend K. I think she likes me.'

'A girl? I didn't know you liked girls.'

Neither did I. 'I'm… not sure I do. I thought I liked you.' I cringe at myself. Why am I telling Joe King this? He's not my journal; he's my crush. The fact that he's here, demon-napped, is proof enough. My desire for him was clearly strong enough for the demons to spot it. I like him. So how can I like K back? She's a lesbian, but I'm not.

'You *have* heard of bisexuality, right? Where you can like both genders?'

'Obviously!' I snap, wondering how he knew what I was thinking. 'But… I don't know if that's me! I've never even thought about liking a girl before! I always just thought about…' I trail off, embarrassed.

'Me.' Joe accurately finishes my sentence. 'I get it. A lot of girls like me. I'm cool. And hot.'

'Modest too.'

He nods, not getting the irony. 'Exactly. I have a lot of

positive qualities. You could have just fallen for them, not the actual me. Or even the idea of me.' His face suddenly plummets. 'Like with me and Hayley.'

'What?!'

'I liked her because she's the girl equivalent of me: hot, popular, successful,' he explains. 'But once we were together, I realised she's actually kind of annoying; clingy and rude. Which isn't me at all. I guess the truth is, I never really liked her for who she is. I just *thought* I liked her because she's what I'm supposed to like. When actually, I like girls like you – unusual ones.' I decide to take this as a compliment. 'So... maybe that's happened to you with me?'

I lean back against the wall. This is the most insightful thing I've ever heard Joe King say. I had no idea he had this much self-awareness. 'Huh. I guess I did always like you because it felt like you were the person I was supposed to like. You're generically hot.'

'Yes. But am I the kind of hot that *you* like, Doomsday? Because this is personal. It's objective. No wait, what's the other one?'

'Subjective. But does that mean that the kind of hot I like is K?' As I say the words out loud, I'm instantly struck by how true they are. I have *always* been attracted

277

to K, from the second I saw those huge mahogany eyes, her delicate mehndi tattoos, and her sexy piercings. I just didn't know it.

Joe sighs ruefully. 'I should have known it was too good to be true. You're way smarter than me. But at least I'm being rejected for a girl.'

I can't believe this is happening. I'm turning down Joe King for K! I fancy a girl! And Joe just helped me realise it. This is possibly even crazier than the fact we're here kidnapped by demons. 'Thanks Joe,' I say. 'For being so chill about all of this demon stuff, and for helping me figure out my… sexuality, I guess.'

'Ah, it's cool. I'll get over it. To be honest, the being held hostage thing gives me a break from Hayley. The demons are nothing compared to her.'

'Have you ever told her you just don't want to be with her?'

Joe nods morosely. 'I've tried. But she tells me I'm wrong and we're meant to be together.' He looks up at me through his long lashes. 'It's kind of why I asked you to the dance. I like you and everything, but I was also hoping Hayley would see us together and leave me alone.'

I put my hand on Joe's arm. 'Hey, if we both get out

of here alive, how about I make it up to you by helping you get Hayley off your back once and for all?'

Joe's eyes light up. 'You'd really do that? Thanks D, you're the best. And if it doesn't work out with the girl, I'm always here. Even if it's just for a casual hook-up.'

I'm speechless, when a demon appears out of nowhere, grunting urgently at me. 'ARGHHH!'

'He wants you to follow him,' translates Joe.

'You speak demon?!'

'I picked up a bit.'

The demon grunts louder, gesturing angrily, and I instinctively cower.

'It's not a big deal Doomsday. They'll just take your blood. It doesn't even hurt! And you get a Meal Deal after.'

It sounds like a pretty big deal to me, but I force myself to stand, swallowing my fear. If Joe can get through this, then so can I.

Chapter 29

The demon takes me to the other side of the warehouse. We pass hundreds of demons on the way, their red skin gleaming, single eyes roving. It's surreal to see so many up close – and to not even try to kill them. The demon leads me to an area with several chairs attached to hospital-like tubes and plastic bags to collect blood. It looks like a pop-up blood drive in a community centre. Only these tubes aren't going into a life-saving fridge or whatever happens at normal blood drives. Instead, they're going into a huge metal vat.

It's the vat we saw from the cameras. Up close it's even bigger than I'd imagined. There are twenty demons surrounding it, stirring feverishly. They mutter as they do so, and as if in response, loud sounds echo back from inside the vat. I feel my blood run cold in horror. This does *not* look good. I need to know more. I try to peer over the edge of the vat, but it's too high and when I get closer, a demon shouts at me, pulling me back towards the chairs. I follow reluctantly but keep my eyes trained on the vat.

The demons are stirring vigorously, and a tiny droplet splashes out onto the floor right next to me. I crouch down eagerly to inspect it. Blood. But then it starts *moving*, sliding across the floor. I recoil, but my gaze stays on the droplet as it slithers back to the vat, all the way up, and then drops itself back inside. It is the creepiest thing I have ever seen – and I've seen K hug a demon to death.

'Grghaghgh.' A demon yanks my arm and shoves me into a chair. Another demon instantly sticks a needle into my arm.

'Owww!!' I can't help crying out in pain – Joe lied about this not hurting – but the demons don't care. Instead, they focus solely on making sure my blood drips into the vat.

I close my eyes, feeling dizzy as the blood steadily pulses out of my arm. I'm glad Joe gave me that wrap. If I'd known this is how I was going to spend the rest of my day, I would have had way more toast at breakfast. But now is not the time for regrets. I need to pay attention to work out what's happening. The demons are clearly doing something to our blood before they drink it. They're putting it all in that big vat, stirring it and whispering weird stuff. Whatever they're doing means it's no longer ordinary blood. The way that droplet moved, it was almost like it was alive…

I can feel the answer to everything somewhere in my mind, but I'm so tired that it won't come to me. Come *on*, Kali. I slow my breathing down, like I would in archery, and allow my mind to relax. It isn't easy given I can see my blood trickling down a tube. I spend way too long just staring at it – the red liquid slowly dripping all the way down to the vat – until it reaches the other blood, and there's a giant BOOM!

I tremble as the vat shakes. I don't know what's happened. But the demons are all grunting excitedly, looking at me with something like… respect? Appreciation? I shudder as I realise my Kali blood has mixed with the crushes' blood and it's all the more powerful for it. I hate that there's nothing I can do to stop any of this. I'm powerless with all these demons surrounding me. I wish I could fight or even run away – but I can't. All I can do is sit here as they take my blood.

So, I force myself to close my eyes again, and go back to trying to slow my thoughts down. I need to use a mantra like K taught me. I try 'let go' but it doesn't work. I need something else, something more relevant. Like… Radha's 'Kali' poem!

I'm not sure I'll remember it all, but the second I begin reciting it, the whole poem comes flooding back. 'Your tongue laps up the blood of demons slain, your naked body dances without shame.' I chant the whole thing to myself, my breath steadying, allowing the words to soothe me, until I get to the final line. 'Pure female power, you are shakti.'

I gasp, jolting upright, eyes open as it hits me. I know *exactly* what the demons are doing with our blood – and it's worse than I thought.

★★★

Everyone's asleep except for me. Even the demon activity has quietened down – I guess they need sleep as much as we do. But there's no way I can sleep right now. I'm too busy thinking. The more I go over my theory, the more convinced I am by it.

The blood in the vat looks alive because… it *is* alive. The demons aren't using the crushes' blood to drink and become stronger – they're using it to resurrect Raktabija.

I know how it sounds, but it makes sense. The blood

in that vat was alive. And the more that time goes on, the more I can hear it spluttering and gurgling. I don't know how this all began – if some part of Raktabija managed to contact the demons, or if they just evolved on their own and figured out a way to get him back. But it doesn't matter. Because either way, Raktabija's growing strength is already making the demons stronger. If they succeed in resurrecting him, then… I don't want to even think about it.

I wish I could share this with the other Kalis. Fireworks aren't going to be enough to take down the OG demon himself – the one that *all the Hindu gods couldn't defeat*. I feel so useless, sat here with this information, unable to tell anybody else. If K was here, she'd know exactly what to do. She always does. She's so smart, and strong, and brave, and beautiful. I can't believe I've resisted my feelings for her for so long – now all I want to do is accept them, and embrace how much I like K.

Suddenly, I bolt up straight. That's it! I'm a Kali! The demons are looking for our crushes. If I fully accept that K is my crush, the demons might be able to sniff her out through my intense desire and bring her here as another hostage! I know this is beyond risky. There is also a very strong chance that K will not appreciate being demon-napped. But if she's here with me, then there'll be two of us Kalis here on the inside, and the demons won't know! We could attack from right inside their lair, catching them unawares while the other Kalis start attacking from outside. It might give us the element of surprise we need to gain the upper hand.

I bite my lip, unsure of whether I should do this or not. There isn't even a guarantee it will work. But it's the only plan I've come up with. And time is running out. It's almost morning and that's when the Kalis are planning to attack. I need to do *something*. If K's here, she'll help me figure out a better plan. And at the very least, I'll be able to hang out with the person I like more than anyone else…

I close my eyes, allowing myself to finally see K the way I've always wanted to. Her beautiful brown eyes. Her lithe, strong body. Her serious, earnest expressions that I find insanely endearing. How cool she is when she battles demons, strangles demons, makes demon-rolls with tarp – and she doesn't even know it. She is the most incredible person I have ever met. When we sat in my room the other night and I apologised to her,

I could feel the chemistry between us. It was so real it freaked me out. But if I'd been brave enough to sit in it, if I'd kept staring into those hypnotic eyes of hers, then maybe we would have been drawn towards each other, and our lips would have touched… I would have felt her lips against mine. Soft. Strong. We'd wrap our arms around each other. And then–

My fantasy is cut off by the sounds of demons chattering excitedly. I let out an involuntary sigh. That was the best kiss of my life, and it hasn't even happened yet. I hope the demons bring K over ASAP so we can do it for real.

Then I let out a cry of excitement. The demons – they must have got a whiff of K's blood during my fantasy! That's why they're suddenly rushing around now! I frown, wishing I could speak demon like Joe. I consider waking him up, but just as I'm about to tug on his tux jacket, the demons start sniffing, racing out of the door. There is no clearer signal – the demons can smell their latest victim and they're on their way to get her.

K is coming, whether she likes it or not.

Chapter 30

'GRGGHH!'

There's a burst of activity as a load of demons rush into the lair. I jolt awake, realising I must have fallen asleep whilst I was waiting. The demons are struggling with something – a black-clad body that's writhing and kicking. I crane forward, praying it's who I think it is.

'Get OFF me!'

I'd recognise that voice anywhere. Relief floods through me as I watch the demons dump the body to the ground, and as soon as they go, I race over. K gets up, scowling, as she dusts herself off.

'K?' My voice sounds shy and small, even to my own ears.

'Kali!!' K wraps her arms around me tight. I squeeze her back just as hard. She's here. Holding me. And it feels so good. We stay there for way too long, until both of us realise how much time has passed and suddenly release each other.

'Hey,' I say nervously. 'Are you… okay?'

She nods, throwing a murderous look behind her at the demons. 'Yeah, no thanks to *them*. What about you? I saw them bringing you in on the cameras. Have they hurt you? Are you okay, Kali?'

I shake my head. 'I'm okay. So are the others. They're over there sleeping.'

K exhales loudly. 'Thank god. I was so worried…'

'There's no need to worry.' Then I pause. 'I mean, there is. We'll get to it. But there's no need to specifically worry about *me*.'

'It's just…' K tucks her hair behind her ear, avoiding my gaze. 'It's… my fault you're here. I'm sorry, Kali.' She looks determinedly at the ground as she speaks with resolve. 'You've probably worked it out already. That I like you. And that's why the demons took you. I'm an idiot. I never should have let myself entertain that thought. Obviously, you're straight and you like Joe. I hope this doesn't make things weird between us. I'll… get over it. I promise.'

I take her hands in mine. They're so soft. It doesn't make any sense considering all the fighting K does. But they are. I look into her shifting eyes and smile gently. 'K. I get it. On every level. Because… you're

288

here for the exact same reason.'

Her forehead creases in confusion. I love how transparent her face is – I can see her every emotion play out. I watch her work it out, her eyes widening with hope and then instantaneous doubt. 'I don't… do you mean…?'

I grin. 'You're here because I like you too. I finally realised how I feel about you. You're my crush.'

K's mouth drops open. She stares at me like she can't believe what I've just said. And to be honest, neither can I. 'But… Joe's your crush. That's why he's here.'

'He was,' I correct. 'He and I had a big chat, and I think maybe I only ever liked the *idea* of him. Because he's the hot, popular guy, and when he chose me, I felt special. I did fancy him – but not like I fancy you.'

'So… you really like… *me*?'

I nod. 'I really like you.'

Her face breaks into a giant beam. She's practically radiating light, and even though she's got a giant smudge of dirt on her cheek, she's never looked more beautiful. 'Really?'

I roll my eyes. 'How many times are you going to make me say it?'

'It's just… I thought you liked Joe.'

'I did like him. But Joe isn't for me. We didn't even have any chemistry when we kissed. It was kind of… bad.'

Her eyes sparkle. 'Is it wrong how happy I am to hear that?'

'Is it wrong how happy I am that it makes you happy?'

She laughs, then her face is serious again. 'Maybe you liking Joe was comphet? You know, compulsive heterosexuality. Where you fancied Joe not because it's what you truly felt, but because it's what society has made you think.'

'Oh my god, maybe! I can't believe there's a name for it.' I want to ask K more, but just then there's a loud bang from the vat. I gulp. It sounds like Raktabija's getting closer to his resurrection. I turn back to K quickly. 'We need to talk about the demons.'

'I know,' she says, instantly alert. 'Tech Kali's found something out. About the blood.'

'Me too! It's worse than we thought. They're using it to resurrect—'

'Raktabija.' K and I say it at the same time. 'You know?!'

'Tech Kali managed to figure it out. It's why they need the blood of our crushes, because it's so potent.'

I nod silently, taking it all in.

'Tech Kali thinks a bit of Raktabija was left behind

and never died,' continues K. 'And that part of him has been growing gradually over all these centuries. He's finally become strong enough to communicate with the clones, and that's what sparked all the changes in them – not a scientific evolving. He's imbuing them with his qualities – the intellect, the planning and so on – and the stronger he gets, the worse it becomes. If he's fully resurrected, then we won't just be fighting him, but an army who are *as strong as him*.'

I shiver with fear. 'K, I think they're close. With the resurrection. When they took my blood, it all sped up.'

'The blood of a Kali that's infused with desire – I'm not surprised,' she says slowly. 'And there's a *lot* of desire in it.'

'K!' I hit her arm playfully. 'You can't flirt while we're trying to kill a major demon.'

'I was being factual!'

'Well, factually, your blood is going to be infused with a lot of *my* desire too. Pent up desire that's finally being released, which probably makes it even more powerful.' I look into her eyes, fully serious. 'We cannot let the demons get your blood. If it gets into the vat, Raktabija will be here in seconds.'

We both gaze over to the vat where the demons are. They're pointing right at us. Things do not look good.

'We need to move the attack forward,' says K. 'We can't wait till morning. We need to do it now – before Raktabija appears. I'll tell the Kalis.'

'How will you–'

But before I've finished my sentence, K is already tapping away on her Apple watch. Of course, she managed to smuggle some tech in.

'I'll do some surveillance video for the others too,' she says. 'Get maximum intel. Then we can attack strategically. Take these demons down.'

I forgot how sexy K is when she's in demon slaying mode. I'm so busy watching her that I only notice the demons when they're almost right by us.

'They're coming!' K whips her head up, tapping even faster. 'We need a plan!' My voice is high with panic, louder than I intended.

It wakes up Joe, with a noisy yawn. 'Doomsday, what up?' He rubs sleep from his eyes, then spots K. 'Whoa. Is this the girl you like? She's hot! High-five!'

K raises her eyebrows at him, temporarily distracted from her typing, and I know she's assessing her old competition. Joe grins, oblivious, his hand still outstretched, waiting for me to high-five it.

And that's when the demons arrive.

They start grunting at K, and Joe translates, 'They want you to go with them to get your blood taken. It's pretty chill, so don't worry about it.'

K raises her fists, and I know she's prepared to fight the demons to stop them taking her blood. It won't work though – there's too many of them.

'Joe,' I whisper urgently. 'If the demons get K's blood, really *really* bad things will happen. Can you… stop it? Please?'

Joe frowns. Then he steps forward decisively, and starts making weird, demonic sounds. 'Grgghh gaahh genn yooo arrrrrvvvvv GAA.'

K and I both stare at him, speechless. He is legit speaking demon.

The demons grunt back, gesturing aggressively. I gulp. This doesn't look like it's going well. K's fists are clenched, ready.

But when Joe grunts one more time, the demons relax. They step away from K and grab Joe instead.

'Joe! What's happening? Are you okay?!'

'It's chill,' he says, before turning to grunt something else at the demons who release their grip on him. 'They're taking my blood again instead.'

'How did you do it?!'

He shrugs. 'Easy. I told them my blood was better than hers. Because, you know, she's a girl.' With that, he rolls up his sleeve, and follows the demons to the vat.

I turn to K, whose lips are still parted in surprise. 'Good to know everyday sexism works on demons too.'

'And that your ex can speak demon.'

'He's not my ex! But he did just do us a huge favour.'

K nods. 'His blood won't even be as potent, now the desire's gone.' She looks at me, a flash of doubt on her face.

'Trust me, it's gone,' I reassure her. 'It went days ago.'

Her expression clears with relief. 'Good. This won't stop the demons resurrecting Raktabija. But it should give us some time. I'm going to use it give the Kalis as much inside info as I can.'

'What shall I do?' I ask.

'Get ready. We fight at dawn.'

Chapter 31

I'm poised, ready to go. K looks at her watch. After a few terse seconds of silence, she nods.

In perfect timing, the windows shatter and the three Kalis burst in on ropes, carrying a giant sheet of plastic between them. 'Hi-yaaaaaaaa!!' they cry out, using the sheet as a parachute to land on the ground.

I grab Joe, Lucia, Kiran and Liam. 'Run!'

We race towards the door. I can hear cries and screams around us as the Kalis attack the demons, but I can't stop to look – not even to check on K. I've been tasked with getting the hostages out and that's exactly what I need to do.

We're almost at the door when a demon launches himself at us. I start fighting, just like K taught me, then I hear Dottoressa's voice from above. 'I'm on it!' She swoops down, grabbing the demon and flying him over to the plastic sheet, before spearing him onto it. She really lucked out, having flying as her superpower.

I lead the crushes out of the building and finally, we're outside, safe. 'Go!!' I tell them. 'Quickly!'

'But what about Kali?' Liam looks worried. 'I can't leave her with them!'

'She can take care of herself. The best way to help her is to get to safety. ASAP.'

Lucia nods. 'It's true. We'll just get in the way here. We need to trust our Kalis.'

'But… I don't understand,' says Kiran, in a daze. 'Kali was… *killing* them at every angle. I've never seen her like that. She was fighting like she had eyes in the back of her head!'

I feel like now is not the time to point out that she basically does – Tech Kali's power is super sight. Instead, I plead, 'Please. Just go. Like we planned. To K's house. You'll be safe there.'

'She's right, come on!' Lucia grips their arms, leading the way.

They follow, except for Joe. He turns to me. 'Can I stay? I can help you. You know I'm almost as good an archer as you.'

I hesitate. He *is* a good shot. And unlike me, he never gets distracted by things going on around him.

'Please Kali?' asks Joe. 'I helped before, didn't I?

By getting the demons to take my blood, not K's?'

I relent. 'Okay, but you're not going inside. You have to stay out here. Okay?'

Joe nods eagerly. Deal!'

I gesture for Lucia to continue without Joe, then show him the weapons the Kalis have stashed for us. I grab Hera, cradling her in my arms. It feels so good to be reunited with her. I reach for the arrows and the lighters, while Joe finds himself another set of bow and arrows. I point to a tree. 'Climb that tree and fight from there, okay? Swear to me you won't leave until I tell you that you can.'

'Yes, sir!'

'It's not a joke, Joe. This is serious. And you need to make sure you only hit the demons when they're on the tarp. Otherwise, if even a drop of their blood hits the ground, more will appear, just like in Mrs Patel's story, okay?'

The smile drops off his face and he gulps, nervous. 'Promise. I… trust you Doomsday.'

I nod. Against the odds, I trust him too. I take a deep breath and race straight towards the screams and explosions coming from the warehouse. It's time to start demon slaying.

★★★

I wipe sweat from my brow, exhausted. I've killed hundreds of demons, but there are more everywhere I look. It's never-ending. The plastic sheet is permanently filled with demon corpses because we're killing them faster than they disappear. It's completely exhausting, but at least there's progress. And none of us are hurt. Yet.

I launch an arrow that burns through two demons at once and I share a victorious glance with K, who has just killed two demons by smashing their heads together. We grin at each other, as Tech Kali launches fireworks on the other side of the warehouse, and I feel a surge of confidence. We can do this.

'AAAAAAAAAAARRRRRRGGGHHH!'

Or maybe I spoke too soon.

A loud, unearthly howl pierces through the air. All of us turn to face its source. The vat. I stare in abject horror as a figure – blood-red, enormous, dripping – hovers in the air directly above the empty, metal vat. It looks exactly like the demons with its one eye, but something about it is different. The air around it is *shimmering*, dark. It stinks of power. And its roar is a hundred times deeper than a normal demon roar.

The demons all drop to their knees in revery, grunting rhythmically. I don't need Joe to translate this: 'Rak-ta-bi-ja. Rak-ta-bi-ja.'

The Kalis are frozen too. None of us know what to do. The biggest demon, the leader of this clone army, the one we've always feared, is *here*. We're all waiting for something, for anything to happen, when Model Kali finally breaks the silence. She slices her long samurai sword through the necks of five praying demons. Their heads loll onto the plastic and Raktabija roars louder than before.

He flies through the air, right towards her, and lands where she was in a split second. Thank god Model Kali's power is invisibility, because if she hadn't just disappeared from sight, he would have killed her. He thrashes around, roaring loudly as he looks for her, and the demon clones spring into action. Battle has officially resumed, and I start shooting fire arrows as fast as I can.

But… something's wrong. My arrows aren't hitting the demons' eyes like they normally do. They're missing, landing on their limbs instead. Only a few of the demons burst into flames and die – the rest are able to pull out the arrows before the fire burns through their blood. I don't understand, until I suddenly do. The demons have got Raktabija's super strength now, and it means they're moving faster than before. It's why I can't hit them as accurately.

I glance around me. It's happening everywhere. K is trying to strangle a demon – and it's trying to strangle her back. Tech Kali is fighting a group of demons with her chain whip and for once, she's *not* winning. Dottoressa is flying demons over to the plastic, but some are escaping. Raktabija is still chasing Model Kali, following a trail of sliced demon heads as her sword flies through the room, and I know she must be exhausted.

We have no choice but to keep on fighting. I quickly fire an arrow at the demon K's battling, and it misses his eye, but gets the back of his head. It's enough to kill him. I barely notice K's grateful glance because I'm having to focus harder than ever. I need to account for the demons' new super speed with my aim. My adjustments aren't perfect. But slowly my aim improves, and I'm able to take down more demons.

We're all fighting harder than we ever have before. We aren't just fighting Raktabija – we're fighting *hundreds* of him. There is no time to pause. No time to do anything other than attack, defend, attack.

'Kali, help!' I whirl around at the sound of K's voice. She's being attacked. By *Raktabija*. I instantly fire an arrow at his heart. He howls in pain as it hits his shoulder and K escapes from him. She's safe. But I'm not. Raktabija rips the arrow out, then comes running right towards me and before I can even blink, he's there, reaching his hand around my throat. He's going to kill me.

'Hiii-yaaa!' I look up to see a glimpse of Model Kali kicking Raktabija so hard his hand slides off me before she disappears again.

K races towards us, attacking Raktabija from behind. Within seconds, his clones are by his side, and she has no choice but to fight them off. I gulp, terrified at the thought of having to face Raktabija alone, but then Tech Kali is right there, her chain whip flying in every single direction. Model Kali is somewhere around, her sword slicing through the air, occasionally hitting Raktabija, though it's not enough to kill him. Dottoressa Kali is flying above us, rounding up demons, and throwing them into the vat. I don't understand her plan, until she grabs a firework and throws it in. They disappear in a burst of flames.

'Yes!!' cries Model Kali, an invisible voice in the distance.

Dottoressa keeps going, flying and weaving as she tries to get more demons into the vat. But they're as fast as Raktabija now so it's no easy task. I use my arrows to help her. I've never fought so hard in my life, but I don't see how it's ever going to end. We're all exhausted. Even with our best efforts, we're only just surviving – not winning. There is a very real possibility that we won't get out of here alive. Unless we do something. Something drastic that could change *everything*. I know the others were against it, but that was before we knew Raktabija was here. I know my plan might not work; but I have to at least try.

Without thinking, I yank one of my arrows out of my bag and shove it into my palm. I don't even wince as blood comes out. I let it drop to the ground, just like invokinghindugoddesses.com said I should. I set the blood on fire with my lighter, watching as somehow, it catches alight. The website said the fire unites all four elements. The water of the blood, the earth of the ground, the fire showing up as itself, and the air the fire needs to burn.

'Kali-ma,' I shout. 'Please come and help us!' Then I remember that I need to chant to invoke her. Should I just chant her name on repeat? With a 'please help us' at the end? It doesn't exactly feel like enough to invoke the most powerful goddess in Hindu history. Unless… I use Radha's poem!

I stand tall, bringing my legs apart, bending my knees and holding my hands high in the air like the goddess herself. I take a deep breath and the words pour out of me.

'Your tongue laps up the blood of demons slain, your naked body dances without shame, your power is yours, though they try in vain, to take it from you, to make you tame. But you refuse to let them define you, tying you down with one narrow, tired view. Instead, you stand female, wild, and free, the goddess I've always wanted to be. Pure female power, you are shakti!'

I recite it again, feeling a pulsating energy throb through my body. Something is happening. I can *feel* it.

Then a hand slips into mine. I open my eyes to see K. She's by my side, offering me her left hand. Wordlessly, I use my arrow to cut her palm. She squeezes the cut, so her blood falls to the ground on top of mine. The flames double, then triple in size.

'Chant with me!'

And she does. Slowly at first, as she learns the words, and then confidently.

We've chanted it three times together – loud – when

Model Kali appears by our side. She cuts her hand too, squeezing the blood onto the flames, and joins in the chant. Dottoressa runs over to do the same, as soon as she's flung another 10 demons into the vat and set them alight with a firework. Tech Kali is still keeping Raktabija busy, fighting him as fast as she can with her whip whirling around her. But when she manages to temporarily wound him, she rushes over to join us. She adds her blood to the mix – she doesn't even need to cut herself because Raktabija has done it for her – and the flames grow to an inhuman size.

We stand, in our goddess warrior poses, chanting, tongues sticking out, invoking the pure female power herself. The flames grow, until they're completely surrounding us. They're burning on every side of us, but the heat isn't painful. When the flames lick against my skin, they don't even singe me. How can they, when we are part of the fire?

The demons, however, cry out in agony when they try to cross the blazing flames and it scorches their skin. We keep on chanting. I can feel the energy rising. This is it. We're resurrecting Kali. She's coming.

But then the power plateaus. It stops growing. I don't know how I know this, but I do. The fire needs more strength, more blood, more *power* to bring the goddess to us.

I don't know what to do. The demons had days to collect blood to resurrect Raktabija. And they had the blood of our crushes, made more potent with our desire. All we have is each other.

We have each other.

I turn to K, and she must have sensed it because she opens her mahogany eyes, looking straight into mine. I feel a flame of desire burn inside me. I want her. So badly. The others are still chanting around us. There are demons desperately raging as they try to find a way through the flames to kill us. But all I can think about is how beautiful K looks right now, with the red light of the fire glowing on her skin.

Slowly, I lean in towards her. She looks surprised — I guess trying to resurrect a goddess surrounded by demons probably isn't the most natural setting for a first kiss — but she locks eyes with me and leans in too. Our lips brush against each other. I gasp at the sensation, my entire body tingling with electricity. From the look on her face, so does K's. But then we kiss again. Properly.

Her lips are as soft as I imagined, but like everything else about K, they're strong too. Every cell in my body comes to life, dripping with desire, as our lips melt over each other's. Our kiss is pure passion. It's *alive*. Blood throbs through me, as K's mouth presses against mine. This is nothing like my kiss with Joe – I have no idea where my tongue is or where hers is – but it doesn't matter. It's almost like we have merged into one, our bodies intuitively moving, the desire overpowering everything else. Every single part of my body feels like it's on fire, in the best of ways. I have never felt so powerful; I have never felt so strong.

And then, gently, I take my lips off, trusting the voice inside me telling me to let go. I think it's the goddess Kali within me, the pure female power, the shakti. K must hear the same voice because she silently offers me her wounded hand and I bring mine to hers. We squeeze them tight, watching as our blood pools together, mingling, as it falls onto the flames. It burns brighter than anything I've seen before. We have to shield our eyes because it's so white-hot. The other Kalis are still chanting around us: 'Your tongue laps up the blood of demons slain, your naked body dances without shame, your power is yours'.

Then there's a violent bang. The flames burst wide throughout the warehouse, burning demons in its wake.

We are still protected from the heat of the fire, but the force of the explosion leaves us sprawling on the floor. None of us speak. We're all too busy staring at the fire in total awe.

There, right in the centre of the flames, on the spot where our blood fell, is Kali-Ma herself. The goddess. Her skin is dark, mesmerising and luminous. Her eyes – all three of them – are wide and alert. Her hair is beyond stunning, a cascading wave of black, thick silk. Her body is covered in jewels and weapons, but not a single item of clothing. She's naked beneath her adornments, her dark skin glowing like she's made of light. I have never seen anything more breath-taking in my entire life.

Suddenly, she roars, revealing her sharp white teeth and that huge, red tongue. Her four arms instantly start slicing through the air, slaying demons everywhere. Just before their blood reaches the ground, Kali-Ma's tongue grows long and wide, lapping it all up. Demons are dropping all around us.

We Kalis just stand there, gaping, watching in total wonder. Our namesake is here and she's more than we could have ever, ever imagined.

And then Raktabija is right there. With a loud war

cry, he leaps on top of Kali-Ma, pushing her to the ground with a sickening crunch. But she springs up instantly, attacking him with every one of her arms. Their fighting is like a dance. The way their bodies are moving so fast, whirling, fighting, grasping. The last of Raktabija's demons are also watching, motionless.

'Come on! Let's fight!' K's call wakes me out of my trance. I join her and we start taking down the demons around us. I try to move like Kali-Ma, imagining my arms are flying through the air as fast as hers, as I launch and fire my arrows at the demons. The others are fighting around me too – slaying demons, fighting, punching, stabbing. Our movements feel synchronised, like clockwork. Kali-Ma's presence has taken our powers to another level; none of us have ever fought like this before. We are united and one. We are all Kalis, and we are in the presence of the goddess we've always wanted to be, standing wild, female and free.

Occasionally, I notice a rogue arrow take a demon down and I grin, knowing it's Joe. He's out there, up in his tree, watching, and joining in. We're doing it. Despite our differences, we are all working together. Inspired by Kali – the goddess who refuses to let anyone define her, the goddess who I always thought of as an outsider, who I saw as weird, ugly and unlovable. But now, as I watch her burn with pure power and unique otherworldly strength, I see how wrong I was. She's the most powerful, beautiful, inspiring goddess out there. Precisely *because* she doesn't conform to any of the standards that women are held to. She's setting her own.

I feel like the best version of myself, the warrior I always wanted to be, as I shoot off flaming arrows into the burning warehouse, slaying demons in my wake. The whole time, I am aware of Kali-Ma. I am in total awe that we are fighting in her presence. That we have resurrected this goddess, this queen, this demon slayer. She is incredible, clawing demons to pieces with her nails, roaring loudly as she fights twenty at a time. They're disappearing faster than ever, and whenever their blood falls towards the ground, her giant tongue darts out and slurps it up before it can birth more clones. Her cries of triumph, victory and rage reverberate around the room. She's not afraid to express herself – her voice is here to be heard, and we are all here to hear it.

It inspires me to be louder too, more vocal as I grunt, exhale, cry out and even warble as I launch my arrows at the demons. I used to be silent when I'd shoot, but Kali-Ma is showing me I don't need to be quiet. I can be loud and make herself heard. I'm not here to disappear – I'm here to slay.

And I do. We all do. Fighting like we've never fought before, doing our best to make Kali-Ma proud. We are her daughters, her descendants, her devout followers until the end.

Then… it is the end. 'We've done it, stop!' Model Kali's voice jolts me out of my trance, and I pause, looking around. There are no more demons left to fight. All the clones are gone. We've killed them all. Their bodies are disappearing by the second, vanishing off the tarp into thin air.

The only one left is Raktabija.

Kali-Ma's cry thunders through the building as she fights him at the speed of light, her limbs whirling as she punches, kicks and slices at Blood-Seed. He's fighting back, just as fast, and I can barely breathe as I watch, my eyes darting around, trying to keep track of their every move.

'Let's help them!' says K.

'How?' asks Tech Kali.

'By chanting,' I say, the answer suddenly clear. 'Like we did before. It gives us strength. It gives

310

Kali-Ma strength.'

So, we stand around the goddess and the demon, bending down into our goddess poses, knees in line with hips like we're in a yoga class, arms high and out to the side in right angles, our tongues sticking out wide, and our backs straight.

Then we chant Radha's poem, reminding Kali of her power. Of her strength. Of her refusal to bow to shame. Because are not what people say we are – we are who *we* say we are. We are Kalis, defined by nobody but ourselves.

The louder our voices get, the more we feel Kali-Ma grow stronger. We don't notice how much time is passing – time is no longer relevant. The only thing we feel is the power of the words. And so we continue, our voices becoming one, our words rising above us.

That's when it happens. Kali-Ma grows bigger, taller and wider, towering over Raktabija, as she doubles, then triples in size. For the first time, he cowers in fear. And she uses that moment to slice off his head with her clawed nails.

It comes off clean, in one deft swipe.

Kali-Ma lifts it high, a moment of triumph, as she roars loud in victory. Then she swallows the head whole. Blood is dripping from her lips but her tongue darts out to lick it up. And then her tongue grows, lengthens, slithering out of her mouth, until it spreads out in front of us, across the entire floor of the warehouse, a red carpet, soaking up all the demon's blood.

Soon, there is nothing left. No blood. No demons. Just us. And Kali-Ma.

Her tongue slowly shrinks back to normal, until she swallows it down. She stands in front of us, her body shimmering with bright, holy light. Her divinity is manifest and none of us can speak. Instinctively, I bow. We all do. United again in our reverence for the mother goddess.

Kali-Ma doesn't speak in response. But she acknowledges us through the magical gift of her touch. She presses her many fingertips to our heads, all at once, and I feel a burst of pure, godly energy rush through my body, setting my every cell alight. In that moment, we all lift our gazes, looking directly at the face of our goddess.

Her eyes – brown, mahogany, gold, black, every single colour all at once – are breath-taking. Literally. Nothing seems to matter as I look into them. She encompasses more than I knew existed. The whole universe is in her eyes. Space. Expansion. Beauty. And life.

The definitions of all these words instantly change for me, and I realise how limited I've been. How small. There's a whole *universe* out there. Who cares what Hayley or Joe think of me? Or even what K thinks of me? The only thing that matters is what *I* think of me. And right now, I think I'm a goddamn warrior. A descendent of the goddess standing right in front of me. A Kali, forever.

Chapter 32

K and I are standing alone in the wood next to the abandoned warehouse. The other Kalis have all rushed off to her house to be reunited with their respective wife, fiancé and work crush. But K and I stayed, together.

'That was… a lot,' I say finally.

She nods, dazed. 'I… can't believe we saw her. Kali-Ma. She was incredible.'

'I know.' I shake my head. 'How was I ever ashamed to be named after her? She's perfect in every single way.'

'It's not your fault.' K lifts her gaze to mine. 'We live in a world with stupid beauty standards and narrow ideas of what attraction is.'

'Well, *my* new definition of beautiful is having four arms, three eyes and iridescent black skin.'

K grins. 'Sounds just as attainable as the Barbie one.'

I grin back, nervously. I don't know what to do with myself now the danger has gone. None of it seems real.

Not Raktabija, Kali-Ma, or even… the kiss. I want to talk about it, only I don't know how. Words seem futile in the face of the divinity we saw.

But K manages to do it for me. 'Is it just me or are you still on a high from earlier? I feel kind of amazing.'

'Me too!' I cry out. 'That kiss—'

'When Kali-Ma touched us—' says K at the exact same time.

I flush, suddenly mortified. Obviously K meant she was on a high from being touched by a *goddess*. Not by *me*! What's wrong with me?! How can I think my first kiss with K is a bigger deal than a goddess coming down to earth to save us?! I'm a total idiot. I wish—

My thoughts are interrupted by K leaning in to kiss me. My skin tingles again when the soft, delicate skin of her lips touches against mine. I can't help groaning aloud in satisfaction. It feels incredible, even without our tongues getting involved. Just the very act of touching K is pure bliss. I wasn't sure if it would still be so special, without the demons and goddess around us. But the chemistry that K and I have is clearly all ours.

'Now I'm on a double high,' she murmurs, slowly, reluctantly, breaking away.

315

'Me too. This is *so* much better than kissing Joe.'

K raises an eyebrow. 'That's not exactly the review I was hoping for.'

'Trust me – this is a 5 star situation. I mean, our kiss invoked *divinity*. My kiss with Joe just invoked demons.' As K laughs, I clamp my hand over my mouth. 'Oh my god. Joe! He's still in the tree!!'

'You left him in a tree?' asks K, confused, as she follows me to Joe's oak. 'Isn't he at mine with the other hostages?'

'I gave him a bow and arrows. He took down a few demons.'

'Hmph.' K sounds reluctantly impressed. 'Why is he still in the tree?'

'I made him promise to stay up there till I arrived. JOE! It's okay to come down!'

'Doomsday? Is that you?' Joe starts making his way down the tree. 'Oh, uh, your crush is here too. Hi.'

'Joe, we did it!!' I cry, hugging him. 'The demons are gone. All of them. Even the OG demon Rakta– I mean, Blood-Seed.' Then I realise I don't *want* to anglicise the demon's name for Joe. I don't ever want to change anything about myself to make it more palatable for white people. I stick my chin in the air proudly. 'Raktabija. He's gone.'

'Wooooo!' Joe cheers loudly and does a little dance. 'We did it!! The demons are defeated!'

K rolls her eyes at Joe's reaction, but I can't help laughing. I even try to join in his celebration dance, but the choreography is more complicated than it looks.

'So, who was that woman with three eyes who took down all the demons?' asks Joe. 'She was *hot*.'

K corrects him. 'She's a goddess, not a woman.'

'Totally,' agrees Joe, and I stifle a giggle. I can't believe Joe has a crush on Kali-Ma. Then he turns to me. 'Also, um, thanks Kali. You saved my life today.'

'I also endangered it… which I am very sorry about.'

Joe shrugs. 'Whatevs. Pierre's going to *freak* when I tell him about this.'

I smile weakly. 'Funny story about Pierre actually…'

But K interrupts, holding up her watch. 'Hey, I just got a message.'

'From the Kalis?' I ask, worried. 'Are they okay? The hostages too?'

'Everyone's fine,' K reassures me. 'It's not that. It's Radha.'

'Radha?!' Then I gasp. 'Oh my god! Her sangeet! I totally forgot – the ceremonies must have started ages ago! She's going to hate me for not being there!'

K clears her throat as she reads the message aloud:

'Hey Kali, K messaged your mum to say you stayed at hers last night.' I give K a grateful glance – she thinks of everything! 'Just wanted to say I'm proud of you for following your dreams and going to the archery competition today. Guessing you turned your phone off to avoid angry messages from your mum, but don't worry, I convinced her to support you. We're all on our way to the competition now! See you there! Can't wait to see your golds.'

'The competition's today?' cries Joe. 'Phil's going to go mad! We need to get there now.'

K sighs. 'As much as I don't want to agree with your former comphet crush, he's got a point. I'm calling an Uber.'

***

I push through the double doors of the auditorium into the main hall of the competition, with K on my left and Joe on my right. The entire auditorium falls silent to stare at us. I assume it's because we've arrived late but then I catch sight of my reflection in a mirrored wall and realise I'm still wearing my Indian outfit. I also have mud, sweat and blood all over my face.

And K and Joe don't look much better…

That's when Phil storms over. 'Kali! Joe! Where have you both been?' He wrinkles his nose. 'Joe, why are you wearing a tuxedo?! And when's the last time you washed it?'

'Sorry Coach,' says Joe. 'We had some trouble getting here.'

'But where have you BEEN?' demands Phil. 'You've missed all the morning events!'

I brandish my bow. 'I… found Hera?'

He splutters, but before he can ask any more unanswerable questions Ri rushes to hug us. But her sudden recoil suggests she regrets it. 'Ew! I mean, uh, what happened to you both?!'

I sigh longingly at Ri in her jeans and cute top, her braids tied back neatly. She looks so *clean*.

Phil frowns. 'I'm going to speak to the organisers and make sure you can both still compete in the last event. Thank god, the biggest one is still to go.'

As he walks away, Ri raises her arms questioningly. 'So? What's going on?!'

'Ri, shit went *down*,' says Joe excitedly. 'There were – ow!' K pinches his arm, and he coughs, returning to the script we decided on in the Uber. 'I mean, yeah.

319

Paris was wild. Kali just got me from the... airport? In her... Indian outfit?'

'The wedding was... yeah,' I say. 'How's the competition, Ri? I've been desperate to find out how you're doing!'

'I won a couple of medals,' she grins.

'A couple of medals?! Uh, that's major!' I cry, as Joe high-fives her, whooping loudly.

K clears her throat awkwardly. 'I'll leave you all to it.'

'You must be K!' beams Ri. 'Kali's told me all about you. Apparently, you love the goddess Kali as much as I do.'

K smiles, surprised. 'Uh, yeah. I'm a big fan. That's... cool you are too.'

'I just love how undefinable she is,' says Ri. 'Powerful as hell.'

'I couldn't agree more,' says K, but just then her watch beeps. 'Oh, it's... my mum. Sorry, I'd better get this.'

Ri drags my wrist, leading me to a corner so we can talk in private. 'Uh, K's so cool! I love her!'

'Me too.' Then I blush. 'Uh, I mean, I like her. We... kind of... kissed.'

Ri's mouth drops open. 'What?! What about Joe??'

'He knows. He actually helped me realise how much

I like K.'

Ri squeals. 'I love that for you!'

I hug her tight. 'Thanks Ri. And thanks for being such a good friend.'

'Right back at you girl!'

'Well, well, well, look who's trying to steal my best friend as well as my boyfriend.' Ri's arms fall limp and I turn slowly to see Hayley, an ice-cold smile on her face. She's clutching Joe's arm, and he looks terrified. 'Nice outfit, *Doomsday*,' she says.

I feel my stomach plummet as it always does in Hayley's presence. I look so gross right now, while she's so perfect. I wish I was facing demons instead of her. And then I remember. I've slayed demons. I'm a legit warrior. A daughter of Kali-Ma. So why am I so scared of Hayley Parker?!

'Thanks,' I reply, drawing my body upright. 'And Joe's *not* your boyfriend.'

She crosses her arms. 'Don't tell me you think he's yours.'

'No. He's not that either. He's his own person. Right, Joe?' I give him an encouraging smile, but his eyes widen in panic.

Hayley scowls at me. 'What's your deal, Kali?'

For a moment, I want to shrivel into myself like the

321

old Kali would have. But I'm not that Kali anymore. I'm a Kali who has kissed a girl and slayed demons. A Kali who resurrected a goddess.

I try to imagine what Kali-Ma would want me to say if she was here.

'What's *your* deal Hayley?' I counter. 'Can't you just let everyone live their own lives? You're always here, trying to control them. Coming to archery, when you *hate* archery. Why can't you just get your own thing?'

Hayley is glaring at me like I'm a one-eyed demon. 'I already have my own thing – Joe and Ri. Or at least, I did, until *you* came along.'

'They can't be your 'thing.' You can't own people. They're not things.'

Hayley takes a step forward as though she's getting ready to push me. But then Ri is between us. 'Hayley. Babe. You're my friend and always will be. But… Kali's right. I need to talk to you.'

'What?' spits out Hayley. 'Kali's brainwashed you too?'

'Kali's my friend,' says Ri firmly. 'And so are you. But the difference is that Kali and I are honest with each other. And… I haven't been with you.'

A hurt look flashes across Hayley's face but she quickly covers it up. 'What are you trying to say, Rihanna?'

'That I haven't always told you the truth.' Ri bites her lip. 'Like, I'm not that big on bao buns. Or those dresses we bought together. Or boys. Or… girls.'

'I… don't understand,' says Hayley, confusion written all over her face.

Ri takes a deep breath. 'I think I'm asexual.'

Hayley's brow furrows. 'What?! But you… I don't… why didn't you TELL me?!'

'I guess because I was scared,' admits Ri. She's being so brave, and it takes every ounce of self-control for me to not cheer aloud as her hype girl.

'I'm scared too,' pipes up Joe. 'I… don't want to date you, Hayley.'

Hayley pales, looking from Joe to Ri. That's when I see how vulnerable she really is. Underneath her cold exterior, she's just as scared as we are. It's weird, but I feel kind of bad for her right now. So, I decide to help her.

'Joe and I aren't dating either,' I offer. 'And earlier he said how cool and popular and hot you are. Just so you know.' Hayley looks a tiny bit more relaxed.

'I… think I just need some time alone,' says Joe. 'It's been a lot with the demons.'

'His personal demons,' clarifies K, who has got off her call. 'Sorry, hi, I'm K. Kali's…'

We both stare at each other. I have no idea what to say. All I know is that I don't want K to say friend, because she's so much more than that, but I'm not ready for her to say girlfriend. She says nothing. Neither do I. The silence grows, threatening to swallow us all.

That's when Hayley groans loudly. 'Are you kidding me?! You two are *dating*?! Is everyone around here suddenly LGBTQIA+ except for me?'

Ri grins at me. 'Let's just say a certain goddess helped us realise who we really are.'

'Tell me about it,' agrees Joe. 'I wish I could date someone like that goddess.'

'Good luck,' snorts K.

Hayley frowns, confused. 'Okay, I have no idea what's going on right now. But… Ri. Can we talk? And work stuff out?'

'Of course! You don't want to… I don't know, talk to Joe first?'

Hayley shakes her head. 'Forget boys – *you* are my priority.' She links arms with Ri, shooting me a 'she's mine, not yours' look.

I roll my eyes, but I don't care. Because I know how important Hayley is to Ri, and if this is the start of Hayley starting to properly accept Ri, then I'm happy for her.

'So, um, Kali?' says K hesitantly. 'I've got some bad news.'

I'm instantly alert. 'Demons?'

'No. That was my mum. She's at your cousin's sangeet. Or at least, she was. And it turns out it's not just your cousin and parents who are coming to the competition to watch you. It's... the entire sangeet party. And they're outside.'

I hear them before I see them. The dhol players are there too, thumping their drums loudly, wedding-style. I can't *believe* they brought dhols to my archery competition! What's everyone going to think?! This is crazy!

K and I look at each other for a moment, silent in shock, then turn our gazes to the door, waiting for the inevitable. But neither of us prepared for when it finally bursts open.

There is so much colour and sparkle that I literally have to shield my eyes. It takes my eyes a few seconds to adjust, and then I gape in total shock. Every single Indian person I know is marching into the archery hall right now, dressed in brightly coloured, shining, gleaming Indian outfits. Not to mention the gold jewellery draped over them.

And my family are right at the front.

'KALIIII!' My mum is running towards me like

she's in a Bollywood movie, her purple saree flying behind her, the family gold weighing her down. I gulp. The expression on her face is more 'furious parent' than 'loving matriarch', which means this is not a happy comedy Bollywood – it's the dramatic kind. My dad is trying to keep up with her in his kurta, and he's sweating so much I can't tell what his mood is. There's Radha – in her emerald green designer saree, struggling in her Jimmy Choos, waving at me in excitement. She's completely mad for doing this. Kevil's behind her, looking confused in his golden kurta, but gazing supportively at his beautiful bride-to-be. All my aunts and uncles are behind them. And a glamorous woman in a sparkly crop top and neon saree who is strutting like she's on a catwalk. Is that–

'K, baby!' Deepa Auntie totters over and air kisses K. 'There you are! Did you know there are a bunch of women all called Kali in our house? They're such angels – one of them fixed the Wi-Fi.' She frowns at K, patting her lips. 'Why are your lips so swollen? Have you been using that lip balm I – oh!!' Her eyes widen and she clutches her heart with her hands. 'Oh my god!'

My family halts their slow-mo Bollywood entrance *just* as Deepa Auntie inspects my lips and squeals out loud. 'Kali *beta*, yours are swollen too!' Oblivious to our audience, she pulls me towards her, in a Dior-scented hug. 'Oh, I knew it! I'm so happy for you both! My favourite girls – yay!'

'I… don't understand,' says my mum slowly, looking from me to K and back again. 'What's happening?'

My entire family is standing behind her – a multi-coloured explosion of silk and taffeta – all with the same question written across their faces.

'Um… it's time for my archery event!' I say desperately. 'Look, there's Phil coming to get us! See you all in there?'

I don't wait for a response. Instead, I run into the hall as fast as I can, my heart racing. I have *no* idea how I'm going to get through this.

Chapter 33

I'm standing at the front of the packed hall, Hera in my arms, remembering Phil's advice. Strong right arm, low left elbow. I breathe deeply, micro-adjusting my position, shifting my chundri out of the way. I'm the last person to compete in this final event. Ri and Joe are the current leads so far, which means that this is a South Bridge victory either way. But if I want to win – and I really do – then I need to get three golds in a row. I glance to the front row where K is beaming, thumbs up. It's impossible to not smile back; her belief in me is contagious.

And then I see Hayley, eyebrows raised, arms crossed, clearly waiting for me to fail. My self-belief wavers. I know I just stood up to her, but I'm still a bit scared of her. I force myself to look away from her. Which means I end up looking at the entire of my family instead. My mum and dad are sitting together – he looks insanely excited, and she looks… serious. I don't know what she knows, but she knows *something's* going on.

There's a flash of movement to the side. Radha. She's winking at me, still in her fancy saree. I don't think I'll ever get over the fact that she left her sangeet for this. All my aunts, uncles and cousins are surrounding them, taking over this whole archery competition. Loads of white people are still giving them weird looks, but my family aren't bothered. Most of them are just whispering and pointing at me, clearly wondering why I'm not doing anything. Phil coughs loudly, suggesting he's thinking the same thing.

I get the hint and reach for an arrow. As I put it into place, Hayley gets out her phone and holds it up to *film me*. I falter. Why is she doing this?! Is she waiting for me to fail? I think back to her sitting in the archery hall, laughing at me, making mean comments. Every single time, I missed the target. It's going to happen again – I know it is. My heart races as I try to resist the panic, but I know I'm going to fail. In front of my entire family. And it's all because of Hayley.

'Cute outfit,' mouths Hayley. 'Wave for the camera, Kali!'

I feel a familiar wave of shame as I look down at my clothes. Why am I different? Why do I look different? Wear different things? Eat different foods?

Behave differently? All I've ever wanted is to be like everyone else, but instead I'm up here in my Indian outfit, with sweaty hair and mud on my legs.

And then I remember that I *am* different. In every single way. Not just because I'm brown, but because I'm a Kali. I was born to stand out. Always. I've spent so long caring about what other people think of me. I've been so terrified of being judged that I spent years hiding myself away at school. I lost myself to please others. I gave my power away to everybody around me, all because I wanted them to think well of me. But my life is my own and the *only* opinion that I need to pay attention to is mine. So why am I letting everyone else stop me?

The truth is that I *like* being Indian. And I like being British. I'm a combination of everything – I'm contrary like Radha said – and I'm proud of it. I'm done hiding parts of myself from people and compartmentalising my life. I want to own it. *All of it.*

I take a deep breath and then I don't let myself think – or even look around me. I just focus on my bow and arrow, lifting my elbow high, getting ready to let go as though I was about to slay a demon. I take a deep inhale, and then as I exhale the arrow away, I let out a loud grunt. Out of the corner of my eye, I see the audience recoil in shock at the sound I just made. But they all burst into a smatter of applause as the arrow lands on gold.

I don't pay attention to any of it though – their shock at my sounds or their praise. I just get ready to go again. I breathe deeply, exhaling even louder as my next arrow soars through the air to the target. It lands on gold again. I know people are clapping again, but I don't really notice it. I don't even turn to look at K for validation and approval. I am focused entirely on myself.

I don't even let my thoughts come in when I line up my third arrow. I just work automatically just like I did when I was demon slaying. I place the arrow in the bow, breathing in the power of shakti, and then I breathe out victory – a loud, Kali-Ma-style roar – as the arrow hits gold.

The roar reverberates around me and I realise it's not just me – the audience are doing it back. Because my results mean I've *won*. Ri and Joe have come joint second. South Bridge Secondary has taken all three medals in the biggest event at the competition. I turn to see Ri and Joe cheering excitedly behind me, Phil wiping away a tear as he says something to me that I'm too spaced out to take in, and my entire community in the stand, cheering and, wait, are they *dancing*?!

The archery audience are staring at them like they're crazy – which they totally are. They seem to have forgotten this is an archery competition, not a sangeet. But then the dhol players start banging out a beat, and it's so infectious that even the white people start to join in. K is dancing with Ri – I love that they're getting on – and I'm about to join them when I see my parents. They're the only ones *not* dancing. My throat goes dry as I realise they're coming over to speak to me. Right now.

My dad is beaming as he wraps his arms around me in a tight hug. 'You won! Kali! I'm so proud of you, *beta*!'

But my mum isn't smiling. She has her arms crossed, and doesn't even try to hug me.

'I'm... sorry I missed Radha's sangeet, Mum. But she told me to. Kind of.'

My mum nods. 'She told me what she told you. All of it. But Kali, this isn't the way things are done.'

I don't know if she means the wedding or things between K and I. I'm about to say something to hide the truth, then I realise I don't *want* to hide anymore. I want to be me. So I stand tall and try to channel Kali-Ma again.

'I… need to tell you both something.' My mum looks worried, like she wants to stop me. But my dad's face is open, ready. 'So, um. I… like K as… more than a friend. In a romantic way. And she likes me too. We're… I don't know. Dating. I guess.'

My dad's mouth drops open in surprise, but he recovers quickly. 'Oh wow! Well, congratulations! K's a lovely girl. You know she's already part of the family for us.'

'Thank you, Dad.' I hug him again, genuinely grateful for his reaction.

My mum is immobile, silent.

'Mum?' I venture.

'I knew something like this would happen,' she says, shaking her head. 'It's the archery. All these manly sports.'

'What?!'

My dad places a hand on her arm and speaks to her in Gujarati. 'Sunita. It's okay. Let her be. She's happy. That's all we want, isn't it?'

'But it's going to make her life so much harder! Kali, you don't know what you're doing.'

'I do!' I force myself to breathe. Shouting at my mum won't do anything. 'Can we… talk properly? Over there?'

My dad gives my mum an encouraging nod,

and she reluctantly follows me to a quieter corner. We both deliberately ignore the Bollywood-archery competition mash-up that's still going strong.

'Mum, I know you think this is something I've chosen and it will make my life harder. But firstly, I haven't chosen it. It just happened.' She looks like she's about to interrupt so I continue quickly. 'And the second thing is that… well… this has actually made my life so much *easier*. I feel so happy with K. When I thought I liked boys, well, boy – I was always so anxious around him. I felt I had to impress him and please him all the time. But with K, I can just… be myself! I'm so glad to have her in my life. It makes me feel stronger. Happier. And less alone. Isn't that a good thing?'

There is a long silence, and I realise my mum is wiping away tears. 'Oh Kali. I'm sorry. I don't want to make you feel like you're not accepted for who you are. I love you and I always will – nothing you can ever do or say would change that. I'm just *scared*.'

'I get it,' I say softly. 'I've spent most of my life being scared.'

'I'm worried things will change for you, and you won't be okay.'

'Mum, things *always* change. And I'm still the same

Kali. I'm just a bit braver. And... happier.'

My mum squeezes my hand, still dabbing her face with a hanky. She's the only person I know who still carries hankies. 'In some ways, I should have expected this,' she laughs ruefully through her tears. 'I always knew that by calling you Kali, you'd have a different life.'

She doesn't know the half of it. 'Why *did* you call me Kali?' I ask, curious.

'It went against the norm,' admits my mum. 'But I knew I had to do it anyway. Because names are important. You know, my name, Sunita – it means obedient. Well-behaved. The perfect name for a good little girl. And that's what I became.'

'I had no idea...'

'I've had a nice life *beta*. I'm happy. But I wanted a better life for you. One where you didn't have to be so obedient and well-behaved. That's why I chose to call you Kali. She's always been my favourite goddess – she's so...'

'Powerful?'

'Yes!' agrees my mum. 'I hoped that by naming you Kali, I was going to raise a strong, independent young woman. And I suppose it's coming true. It just took me by surprise.' She smiles, dabbing tears away. 'I am proud of you Kali, always. It's just the older you get, the more scared I become. Because you're doing things I never could. I worry I won't be able to keep you safe anymore.'

Tears sting my eyelids. 'Mum, I am *so* glad you named me Kali.' And it's true. Even with the demons. 'It's helped make me who I am. Thank you for being brave enough to do it. And I know life might be harder if I'm different. But at least it makes me stronger.'

Tears slide down my mum's face as she wraps her arms around me. 'Oh *beta*. You're already the strongest person I know. You deserve a hundred gold medals. And...' She coughs awkwardly. 'You deserve a... girlfriend like K.'

I hug her tight. 'I love you for saying that, Mum. But K and I haven't exactly had the 'what are we' chat yet.'

She frowns, confused. 'Oh, your generation. There's always something new!'

I laugh, and then inhale an overwhelming amount of Dior. I look up to see Deepa Auntie and Radha. 'Sunita!' cries Deepa Auntie. 'Have you heard about our girls? Isn't it wonderful? Imagine, we could be sisters-in-law!'

'Yes, well, it's all very new for me,' says my mum delicately, as Radha's face breaks into a massive grin.

'Oh, I'll fill you in!' Deepa Auntie threads her arm through my mums and leads her away. 'Now, the best thing about being the mum of a teen lesbian is you never have to worry about them getting pregnant!'

Radha and I catch each other's eye and burst out laughing. 'Oh my god, your poor mum! Deepa is going to shake up her mind in ways she did not see coming.' Then Radha pulls me into an unexpected hug. 'Also, hello, someone came out! I'm so proud of you Kali. And you won! Look at you!'

I manage to free myself from her silk and chiffon embrace. I don't think I've ever been hugged so much in one day before. 'Uh, thanks Radha. I didn't expect you all to come down...'

She shrugs. 'Oh, why not? What's a venue? We may as well have the rest of the sangeet here.'

'Wait, what?!'

She points to the entrance, where I see a load of caterers setting up silver buffet containers. 'Deepa sorted it all. We've moving the party here. And the band will be here soon.'

I shake my head, laughing. 'Wow. I can't believe you did all this for me.'

'You're my family,' says Radha simply. 'I'd do anything for you.'

337

Chapter 34

I yawn loudly as my mum sticks pins into my saree, adjusting the folds of silk.

'Stay still,' she admonishes. 'And stand up straight!'

I'm trying, but honestly, I'm *exhausted*. I've been up since 7am because apparently that's what time girls and women of the bride's household should be up to get ready. Ri and Hayley were shocked when I told them the wedding starts at 11am – apparently that's weirdly early for non-Indian people, or in Hayley's words, 'uncivilised'. But it's even worse for me; I've been prodded, made up, tonged and massaged for *hours*.

But that's not even the main reason I'm so tired. Every muscle of my body aches from yesterday's demon massacre and I didn't even get an early night to recover! I ended up dancing to Bollywood mash-ups 'til midnight in the archery hall, with the entire of Radha and Kevil's wedding party, *and* everyone who'd come to the competition. It could have been a total disaster – both sides of my life colliding spectacularly – but actually, it was the most fun I've had in forever.

It's why I made the potentially life-ruinous decision to invite all my friends to Radha's wedding today (she drunkenly gave me permission on the archery dance floor). K's going to come, of course, but so are Ri, Joe, Jack *and* Hayley. In the cold light of day, this no longer feels like the brilliant idea it did last night when I was high on endorphins and excitement. But it's time I stopped trying to keep my life so separate. I am a mash-up of contradictions – Bollywood and archery and so much more – so why can't I celebrate that?

'All done!' says my mum, smiling proudly as she leads me over to the floor-length mirror. 'Beautiful!'

And for once, I agree. Radha said I could wear whatever I wanted today, instead of the pink saree she chose for me, so I raided her cupboards and picked out a black and gold saree in honour of Kali-Ma, to wear with a gold crop top. It felt appropriate, considering everything that's been happening lately, but I also look *good* in it. Not just because I've spent the last three hours getting my hair and make-up done, but because I look like myself. And I'm realising that's the most important thing of all.

'Now for the nariyal…' My mum walks over to me carrying a coconut decorated with red patterns, nestled into a plump cushion. It's the fanciest coconut I've ever seen. 'Let's just gently place this on your head. And you can use your hand to support it. Perfect!'

I thought I'd feel ridiculous with the coconut on my head, but actually, it feels kind of cool. Plus, it means everyone can see the mehndi designs on my hands, creeping up my forearms, under the stacks of gold bangles my mum shoved onto my wrists.

'Ready?' asks my mum. 'Kevil's family are here already. The dhol players are making that pretty clear!'

I nod in reply, nervous about what I'm about to do. I carefully follow my mum out of the room – she looks stunning in a silky silver saree – towards the din of out-of-tune voices and loud drums coming from outside the hotel.

It's even more deafening when we get there. Kevil is standing at the bottom of the hotel steps, in an amazing gold outfit with a matching turban on his head, dancing confidently, surrounded by his family and friends, who are all singing Indian wedding songs to the beat of the dhols. I can't help laughing at the sight – he looks so happy!

He stops when he sees me and lets out a piercing whistle. Everyone stops dancing, the dhol players cease their banging, and *everyone* turns to look at me. I feel myself blush, uncomfortable in the limelight, gazing around at the sea of brown faces. And then – in the corner of the car park, coming out of an Uber – some non-brown ones. My guests have arrived.

There's Ri, in an amazing purple lehenga courtesy of Radha's wardrobe, Joe and Jack in matching fuchsia kurtas from Kevil's wardrobe, and Hayley, in the pink saree I was supposed to wear. It looks miles better on her than it ever did on me, and for a second, I feel embarrassed to be standing on the steps of the hotel, in my black and gold saree, dripping in jewellery, holding a coconut on my head. I couldn't look more Indian – more *different* – right now.

But then I realise I'm *glad* they get to see me like this! It's part of who I am and I'm proud of it all. If they don't like it, they're not my friends. I stick my head defiantly into the air, hitch up my saree skirts with my right hand, and slowly walk towards Kevil like my mum told me to. I can feel her right behind me as I reach Kevil, gently marking a red dot on his forehead with my ring finger, in a sign of blessing to welcome him to the wedding.

Kevil spontaneously hugs me – that was not in the wedding planner's ringbinder – and whispers in my ear. 'Thanks Kali. I can't wait for you to be my sister!'

I hug him back, surprised he feels that way. I feel a bit guilty as I've never thought about Kevil becoming my cousin-brother; I've always just avoided him, assuming he was a basic Radha fanboy, with his puppy-dog eyes. But liking Radha is not his whole personality, in the same way that Radha's beauty and brains aren't hers. There's so much more to both of them, and I'm looking forward to getting to know who they *really* are, beneath the outer layers.

Just then, the dhol players bang their drums into life again, and someone lets off multicoloured streams of powder. Kevil's family starts singing, clapping and dancing again, and the wedding is officially back in action.

'You were amazing,' says a voice behind me. K. In her emerald green lehenga. She looks so hot it takes my breath away. 'Great balancing with the coconut.'

I laugh, hugging her. 'Thanks. I'm so glad you're here! And you look incredible.'

'You too. Kali-Ma would be proud of the homage.'

We're interrupted by a cry of 'Doomsday!' Joe, obviously. 'Sick coconut skills – your balance was on fire.'

K scrunches up her face in reluctant agreement. She doesn't want to like Joe, but somehow, she can't help it.

'And you look sooo cool,' says Ri. 'The black and gold is amazing!'

Hayley coughs. 'Yeah. Uh… can we talk a sec, Kali? Privately?'

I don't know whether to be more surprised that Hayley just used my actual name or that she wants to speak to me alone.

'You don't have to look so scared,' she scowls. 'It's not major.'

I'm not scared – not now I know what I'm capable of. 'Okay. Let's do it.'

Hayley clicks her fingers and Jack is right by her side. 'Babe, go inside with the others and save me a seat?'

He kisses her cheek. 'Of course. Come on everyone!'

K and I exchange a grin before she follows the others into the hotel, and then I'm alone with Hayley.

'So, you and Jack?' I ask. 'That was quick!'

'He always liked me, he just couldn't go there because of Joe,' says Hayley matter-of-factly. 'But now Joe and I are over, he was free to make a move. And Jack's a *way* better boyfriend than Joe ever was.'

343

'I'm… glad you're happy!' And I really am. I don't see Hayley as a scary mean girl anymore – she's just like the rest of us, with hopes, dreams, and a whole load of insecurities on top.

'Thanks.' She fidgets with the edge of the saree. 'Also, uh, Kali, I wanted to say sorry. Ri made me see that I was awful to you. I was critical of your culture which isn't cool. And to be honest, it was also kind of dumb, because your culture is insanely cool. I did a video of me in this saree and it got way more likes than *anything* I've ever done!'

I can't help but laugh. That's the most Hayley apology I've ever heard. But I know what she's trying to say. 'Thanks Hayley. I appreciate that. But my culture isn't a trend. It's who I am. And I never should have cared so much about your opinion anyway – it doesn't even matter.'

Hayley looks disconcerted by this, then shrugs. 'Okay. See you in there!'

***

K and I have our arms wrapped around each other, and we're dancing slowly in the middle of the dance

344

floor. This is officially the best wedding I've been to in every single way. Even the ceremony was unexpectedly moving, as the priest explained *why* Radha and Kevil had to walk around a fire, tie their flower garlands together, and do all the other traditions that normally make me yawn with boredom. I'd never heard the reasoning behind them before, and it was actually kind of beautiful to hear all about the importance of hope, love and union.

But my favourite part was at the reception, when Radha stood up and announced that she, the bride, was going to do a speech, which is unheard of at an Indian wedding. It was a major feminist moment in itself – and then processed to surpass all my expectations. She started with the normal bits first, thanking everyone for making the wedding happen. Deepa Auntie got a shout-out, of course. Then she moved on to the emotional parts, thanking my mum and dad for being a second family to her, and thanking Kevil for giving her a sense of love and safety, for feeling like home. I would have vommed if it wasn't for the fact I know exactly how she feels because… it's how I'm starting to feel about K.

And then Radha thanked me – Kali Kadia, coconut

carrier and archery queen – for inspiring her for what she was about to do. I had no idea what was going to happen next, but that was when she pulled out her phone and read out her poems. *All of them*. I don't think I've ever cheered so loudly in my life. I was so proud of her and the whole wedding loved them (except for the old Masi who fainted when she read the bit about Kali's naked body, but my dad revived her with a mockito).

My opinion of Kevil skyrocketed when it was time for him to do his speech and he said there was no need because his incredible wife had already showed us how it was done, and there was no point in trying to out-do her. I always thought he was a bit simple for only ever going on about how amazing Radha was, but now I see he's actually very smart for seeing her worth.

Then my dad did a speech, and it was so heartfelt I burst into tears. He spoke about how Radha is like a daughter to him – but then he spoke about his other daughter too. And how proud he was of us, his brave, strong, independent girls. He had his arm around my mum the whole time too, and I realised how lucky I am to have parents like them. They didn't just give me the name Kali; they encouraged me to be the Kali I am.

I had loads of fun hanging with Ri and Joe too (Hayley and Jack were too busy kissing each other behind the catering van). Ri was in total heaven – it turns out Radha's wedding outshone her wildest dreams of an Indian wedding. When we were queuing for the buffet, she filled me in on her conversation with Hayley and how she feels so much better now she can be her true self with her; and it's given her the confidence to come out to her family. Apparently, Hayley made a real effort to apologise, and has decided she now identifies as an 'ace ally' so she's going to set up an LGBTQIA+ club on Wednesdays. It's not exactly what I meant about her getting her own thing, but at least she's supporting Ri.

I had an amazing time with K and the other Kalis too (Deepa Auntie pulled another favour and squeezed in an extra table so they could all come). I know we only met properly for the first time this week, but there's nothing like slaying thousands of demons and resurrecting a goddess to create a lifelong bond. They see and accept every part of me, and I do the same with them. It's inspiring me to try and do the same with my family and my friends as well. And it's already working. Being here at this wedding is the first time I don't feel like an outsider with the Indian community or with my school friends. Instead, I feel like I'm exactly where I need to be – and that I belong.

I invited Mrs Patel to Radha's wedding as well. She came to the competition yesterday to see if Joe was okay, and I updated her on everything about the battle. She burst into tears, and said that hearing how I'd invoked Kali-Ma helped her release the last remnants of guilt she was holding onto, because she knew that on some level, she'd helped us Kalis defeat Raktabija. And in helping us, she'd helped her sister too. I discussed it all with the other Kalis straight afterwards, and we decided Mrs Patel is definitely one of us. We're going to hold a special ceremony to honour our fallen Kali sisters so Mrs Patel can finally lay her grief to rest – and we're adding her to the WhatsApp group. She's earned her place.

'Kali, how are you feeling?' K's soft voice interrupts my thoughts.

I smile into those perfect mahogany eyes, our bodies swaying in time together to the music. 'Honestly? I've never felt better. This is the best weekend of my entire life.'

'The weekend you were demon-napped, saw

Raktabija come back from the dead, and had thousands of demons try to kill you?'

'It's *also* the same weekend we saw the goddess Kali, I realised I liked you, we had our first kiss, I won gold at archery, I stood up to Hayley, *and* I told my family I like you. Not to mention the fact we slayed all those demons.'

K grins, and her face lights up so bright that my heart starts thudding. I don't think I'll ever get over how magnetic she is. 'That does sound like a pretty good weekend. You know, yesterday, when I was introducing myself to your friends, and I said I'm your... well, I didn't say anything.'

I nod, nervous. 'Yes?'

'It's because I didn't want to say friend.'

'I didn't want you to say friend either!' I burst out. 'You're so much more than that!'

'Same for you, but I'm not ready to say girlfriend either,' admits K. 'I like you *so* much Kali. But I need to go slowly. I... didn't want you to know this, but Lola had a boyfriend before she met me. And when we got together, things were so great.'

I ask the inevitable. 'Until?'

'I got my period. I told her, and I made the mistake

of telling her about the demons too. She totally freaked out.' K pauses, and I wait, giving her the space she needs. 'She left me and went back to her boyfriend from before. Ever since, I've found it hard to trust. And I think it will take time for me to do that.'

'Oh, K.' I hold her hands, my fingers tracing the tattoos on her wrists. 'I understand. But I need to you to know I'm not Lola. I'm not going anywhere. You're the one I choose.'

She smiles hesitantly. 'So, you're up for dating? Going slowly?'

'Definitely. I need to go slow as well – unlike you, I've never even had a relationship! But I'm not sure I could cope if you were seeing anyone else too. Could we, maybe, be exclusive?'

'I wouldn't have it any other way.' K leans in to kiss me and my breath catches. I can't believe I'm kissing her at Radha's wedding, in the middle of the dancefloor surrounded by aunties and uncles. But it feels like the most natural thing in the world.

'I'm so glad I met you,' I whisper. 'I'll always be grateful to the demons for bringing us together.'

'We would have found each other anyway. Although, it was nice having a demon–cleaner–upper.'

'Hey, I upgraded pretty quickly to demon slayer!'

'Oh fine, I suppose so. And goddess resurrector.'

'I'll take that! But now the demons are all gone, does this mean we're not demon slayers anymore?'

'We'll always be demon slayers. It's in our blood.'

We wrap our arms tight around each other and keep on dancing. I am so grateful for everything. I'm *exclusively* dating the person I like most in the whole world. My parents are slow-dancing in the corner. Ri and Joe are trying to start up a congo line. Hayley and Jack are kissing so intensely on the dance floor that all the masis and masas are freaking out. And Radha and Kevil are so blissfully happy that it's radiating off them to all the rest of us.

I'm so happy it almost hurts. I'm surrounded by everyone I love and life has never been so good. I rest my head on K's shoulder, smiling down at the floor. I catch a glimpse of her trainers beneath her lehenga and laugh out loud. 'Are you wearing trainers with your Indian outfit? That's so you!'

'They're comfy,' protests K, pointing out her feet to show me her trainers. They're the same ones she was wearing yesterday. Limited edition navy Nikes. She angles them like she's modelling, and we're both laughing, until we stop at the exact same time.

Because we've seen something on the bottom of her shoe.

She slowly lifts it higher towards us, and we both gasp in horror. There's a small splodge of red on the bottom of her shoe. Glistening. Shiny. Dark.

Blood.

My throat is dry and voice croaking when I speak. 'K. There's a drop of blood on the sole of your shoe. The part that has touched the ground.'

K lifts her wide, worried mahogany eyes to mine. I know exactly what she's feeling, because I'm feeling it too: a mix of fear, confusion and serious adrenaline. She swallows it all down. 'You know what this means, right, Kali?'

I nod, my heart racing and blood fizzing with everything this could mean. I don't want to say it out loud, but I know I have to.

'Yes. Out there, there might still be…' I take a moment to breathe before I say something I thought I'd never have to say again. 'A demon left to slay.'

Acknowledgements

I love this book so much and I'm so grateful to everyone who has worked on it!!

Thank you to my agent Chloe Seager for being so brilliant and supportive. I remember emailing you an over-excited, way too long message about this new idea that had just come to me on a bus journey (shoutout to the 113). I'm so glad you were as enthusiastic about it as I was!

Thank you to my editor Eishar Brar for loving Kali and K as much as I do. And thanks to the rest of the team at Knights Of, including Jade for your illustrations and George for your design. You've all brought my characters to life just as I imagined and I'm so glad I get to publish this book with you all.

Thank you to my cousin Prisha for being my first reader and giving me lots of (very honest) feedback. It really helped!

Thank you to Buffy The Vampire Slayer for being such a major inspiration to me – I loved that show and always will.

Thanks to my friends and family for all your support.

And finally, thank you to all the readers out there who are battling their own demons. I hope this book helps you in some way.

Radhika Sanghani

Author

Radhika Sanghani is an award-winning features journalist, acclaimed author, screenwriter, influential body positivity campaigner and a BBC Writers Room graduate. She regularly writes for the Daily Telegraph, Daily Mail, Guardian and Glamour, and regularly appears on the TV and radio. She is also a TedX speaker on body positivity and a yoga teacher. She's written four adult novels and her middle-grade debut *The Girl Who Couldn't Lie* (Usborne) published May 2024. You can find her @radhikasanghani on social media.

Jade Deo

Illustrator

Jade is an Indo-Caribbean American illustrator from NYC with a love of storytelling. Though an emerging interdisciplinary tech professional by trade, she is a lifelong reader who often freelances within the book community. She frequently draws on cultural and political influences for her work, and enjoys using art as a means of fostering discussions around representation and various social causes. To learn more about Jade, find her on Instagram @jaded.draws.